MY KIND
OF
Perfect

A Finding Love Novel

NIKKI ASH

MY KIND OF PERFECT'S PLAYLIST

Feels Great - Cheat Codes

House Party - Sam Hunt

Ain't My Fault – Zara Larsson

Blue Tacoma – Russell Dickerson

Sorry – Justin Bieber

Eenie Meenie – Justin Bieber & Sean Kingston

Feelings Show – Colbie Caillat

This Feeling – The Chainsmokers

I'm Yours – Alessia Cara

Behind These Hazel Eyes – Kelly Clarkson

Just the Way You Are – Bruno Mars

The Difference – Tyler Rich

I Don't Care – Ed Sheeran & Justin Bieber

Gold – Britt Nicole

Take Back Home Girl- Chris Lane

Give Your Heart a Break – Demi Lovato

Wanted – Hunter Hayes

There's No Way – Lauv

What Do You Mean? – Justin Bieber

Can't Take Her Anywhere – Dylan Scott

Tie Me Down – Gryffin & Elley Duh

To Bret, for loving me imperfectly perfect.

One

CHASE

"Hey...Yeah, I'm on my way," my wife whispers into the phone, thinking I'm asleep.

I had to pull an extra shift at work because two of the guys called out, and then we were up all night putting out a fire that resulted in a mom and her baby both losing their lives. I love my job as a firefighter, but some days it's harder than others. We want to save them all, and it sucks when we can't.

"I'll see you soon," she says softly, using a tone very unlike her. I crack an eye open and see her standing in front of our dresser, putting her big hoop earrings into her ears. She's dressed in a short, tight, leopard dress and tall as fuck heels that show off her mile long legs. Her long, dyed, black hair has been straightened, and her face, which is being reflected in the mirror, is covered in makeup.

She's going out without me...again.

I take a moment to assess her features. My wife is hot. Always has been. And dressed the way she is right now, she looks every bit like the model she once was—before fame got to her head and destroyed her career. But if you remove the makeup, you'll see the wrinkles around her mouth from years of smoking. And if you look closely at the creases in her arms, you'll see the scars from the needles. She's been clean for a while now, but those scars are permanent. Just like the damage she's causing to our marriage by the choices she's making.

Before she can escape, I roll over and sit up. She doesn't notice me right away, so I clear my throat. She jumps, startled, and swivels around. "Chase... you're awake." Her striking blue eyes meet mine.

"I am. Where are we going?" I throw the freshly washed blanket off me—noting how she's been doing the sheets several times a week, when she used to barely wash them once a month—and stand. I don't really have any intention of going anywhere. I have to be back at work at 8:00 a.m., but my fake threat forces a reaction out of Victoria—shock tinged with a little bit of guilt—that tells me everything I need to know—something I've been suspecting for a while now.

My wife, the woman I've been married to for almost ten years, have been friends with for even longer, have been through ups and downs with, was by her side every time she fell off the wagon and needed help getting back on, is having an affair.

When she came home the first time smelling like another man's scent, I questioned her. She told me I was crazy, that I was starting shit for no reason. The next time, she said the club she and her friends were at was crowded and a guy probably rubbed up against her. It was a dumb as fuck excuse, but I swallowed it down, not wanting to believe my wife would cheat on me.

But now, it's time I open my eyes and stop being a dumbass.

"I'm going out with Fiona and Jezibel," she says, referring to her washed-up model friends.

"Cool. I'll join you."

Her eyes widen, but she quickly schools her features. "It's a girls' night," she retorts.

"I don't think they'll mind me crashing... Plus, I miss you." I walk over to her and cage her in my arms.

"Don't you have to work tomorrow morning?" She moves my arm and steps away like she's repulsed by me. I can still remember the days when we would spend hours at a time with me inside her. Even the last year, since she's been pushing me away, we haven't gone more than a couple days without having sex. But the last couple months it's gotten worse. I can count on one hand the amount of times I've been intimate with my wife. She starts fights all the time, which end in me sleeping on my friend Alec's couch. And when I'm home, she's either out with her friends or doesn't feel well and wants to be left alone. Something is definitely up, and I'm going to find out what—or who—it is.

"I do," I tell her, answering her question. "I actually have to work a double." A lie.

She chews the inside of her mouth. "Then you better get some sleep."

"Yeah, you're right," I say, a plan forming in my head. "Guess I'll see you in a few days." I step close to her and kiss her cheek. "I love you."

"Me too," she chokes out. "I, uh, I gotta go."

I watch as she grabs her purse and rushes out the door, and then I fall back into bed, knowing if I don't get some sleep, I'm going to be useless tomorrow, and as much as I want to follow my wife and catch her in the act, I have a crew of men who need me to lead. I worked hard to get to where I am, and I can't lose everything I've accomplished—especially since there's a good chance I'm going to lose my wife anyway.

———

"YOU'RE MORE THAN WELCOME TO CRASH AT MY PLACE," Alec says as we walk to our vehicles. It's finally eight in the morning, which means our twenty-four-hour shift is over and we're off for the next four days—unless another guy calls out and I have to come in. This has been one long as hell week. "I was only fucking with you yesterday about squatting on my couch," he adds.

I laugh at his remark. Yesterday I was fucking with him about not owning up to his feelings for Lexi, his best friend whom he's in love with but won't admit to. And in return, he called me out on sleeping on his couch several times the last few weeks.

"I know, man, and I appreciate it, but... I need to go home." I don't bother mentioning that my wife has no idea I'll be home in a few minutes, and if I'm right about my suspicions, there's a good chance I'll catch her with another man, in our home, dirtying those clean fucking sheets. "I'll see you tomorrow night." Alec's birthday is today, and we're all going out tomorrow night to celebrate.

I jump into my charcoal gray BMW 3 series—a gift to myself last year when I got my promotion as Battalion Chief—and head the few blocks home. I pull through the gate of our community and smile to myself at how far I've come. Victoria and I grew up in a small, poor neighborhood in South LA. We would talk of one day getting out of the ghetto. She would become a huge model and I would fight fires. We both achieved our dreams, but unlike Victoria, who couldn't deal with the dark parts of your dreams coming true, I remained grounded. She wanted to purchase a mansion in Hollywood Hills with the money she was making, but I refused, instead telling her we could do that in a few years.

It's a good thing I won that argument, because not too long after, she was caught with blow up her nostrils during a fashion show. Her career tanked, and I found out she spent all her money on partying and getting high.

When I got my promotion, I moved us away from Hollywood and into a two-bedroom apartment near UCLA. It's more laid back—less temptations for her. I paid for her to go to rehab and when she got out, I had everything set up and ready. At first when she got out, she was on board, focusing on herself and us, but all too quickly, she was back to her old self. Going out and partying.

She swears she hasn't done any drugs, but I wouldn't doubt she's lying.

I go to pull into my designated parking spot, but there's already a newer-looking Porsche parked in it. I glance over and see Victoria's Mercedes in hers. I bought it for her when I got my promotion, hoping it would make her happy. Spoiler alert, it didn't.

I park in a guest parking spot and then head up to our second floor apartment. After unlocking the door, I open it slowly and quietly, and then close it the same way. I walk through our foyer and living room and stop in the doorway of our bedroom. The door is wide-open and she's in bed, sleeping on her side. Her hair is splayed out across the pillow, and her lips are forming a little pout. And behind her is a man I've never seen before with his arm thrown over the side of her, his hand resting on her bare, fake breast—something else she wasted her money on, thinking she needed them to be successful.

I knew there was a damn good chance this was what I would find when I walked through the door, but I wasn't prepared for the hurt and betrayal I would feel seeing my wife in another man's arms.

I met Victoria when we were ten, fell in love with her when we were seventeen, and we were married when we were twenty. Now, at twenty-nine years old, we're about to be divorced. Because there's no coming back from this. I could forgive her for just about anything, but fucking another man... I can't do it. No matter how much I love her.

I clear my throat and Victoria's eyes pop open. It takes her a second for it to click: her husband is home and she's in bed with another man. But once it does, she jumps out of bed, in nothing but a tiny G-string.

The guy groans, stretching out his arms. He has no clue what's happening.

"Chase," she squeaks, her eyes darting between me and her fuck buddy. She runs over to the bathroom door and grabs her robe, throwing it on.

"Huh?" the guys says, opening his eyes and meeting mine. "Oh, shit. Look, man... I don't want any problems." He climbs out of bed, wearing only a pair of boxers. Human nature has me checking him out. He's about the same height as me, has tattoos donning his arms, whereas I'm tattoo free. He's skinny, tiny abs, but nothing like the muscle I have from working out daily. I'm not sure what's drawn Victoria to him, until he sniffs and wipes his hand back and forth under his nose. And then it hits me: he's a druggie, like my wife.

"Look, Chase, I wanted to tell you, but I didn't want to hurt you," she says, stepping over next to the guy.

"You told me you two were over," he says to her.

At this point, most guys would've pummeled the man who was sleeping in his bed, but that's not who I am. I'm married to Victoria, not this guy. Should he have been fucking a married woman? Hell no. But I got a glimpse at her left hand and saw she removed her ring. She's been lying to both of us.

"We are now," I tell him calmly, refusing to go ballistic and throw shit. I gave this woman my all. I loved her and supported her. I was faithful to her. And in return, she cheated on me God knows how many times.

My gaze meets Victoria's. "Let me know when I can come back and pack my shit. I don't want you to be here. And I'll file for divorce... you know, since you don't have any money to file yourself."

I turn my back on my cheating wife and walk out the door. She doesn't bother to chase after me, and I don't expect her to. She made her decision a long time ago.

A few minutes later, I'm pulling into Alec's complex. It's nicer than mine, located in a wealthy neighborhood. He comes from a well-off family—stepdad is a retired UFC fighter—and was given the place as a gift after he graduated from the fire academy.

I knock on the door, and Georgia answers. She's Alec's roommate, along with her sister, Lexi. She's holding her laptop in one hand and the door with the other. Her brown hair is up in a messy bun, and her eyes, green like the grass after a good rain, shine in sympathy.

"Hey," I mutter, "Alec mentioned..."

"Yeah, of course," she says, thankfully not making me finish my sentence. If I had to, I might fucking lose it. I'm barely holding it together as it is.

I grab the door from her and walk through it, closing it behind me.

"The pillow and blanket are where you left them," she tells me. "Lexi is at the beach, surfing, and Alec is asleep."

"Thanks." I fall onto the couch and drop my face into my hands, trying to figure out how the hell my life has come to this.

My phone dings and I pull it out.

Victoria: You can come by and get your stuff tomorrow. And I'll file for the divorce. I want it done ASAP.

She'll file for divorce?

Me: With what money?

There's no way her cheating ass is getting a dime from me.

Victoria: Raymond said he'd pay.

Raymond... Guess that's the guy's name. Must've been his Porsche parked in my spot. What a fucking dumbass. He finds out the woman he's fucking is a liar and offers to pay for her divorce? Must be the powder he's been snorting.

Me: Cool, he paying for your apartment and Mercedes too?

We both know her broke ass can't afford to pay for either one. Speaking of which... I pull up my bank app and quickly transfer my money from our joint checking to my sole savings account. I'll need to visit the bank as soon as possible to close that checking account and open a new one.

I wait a few minutes for her to answer, and when she doesn't,

I put my phone on silent and throw it onto the coffee table. Fuck her and her cheating ass.

Grabbing the pillow and blanket next to the couch, I lie down and close my eyes, trying not to let myself get worked up. But fuck, it's hard. I gave her everything, all of me. My money, my time, my love. And what did I get in return? A cheating wife. At least we didn't have any kids. The divorce will go through quickly and then I can move on, start my life over again. I can tell you one thing, there's no way in hell I'm ever giving a woman that much of myself again.

Lesson. Fucking. Learned.

Two

CHASE

Fifteen Months Later

"Hey, what are you up to tonight?" I pop my head into Georgia's room and ask, even though I already know what she's up to... the same thing she's *always* up to.

She looks up from her laptop, and her emerald eyes meet mine. "Working." She lifts her laptop slightly.

"Any chance you want to go to Club Illusion with me?"

In the last two years, since I've known Georgia, I've only seen her actually go out a handful of times—usually when Lexi would drag her out for a celebration. But since Lexi and Alec moved out—after getting married and having a baby—Lexi has been too busy to go out, which means Georgia hasn't been out either.

"No, thank you," she says softly, shaking her head to emphasize her answer. She glances back down at her laptop, resuming her work. The woman practically lives in her room, on that thing. The only time she ever leaves it is to either visit her family or check on the art gallery she helps Lexi run. Hell, she even has her groceries delivered.

"All right. Not sure if I'll be home tonight, but text or call if you need anything, okay?" I tell her the same thing every night before I go out, or before I leave for work. In the several months we've been living together, she's never once texted or called me.

"Will do." She smiles sweetly up at me. "Have a good night."

As I'm about to dip out, I notice her smile quickly fades into a frown. I do a double take, and her eyes are already back on her laptop, but something about the way her lips quirk down rubs me the wrong way. I should probably ignore it. My friends are waiting, and while Georgia and I get along, we aren't exactly friends. The only reason we ended up living together was out of circumstance—Alec was too lazy to sell the place, Georgia wanted to give her sister some space, and I didn't want to deal with finding a new place to live.

"Hey," I say, getting her attention.

She glances back up at me, her eyes slightly glassy.

"You okay?"

"Mmhmm." Her gaze goes back to her laptop.

"You sure?" I assess her features, not buying her noise of an answer.

"Yeah," she chokes out, her voice contradicting her response.

"No, you're not," I say, stepping into her room.

I glance around, realizing in all the time we've been living together, I've never actually stepped foot in her room. After Lexi and Alec moved out, she took over the master bedroom. The walls are filled with a mixture of art her sister has created over the years and family pictures. Her furniture is all feminine, white-wash wood, and her area is clean and organized, barely lived in.

"Umm...yes, I am," she volleys without looking up.

"Look at me," I demand. When she ignores me, I step closer and pull her laptop away from her.

"Hey! What are you doing?" She scampers off the bed and comes after me.

I hold it over my head, and she tries to jump to grab it, but she's a good half-foot shorter than my six-foot self, and with my reach being longer, she doesn't stand a chance.

"Chase," she whines. "I have work to do.

"First tell me why you're upset."

"I'm not upset." She huffs.

I can't help but chuckle at the way her lips form the most adorable pout.

"Are you laughing at me?" she accuses, her eyes turning into thin slits. It's not often Georgia gets mad, but when she does, it's sexy as hell.

The first few months of us living together were rough. Our rooms were butted up next to each other and when I would have women over, they would be a bit...vocal. Georgia would get hella pissed and let me know. And then there was this one time when a woman used her shaver... Yeah, she damn near killed me.

It wasn't until I agreed to stop bringing women around that things calmed now. Then, after Alec and Lexi moved out, she moved to the master bedroom, which gave her her own bathroom. She told me I could bring women over again, but for the most part, I prefer going to their place. That way I can leave the morning after.

"Chase! My laptop!" she complains, jumping up to grab it.

"Not until you tell me what's wrong."

She drops her hands and sighs. "I just... I miss my sister," she admits with a shrug. "I guess... I'm kind of lonely." Tears fill her eyes, but she quickly blinks them away. "Now can I have my laptop back, please?" she whispers.

I knew she and Lexi were close, but I didn't consider that Lexi moving out would be this hard for her. I've been so busy focusing on my own shit, like moving forward after my divorce, that I haven't paid attention.

"Come out with me tonight," I suggest.

"So I can play third wheel to whichever woman you're planning to dick tonight?" Her face scrunches up in disgust. "I'm good."

I bark out a laugh, shocked and kind of turned on that she said dick. How very unlike Georgia. "I'm not going to *dick* anyone. I'm just going to have a drink with the guys." I had every intention of getting my dick wet tonight, but I can hold off one night to get Georgia out of the house.

"C'mon," I press. "You might even have fun." I mock gasp and she rolls her eyes.

"Fine." She sighs, trying to sound like going out is such a hardship. "I guess I could use the change of scenery."

"And an alcoholic beverage," I add. "Get dressed, so we can go."

I head out to the living room and drop onto the couch to wait for her. Women take hours to get ready, so I text the guys I'm meeting that I'm running late and warn them Georgia will be tagging along, so they know to be on their best behavior. Since Georgia sometimes stops by the fire station with Lexi to visit Alec, they know her. But since she's kind of a recluse, nobody besides her family *really* knows her.

I'm texting Carter back, when I hear the click-clack of heels on the wood floor. I look up, mid-text, and am shocked as shit by the sight in front of me. For one, I swear she's gotten ready in under twenty minutes. Something I've never seen a woman do before. But also, I've seen her occasionally dress up, and it's always on the conservative side. However, right now, what she's wearing is anything but.

Her black tank top is a turtleneck, hiding her cleavage, yet it's form-fitting, showing off the outline of her perky tits and slim waist. You can't technically see anything, but you can damn sure imagine what's underneath. She's wearing tiny—and I mean *tiny*—white shorts that show off her creamy, toned legs. Holy shit! My eyes land on her feet, and she's donning black open-toed heels with little ribbons on the tops and red soles on the bottoms. My mind immediately goes to her legs wrapped around my waist with those heels digging into my back as I fuck—

Jesus! I. Cannot. Go. There.

"Do I look stupid?" she asks, forcing my eyes to go to her face. Her hair is down in waves, and the glasses she wears when she's reading or working on the computer are absent. Her lashes are coated in a thin layer of mascara and her lips are shiny. But aside from that, she's all natural, and fucking beautiful. I knew she was pretty. Once upon a time, I even considered trying to hook up with her, but Alec pulled the best friend card, and I never bothered to look again. I mean, she's always in sweats and oversized shirts when she's lounging around the house. And when she leaves, jeans and a T-shirt. I had no fucking clue what was hiding under there.

"I'm going to go change," she says with a sigh, knocking me out of my thoughts.

"No!" I yell too loudly, causing her brows to rise in confusion. "I mean, no," I choke out, clearing my throat. "You look good."

Every night I go out, I come across women in expensive outfits and caked-on makeup trying way too hard—which is the norm in LA—yet here she is, wearing shorts, a simple top, and a pair of heels, and she blows any woman I've ever come across away.

And the worst part... she has no damn clue.

"Are you sure?" she asks cautiously. "Lexi left these here... Well, except the shoes. These are mine. Lexi bought them for me..." She rambles on, and all I can do is stare at her pouty pink lips. "I don't really have any going out clothes, and I didn't want to embarrass you, or myself."

Huh? This shakes me out of my trance.

"One," I say, standing, hating that she thinks she would embarrass me based on her wardrobe. "You could wear a burlap sack and look sexy as hell."

She snorts. "You're such a liar."

"No, I'm not," I tell her truthfully. "And whatever you want to wear is up to you. Nothing you put on would embarrass me."

She flinches, quickly trying to hide it with a smile.

"What were you just thinking?" I ask, needing to know what's going through her head. She's the most soft-spoken person I know. Aside from getting upset about the women I used to bring home, she never complains about anything.

"Robert hated the way I dressed."

"Fuck Robert."

Robert was her short-term boyfriend. He thought he was fucking special because he worked for Daddy's law firm, and he treated Georgia like shit. A few times I considered letting him in on a little secret: Georgia was way too fucking good for him. But I didn't want to start shit that wasn't my business. Luckily, she's smart and dumped his ass.

"You ready to go?"

She takes a deep breath, then exhales harshly. "Yeah."

We take an Uber to the club because I'm planning to drink, and when we arrive, since I'm friends with the guy at the door, we get right in without having to wait in line.

"What do you want to drink?" I ask her when we reach the bar.

Her brows furrow in thought. "A lemon drop, I guess." She shrugs and squints, and I can tell she's uncomfortable. But this will be good for her. She's a young, single woman. She should be out having a good time, not cooped up in her room.

I shout our order to the bartender, and a minute later, he returns with my beer and her lemon drop. "Let's go find the guys," I tell her, handing her her drink.

As we make our way through the throng of people, several of them stop me to talk. Since my divorce last year, I've been making up for all the years I was home, trying to be a good husband. At first I was worried I'd run into Victoria at the clubs, but I've yet to see her since the day I picked up my shit. Given I agreed to what she wanted in the divorce, I had my attorney stand in my place to have it all finalized, and from what he told me, she had hers do the same.

I spot Carter and Luke, and grab Georgia's hand to guide her over to them, so she doesn't get lost in the crowd. Her hand is small inside mine, and I think about how long it's been since I've held a woman's hand. Victoria was never really the touchy-feely type, unless she wanted something, and the women I hook up with are just that—a hookup.

When I glance back at Georgia, she smiles weakly, looking completely out of her element, and I vow to show her a good time tonight, to make her see there's more to life outside of her four safe walls.

"What's up!" Carter yells over the music. He extends his hand and reluctantly I drop Georgia's.

"Georgia, you remember Carter?" Carter works with me on the same shift at the fire station.

"Yes," she says shyly, making him grin wide. In LA, we're used to women who are coy or have an agenda. Almost all of them are here to be the next big model or actress, and they'll soak up attention anywhere they can get it. A woman who is genuinely sweet and innocent like Georgia is rare.

"Nice to see you again," Carter says with that look in his eye he gets when he's interested in a woman. "Would you like to dance?"

At his bluntness, Georgia's eyes comically bug out. "Oh... umm..."

"We just got here," I cut in. "We're going to have a seat for a few minutes."

Georgia smiles up at me, liking that idea, and the way she looks at me like I'm some sort of white knight has me chugging my beer. Georgia is off-limits. For one, she's Alec's best friend, and he would kill me for going there. But also, I have no desire to settle down. I was tied down for twelve years, and look how that worked out for me. I just don't think I have it in me to give myself over to another woman. And Georgia is the kind of woman who deserves it all.

We slide into the booth, just as Luke and Scott walk over, each with a beer in their hands and a woman tucked under their arms. Both of them work the same shift as Alec, Carter, and me. Since we all have the same days off, we've gotten close. There's one other guy, Thomas, who works with us as well, but he's married with kids.

"Georgia... Luke and Scott," I tell her, ignoring the women. They won't be with them tomorrow, so there's no point in introducing them.

"Nice to see you again," she tells both of them, taking a sip of her drink.

"You too," they both shout over the music. Luke's eyes meet mine, and his brows go up in a silent question. I shake my head, and he nods with a laugh.

The guys all excuse themselves to go dance, leaving Georgia and me at the table alone. "Is your drink good?" I ask, making conversation.

"Yeah. If you want to go dance or whatever, you can."

"Nah, I'd rather chill with you." I shoot her a playful wink and her entire face turns pink. Fuck, she's adorable. "So, tell me about you."

"You know me." She laughs, bumping my shoulder with hers. The sound shouldn't affect me the way it does, hitting me straight in the chest. It's genuine and sweet. No motives behind it.

"Yeah, I know you, but I don't *know* you. Aside from the fact that you do web design for a living, I don't really know anything else."

She thinks about this for a second. "That's really all I do," she admits, so softly that if I wasn't sitting so close to her, I wouldn't have heard her. "I design websites for different businesses, maintain them... I do some graphic design..."

"What do you do for fun?"

Her eyes meet mine, and her pink lips form a frown that has me wanting to put a smile back on her face. "I guess nothing," she says, lifting her cup and downing the rest of her drink. She cringes as she swallows, then sets the glass down. "I had this plan," she admits. "Well, Lexi and I had this plan... We were going to find our perfect paths."

I want to laugh at that. I learned a long time ago there's no such thing as perfect, but from what I've seen, Georgia, Lexi, and Alec were raised in a sheltered, cushy life, so it makes sense she would believe perfect exists.

Not wanting to jade her with my truth, I keep my thoughts to myself. "And how's that going?"

"Lexi found hers. She and Alec fell in love and got married and had Abigail..." She smiles brightly, genuinely happy for her sister. "And she found her calling with Through Their Eyes."

Through Their Eyes is an art gallery that's set to open soon. It'll help raise money for autistic children and adults, focusing on those who are low income or homeless.

"You're the reason Through Their Eyes even exists," I point out. Georgia inherited an oil company from her biological father who died when she was little. She sold it for millions of dollars, making her a millionaire at twenty-one years old. You would never know it, though, when you're around her. Especially since she still works like she needs the money—something I respect the hell out of her for.

"I provided the money, sure," she says. "But the rest is all Lexi. From the second I shared my idea with her, she made it her own, which is what I wanted. That gallery is going to do amazing things for a lot of people."

"But…" I prompt, sensing one coming.

"It's hers, not mine. She found her path, but I haven't found mine. And since she moved out, I haven't really been looking."

"What interests you? Besides web design."

She ponders my question for a few seconds. "I like reading… and watching cooking shows," she says with a laugh. "And eating."

"So, you should try cooking." I cringe when I say the words, thinking about all the times her sister tried to cook and the fire department was called because of the smoke alarm going off. Hopefully being a horrible cook doesn't run in their family.

As if she can hear my thoughts, she laughs. "I've cooked a few times with my mom and I've never burned anything." She winks, actually fucking winks, and my dick flexes in my pants. My guess is there's more to Georgia, but she hasn't allowed her true self to come out.

"Then you should definitely cook. I can be your taste tester." I can't even remember the last time I had a home-cooked meal, aside from the food the guys grill at the station. I can't cook for shit, and Victoria would never even attempt it.

"What else?"

"I don't know. I guess it's something I need to think about."

"Well, while you're thinking, what do you say we dance?" I stand and extend my hand.

"I don't know..." She eyes my hand speculatively.

"C'mon," I push. "We've danced together before and I was a complete gentleman."

"All right," she says, giving in and placing her hand in mine.

As I escort her to the middle of the dance floor, I push away any thoughts of how perfect her hand fits in mine, wondering what the hell I'm doing.

Three

GEORGIA

What the heck am I doing? One minute, I was updating a website, considering if I should order Chinese or Thai, and the next, I'm at a club, talking to Chase about my path. And now, I'm in his freaking arms, dancing with him to some old Jason Derulo song.

I'm so out of my element here. I can feel the panic attack creeping up, and I mentally beg it to stand down. My body and mind are confused, wondering what the hell I was thinking coming here—without Lexi, no less. She's the only person who really knows me, knows every one of my weird quirks, and doesn't judge me for them.

I'm not good at this—being in public, *peopling*. That's Lexi, she's the life of the party. And I'm good at standing behind her.

"Hey," Chase says to get my attention. "You okay?" He has his arms wrapped around my waist, and we're swaying to the music. He's so confident in everything he does. So good at fitting in.

When I don't answer quickly enough, he pulls me off the dance floor and over to a small, darker corner away from everyone. "Georgia, what's wrong?" he asks. "Your heart..." He presses his palm to my chest. "It's beating so hard."

That's because I'm in the middle of a panic attack. Because I'm a freaking loser and can't handle being in crowded places.

I try to open my mouth to explain, but I can't speak. I'm too worked up. From the outside, I look like a normal woman standing close to a man, but on the inside, my heart is thumping in my throat. It's hard to catch my breath. Tears are burning behind my lids. I close my eyes, trying to calm myself down, but it only makes it worse when memories from when I was younger surface, like they always do. Of my biological father yelling at me and throwing me in my room because I was crying for my mom. Of me being forced to stay there for days, by myself, all alone. Begging my grandmother to let me out while he was at work. I didn't know where my mom was at the time, but I knew she wasn't there with me.

I was little, too little. I shouldn't even remember what happened, but I do. I used to think they were nightmares, but the older I got, the more I realized they were memories. Memories I've never told anyone about—not even Lexi.

"Shit, Georgia, you're shaking," Chase says, rubbing his palms up and down my arms.

"I need..." I croak out. "I need to leave."

I take off running through the crowded club in search of the entrance. I don't stop until I push the door open and fall outside, gulping down pockets of air, finally able to breathe a little easier.

Jesus, I'm so messed up. I need to grow the hell up. I'm almost twenty-two, for God's sake. My biological father is dead, and I've been safe and loved for years. Tristan, the man who adopted me—and is my dad in every way that counts—and my mom love me more than anything. I've lived a life most dream of. I should be normal—like Lexi.

But I'm not.

"Georgia!" Chase yells, catching up to me. "What the hell happened back there?"

Not wanting to embarrass myself any further, I shrug. "I'm not feeling well."

"Bullshit," he hisses. "I felt your heart. You were shaking and—"

"Can you just drop it?" I snap. "I never should've come here."

Chase steps closer to me. "You were having a panic attack. Being in that club, with all those people..." His hazel eyes lock with mine as the pieces fall into place. "That's why you don't go out and stay in your room all the time..."

"Yeah, I'm weird. I'm going to catch a cab home. You should stay and have a good time." I turn to leave, but Chase grabs my forearm, stopping me.

"You're not weird. You have social anxiety. Have you talked to anyone about it?"

No because that would mean telling my family...

I shake my head. "I'm okay now. Really, you should go back

in. I'm sorry for ruining your night. At least next time you'll know better than to invite me," I half-joke.

Chase doesn't laugh. "You didn't ruin anything." He flags down a cab and opens the door for me. I slide in, and then he gets in as well.

"You don't have to—"

"I'm not sending you home alone," he scoffs. "It's fine."

The ride home is quiet. When we get up to our place, which is on the second floor, we go our separate ways. I take a quick shower, then get dressed in a tank top and sweats.

I'm standing in the kitchen, getting a drink of water and checking my phone, when Chase walks in. He's dressed in black basketball shorts sans shirt. My eyes trail down his body. He works out almost every day, and his muscular body is proof of that. His skin is tattoo free, with only a light spattering of hair across his hard chest. His six-pack abs look almost airbrushed on. And the V that disappears beneath the waistband of his shorts... Jesus. My hand tingles, wanting to run my fingers down them to make sure they're real.

Chase clears his throat, and my eyes pop up to meet his, which are dancing with laughter because he just caught me blatantly checking him out. His chocolate brown hair is wet and messy from his shower, and a few droplets of water drip down his temple.

My phone pings with a text, and I glance down at it. I must frown at it because Chase says, "Something wrong?"

"No, I'm—"

"Can you please not lie to me?"

I look up and his jaw is ticking.

"I was lied to by my ex-wife for years. If you don't want to tell me something, just say that, but don't lie."

I swallow thickly at his request. I'm so used to saying I'm okay, it's become my go-to answer. I didn't intentionally lie to him.

"Lexi and I were supposed to meet tomorrow for lunch and to get our nails done. It's our thing..." Or at least it was until she had her daughter. Now I feel like I barely see her anymore. "She has to meet with the event coordinator for the gallery opening. It's not a big deal," I say flippantly, hoping my tone matches my words.

I send Lexi a text back, telling her it's okay and we'll get together soon. When I glance back up, Chase is staring at me. "What?"

"I never realized how often you lie. Do you ever tell the truth?"

"I'm going to bed," I mutter, not wanting to argue with him. I don't do well with confrontation and I'm finally not feeling like I'm going to hyperventilate, so I'd like it to stay that way. Before he can argue, I hurry into my room, shutting the door behind me.

"HEY, SLEEPYHEAD," A DEEP VOICE SAYS. "TIME TO GET up."

I groan and roll over, coming face to face with Chase, who's sitting on the edge of my bed. "What time is it?" I ask, my voice gravelly with sleep.

"Nine o'clock."

"Ugh! I'm sleeping. Wasn't my door closed?"

"Yeah, but I knocked and you didn't answer."

"Because I was sleeping," I whine. I was up until almost four o'clock working on a large website I'm creating for a fortune five hundred company.

"And now you're up. Let's go. We have things to do today."

I sit up, confused. "I don't have anything to do today." I glance at him and he's dressed in a Station 115 shirt, which is the fire station number he works at, and a pair of jeans.

"Yes, we do," he argues. "Now, up." He pats my thigh. "The day is a wasting."

He stands and grins. "I'll meet you in the living room when you're done getting ready." Then he disappears.

Twenty minutes later, I'm dressed in a pair of jeans and a shirt, ready to go. "Want to tell me where we're going now?"

"Who's your book boyfriend?" he asks, his eyes on my chest.

I glance down and then laugh. My shirt reads: My book boyfriend is better than yours. "It's a joke. I got it at a book signing I went to last year in San Francisco. A book boyfriend is a fake boyfriend from a book."

I turn around so he can see the list of names on the back of my shirt. "It's all my favorite heroes from the books I've read."

"Carson Matthews, Ridge Beckett, Kostas Demetriou, Reece Hatfield." Chase tilts his head to the side slightly in confusion.

"I told you I'm weird. The only serious relationships I've ever had were with fake guys."

"Stop saying that. You're not weird. I was just wondering how good those guys can be if they can't even really please you." He shrugs.

If I were drinking, the liquid would be all over him. "Well, I've only been with one guy," I admit, "and he was selfish in bed, so I think I'll take my fake men over real ones." The second the words are out, I immediately regret them.

"Wait... you slept with that douchebag Robert?" he asks incredulously.

"Not that it's your business..." But since I did bring it up first... "No, but we did stuff." He attempted to finger me, but nothing happened, and when I asked him about it, he got defensive and said sex would be better.

Chase's mouth gapes open. "You do *not* get to judge all men based on that asshole."

"Whatever, I'm dressed. Now where are we going?"

"It's a surprise." He grins mischievously.

Since I don't know where we're going, we take his car. It's a newer BMW, the interior all leather, and the gadgets all high-tech.

"This is a nice car," I say, realizing it's the first time I've been in his vehicle.

"Thanks."

"Too bad it's probably overpriced and will break down on you soon."

His head whips around to look at me. "What?"

"Yeah, don't you know what BMW stands for?" I ask, remembering all the jokes my dad threw at my godfather, Mason, over the years about his love of BMWs. My dad is a Ford man through and through, and Mason only buys BMWs. At first, I wanted a cute little car, but my dad wanted me to have a Ford truck so I would be safe. It took some getting used to, but it's kind of cool knowing I could run over any vehicle on the road—yes, my truck is that damn big.

"Really?" he scoffs. "You're going there? You drive a Ford," he accuses.

"First on Race Day."

Chase snorts. "Just don't be calling me when your truck is stuck on the side of the road, dead, to come pick your ass up in my BMW."

I laugh and turn the volume up on his radio, liking the song that's playing. When we drive into Larchmont, a small neighborhood I know well, since my parents both have businesses here, I glance around curiously.

"Coffee first," Chase says, pulling through the drive-thru of Jumpin' Java, my favorite coffee place. I smile on the inside that he knows this. I was with Robert for months and he didn't pay attention to anything. I hate mushrooms, yet every time he would order our food—because he insisted on ordering—he would forget to mention to the waitress to leave them off for me. And when I would complain, he would tell me that adults eat vegetables and to stop acting like a little girl.

A few minutes later Chase pulls into a parking lot and turns off his engine. I'm not sure why we're here, but I don't ask, instead, grabbing my coffee and following him.

When he steps up to a nail salon, I grin. "You're taking me to get my nails done?"

"*We're* getting our nails done." He winks playfully. "Just call me Lexi 2.0."

"Oh my God." I laugh. "Really? You're getting your nails done?"

"Whatever you two were supposed to do, I'm doing it too."

My heart swells. "Thank you, but you don't have to do that." And then without thought, I wrap my arms around him for a hug. I'm not expecting him to return the hug, so I'm taken aback when his hands slide around my waist and rest on the small of my back. I should back up... end the hug. But instead, I stay where I am, with my face pressed against Chase's chest. When I breathe in, I catch a whiff of his scent. It's clean and masculine and oddly enough smells like comfort.

I glance up, and our faces are close... too close. He looks down, his eyes landing on my lips, and I think for a second he's going to kiss me, which causes me to panic, unsure if I want him to. On one hand, I bet he'd be a good kisser... He definitely has the experience. On the other hand, he has all that experience because he's been with a lot of women, and I can't become one of those women... That's not who I am.

Before I can decide if I want him to kiss me, he retreats,

clearing his throat.

"I want to," he says.

He wants to, what?

Kiss me?

Did I voice my question out loud?

Then he adds, "Plus, I've been needing to get a good pedicure." Oh! He's referring to wanting to get his nails done with me. I sigh in relief.

"Well, if you insist... This should be fun."

We walk inside and Chase surprises me when he tells the guy he has an appointment for us. We're told to pick out our colors. I go with my usual: pink, and Chase chooses blue.

"You can get clear, you know," I point out.

"Eh, what's the fun in that?"

We sit in our assigned chairs and the lady shows him how to turn his chair massager on. "Damn, this feels good," he moans loudly, his eyes rolling back.

Several of the employees and customers look over, making me laugh under my breath at how crazy he is. He glances over at me with a dreamy look in his eyes and shrugs, not giving a shit what anybody thinks.

I try to imagine Robert here with me and I can't do it. He would've scoffed at even the idea of a man getting a pedicure. Yet, Chase is one of the manliest guys I know—I mean, he runs into burning buildings for a living—and he's completely okay with sitting in a salon getting his toes painted.

Chase has made me laugh more this morning than I ever laughed with Robert. I was so stuck on the fact that I wasn't right for Robert... that I wasn't enough. When the truth is, Robert wasn't right for me.

"What's going through your head?" Chase asks.

"I want to find someone," I admit.

When his brows dip in confusion, I explain. "I want to find a guy who's right for me. Robert wasn't."

Chase nods in understanding. "You'll find him, Georgia, you just have to get out of the house to look."

He's right, and for most women that would be easy, but for me, it's a bit more difficult. It's probably why I settled so quickly for Robert. He was the first guy to give me attention. I was searching for that perfect path and there he was standing there. I thought at the time it meant something... And I guess in a way it did: a lesson learned.

"Damn, they massage your feet too?" Chase moans. "I'm going to have to get a pedicure every month."

I giggle and snap a picture of him. Since his head is back and his eyes are closed, he doesn't notice. I send a group text to Lexi and Alec.

Me: Look who's replaced Lexi! <insert winky face with tongue sticking out>

Alec: LOL How the hell did you get him to do that?

Me: His idea...

Lexi: Nobody can replace me! <insert side-eye>

Me: Well, he did. <insert shrugging brown-haired woman>

Lexi: Tomorrow, let's do breakfast!

Me: Sure! Sounds good.

"Did you tell Alec I'm getting my toes done?" Chase asks.

I look up and laugh. "Maybe..."

"You're lucky I can't get up right now, but once I can, you're dead, woman."

I laugh harder. "Okay, whatever you say. Lexi and I are meeting for breakfast tomorrow."

"That's good. See? You have nothing to be worried about with your relationship with your sister."

After getting our toes done, Chase gets a manicure, this time forgoing any polish, while I get my fills done on my acrylics. I get my eyebrows threaded, and he gets his trimmed. When the technician waxes the middle of his brows and he squawks like a duck, I crack up.

"Thank you for doing this," I tell him, once we're back in the car on the way home.

"You don't have to thank me. I had a good time, and I feel like a whole new man." He wiggles his clean fingers, making me giggle.

"So, there's this bonfire tonight," he says. I open my mouth to tell him no, but before I can, he adds, "And before you say no..." He side-eyes me. "It's at Carter's house. He's on a couple acres, has a big backyard that's backed up to the water. There won't be a lot of people there. Just a few. It'll be fun. We'll cook some hot dogs, roast some marshmallows, and I'll be with you the entire time."

It actually sounds fun, and before I can come up with an excuse not to go, I find myself saying, "I'll go... But if you want to leave me to do your own thing, I'll understand."

"My own thing?"

"You know... if you meet a woman and want to hang out with her..." The words taste bitter as they leave my mouth, but I push the thought aside. Chase is just being nice to me because I told him I miss Lexi and am lonely.

"If I wanted to hang out with some other woman I wouldn't have invited you," he says, leaving no room for argument in his tone.

CHASE

We arrive at Carter's place, and there are a few cars parked in his driveway and along his front yard. Georgia is dressed in a pair of skintight jeans, a black hoodie that reads Fight Club, and black Vans. I love how low-key she is. Most women would be dolled up, but not her... She's dressed casual and it makes her that much sexier. Her eyes are scanning the area, and I can tell she's nervous about being here. I promised her there wouldn't be too many people, but she's still scared. I told Carter a little about her condition and he ensured me there would only be a handful of people hanging out.

"He has a nice home," she notes absentmindedly.

"His parents left it to him." Carter lost both of his parents in a hotel fire when he was younger, which is the reason he decided to become a firefighter.

Taking Georgia's hand in mine—something I've grown to enjoy doing the last couple days—I walk us around the side of the house. The closer we get, the louder the music gets.

When we reach the backyard, Georgia comes to a halt so she can take everything in. There's a patio with tables and chairs, a decent size swimming pool, and a hot tub. Farther out, there are several lounge chairs facing the Pacific Ocean, and when you walk along the wooden path, it leads to his private beach where he has a bonfire going with chairs forming a circle around it.

If I had to guess, there are probably about fifty people here, a little more than I thought, but because he has so much room, it's not stifling like a club, so I think Georgia will be okay.

"There are a lot of people here," she says, mimicking my thoughts.

"They're spread out, though. Let's go find Carter to say hi, and then get drinks."

She nods, her hand tightening in mine.

"Hey, man." Carter extends his hand to fist bump me. "Nice to see you again, Georgia. Mi casa is your casa. Drinks are on the patio in the fridge and on the counters... food's cooking. You can also grab something to grill over the bonfire."

"Thank you," Georgia says politely.

"Of course," Carter says back with a smile.

We stop at the drink area and since I'm driving I grab a Gatorade. Georgia shocks me when she goes with a Mike's Hard Lemonade.

"I'm hoping a little alcohol will help with my nerves," she admits.

"Hot dog?" I point at the food.

"Yeah, can we grill it on the fire?" she asks, her face lighting up.

I chuckle. "Of course."

I pile a couple dogs on one plate and the ingredients to make s'mores on another so I won't have to come back up. Georgia makes us a plate of sides, and then we head down to the beach.

It's a nice night out, with only just enough breeze to make it cool and comfortable. We find two open seats and get situated. Thomas is sitting next to us with his wife in his lap. They must've gotten a babysitter because I don't see either of their kids running around.

"What's up?" I say, jutting my chin toward him.

"Date night." He grins.

After making introductions between Georgia, Thomas, and his wife, Hilary, we stick our dogs on a couple of skewers and hold them over the fire.

"You okay?" I ask Georgia quietly.

"Yeah." She glances over at me and smiles. "This is nice."

We watch our dogs cook, turning them until they're wrinkly and dark brown, then we remove them and drop them into our buns.

"Mmm," she moans, taking a bite of her hot dog. "How is it that it tastes better cooked like this?"

I laugh and take my own bite, ignoring the way her moaning hits me straight in the dick. It's damn good. Crispy and cooked through.

"Looks like your first cooking mission was a success," I joke.

Georgia laughs. "I saved a couple of recipes online that I want to try."

"Once you know they're good, remember I'm your taste tester."

She cracks up. "You're supposed to try them to tell me if they're good."

I just shrug, taking another bite.

"Want some potato salad?" she asks, holding a forkful up.

"Sure." I'm about to set my hot dog down, when Georgia leans over and feeds me the bite, before taking her own. I watch as she enjoys the food, moaning and smiling with every bite. Georgia was right, she loves food.

"I'm going to make a s'more," she says, pushing a marshmallow onto the skewer and then hanging it over the fire. I watch her while she watches the marshmallow. I don't know what the hell is going on with me, but I can't take my eyes off her. The way she scrunches her nose up in concentration. How every once in a while, she drags her tongue across the seam of her plump lips, wetting them. I've been with several women in the last year, in more intimate positions, but none of them entranced me the way Georgia does without even trying.

"Shit," she hisses. "I burned it."

Reluctantly, I tear my gaze from her to see what she's talking about and find a charcoal black marshmallow engulfed in flames at the end of her skewer. "Here, let me help you," I say, taking the skewer from her and flicking the burned marshmallow off, then adding a new one.

"I wanted to do it." She huffs, her mouth forming a cute as fuck pout.

"C'mere." I nod toward my chair. She stands, unsure where I want her, and I grab her around the waist, pulling her into my lap. "Now, the key to making the perfect marshmallow is to cook it evenly," I explain.

Placing the skewer in her hand, I wrap mine around hers. She leans back slightly to get comfortable, and with her face near mine, I can smell her sweet scent. I don't know what it is, but it's soft and feminine. Without thinking about what I'm doing, I run my nose along her neck.

Georgia stiffens, and I immediately stop. "Sorry," I murmur. "You smell good."

"It's Moonlit Path."

"Moonlit Path has a scent?" Weird.

She giggles. "Yes, it's what you're smelling."

"Well, okay then." I extend her skewer. "To make it perfect, you have to constantly turn the marshmallow in a three hundred and sixty degree circle. If you stop too long, the fire will attack it."

"And then burn it," she adds, like the fire has personally offended her by burning her marshmallow.

Slowly, we turn the skewer around and around until the entire marshmallow is a perfect golden brown. "All right, grab the graham cracker and chocolate," I tell her, pulling the skewer back.

She bends over to grab the plate and pushes against my dick. I let out a grunt and she pops up. "Sorry, did I hurt you?"

No, you just woke up my cock and now it wants some attention... "I'm okay," I croak out.

"Here you go." She holds up the plate, and I lay the marshmallow on the chocolate.

"Close it." She places the graham cracker on top, holding it down, so I can pull the skewer out. "All right, try it." I nod toward the snack. She lifts it up and takes a big bite, then sets it back down. Because of the hot marshmallow, melted chocolate drips out and coats her lips. It takes every ounce of restraint I have not to swipe my tongue across her chocolate-covered lips and taste her.

"Oh my God," she moans. "So good!" Her tongue darts out and licks up the chocolate, cleaning the mess from her mouth, and the entire time I wish I were doing it for her.

"Here, try it." She lifts it back up and shoves it toward my mouth. I open wide and take a bite. When she drops it onto the plate, her gaze zeroes in on my lips, and based on the way her eyes are now hooded, I would bet she's thinking the same thing I was just thinking a second ago—she wants to taste me.

Not giving a shit about anything besides tasting her, I lean in to do just that, but before our mouths touch, my name is called out, breaking the moment. Georgia scrambles off my lap and I stand.

"Hey, I thought it was you," Fiona says, walking over. She's dressed in a skimpy bikini and is holding a martini glass in her hand. She must've been walking down the beach from one of the bars. She looks the same as she did a year ago. Same fake face, hair, and tits spilling out of her top. Her skin is so tan, it's almost leathery looking.

"It's me," I say, plastering on a fake smile.

"How are you?" she asks, her enhanced lips forming a fake pout. Fuck, everything about her is so damn fake.

"I'm good. At a buddy of mine's bonfire."

"That's fun. I was so sad for you when Victoria divorced you. I always thought you were a good guy, but you know Victoria... So materialistic."

She rolls her eyes, and I stifle a humorless laugh at the irony of her words. She gained most of her money from marrying a guy three times her age and then getting everything of his when he died.

"I was worried about you, but I'm glad you're doing good... Oh," she says, looking around me at Georgia. "Who's this?"

I glance back and Georgia is nervously shuffling her feet, unsure whether to step forward or run away. "A friend," I tell her, giving her nothing more.

"Girlfriend?" Fiona asks, false sweetness dripping from her words.

"No," I tell her truthfully.

"That's too bad. With Victoria getting married and having a baby, I was hoping you would've moved on as well."

Her words hit me straight in the gut. Not because I'm jealous, but because it conjures up old memories of me begging Victoria to have a baby with me. I wanted nothing more than to start a family. When we first got married, she wanted that too. But then she let the modeling world get inside her head and changed her mind, telling me she didn't want a child to ruin her perfect body or life. It's crazy how much someone can change. Who we were in our teens and early twenties is nothing like who we were when we parted ways.

"Such a cute little thing," she continues.

"So, she's good, then... Clean?" I shouldn't care, but it's hard not to. In some capacity, Victoria was a part of my life for damn near twenty years.

"Is anybody really clean in LA?" Fiona cackles. In other words, she's still a druggie. My heart goes out for that baby. I'm just glad it's not me who has to deal with that shit. Her cheating on me turned out to be a blessing in disguise. It saved me from years of heartache.

Which is exactly why I'm single.

I glance at Georgia, who looks uncomfortable as fuck, and sigh, thankful I didn't kiss her. It would've crossed us over a line I'm not prepared to step over. Sure, she's nothing like Victoria, but she's young and people change. No matter how sweet she is, I just can't risk my heart again. Not now... maybe not ever.

"We better get going," I tell Fiona.

"Okay, good seeing you." She waves, then traipses over to her friends, who were standing back, drinking and talking, while waiting for her.

"I'm not feeling well," I mutter to Georgia as we walk back.

She doesn't say anything and I feel like an ass for my change in mood. But it's for the best. Nothing can happen between us. We're friends, and that's the way it needs to stay.

Five

GEORGIA

It was like watching someone flip a switch. One minute I was in Chase's lap, inches away from being kissed by him, and the next, he's barely acknowledging me as he talks to some fake wanna-be Barbie about how his ex-wife is married with a baby. I watched as his entire demeanor changed. It was as if he completely shut down. Gone was the playful, fun, flirty Chase, and in his place was the closed-off, broken-hearted shell of a man.

I knew he wasn't available. He's made it clear so many times when he talks to Alec. He was with his wife for years, gave her all of himself, and when she cheated on him, it destroyed him. In the last year, he's never been with the same woman more than a few times. I would know since I would see them coming in and out of his room—until he agreed to take it to their place instead. Maybe that's changed in the last few months, but I would think if he were serious with someone, he would've brought her around or, at the very least, mentioned her.

The fact is, Chase has never pretended to be someone he's not. He's mentioned on more than one occasion he doesn't want to get married again. Alec told him he'd think differently once he met someone worth putting his heart on the line for, but Chase disagreed.

The ride home was quiet, Chase obviously in his own head. I tried to talk to him, but he cut me off, telling me he didn't want to talk. And once we were through the door, without so much as a good night, he retreated to his room.

I was a little upset when he refused to introduce me to his... whatever she was... friend of his ex-wife? But what hurt even worse was the way he raised up a wall between us afterward. I thought we were friends, but the way he treated me on the way home was like I was nothing to him. I opened up to him, and he couldn't do the same for me.

Needing to take my mind off Chase, I lose myself in my work, and before I know it, it's already six in the morning and my phone is going off.

Lexi: Abigail was up all night. I'm exhausted. Raincheck?

My heart hurts, and the loneliness I feel has me wanting to throw my blanket over my head and disappear. So, after I text Lexi back that it's okay and we'll get together another time, that's exactly what I do.

CHASE

Fuck, I'm such an asshole. I was stuck in my own head last night and I completely shut Georgia out. I went straight to bed and passed out, just needing to shake off everything Fiona said. I'm so used to keeping women at a distance, I didn't even consider Georgia's feelings, just pushed her away and slammed the door on her face—literally and figuratively.

Now I'm pacing the floor, waiting for her to get home. She had breakfast plans with Lexi, and when I woke up she was already gone. I texted her, asking if we could talk so I could apologize, but she hasn't responded.

Figuring she's busy with her sister and might be a while, I get dressed to go for a run. I can use the fresh air and time to think. But when I get downstairs, I notice Georgia's monster of a truck is in her parking spot. I pull out my phone and text Lexi.

Me: Is Georgia with you?

Maybe Lexi picked her up.

Lexi: No, I had to cancel breakfast. Abigail was up all night...

Fuck, does that mean she's still in her room? It's almost noon.

Lexi: Everything okay?

I should probably mind my own business, but my guilt over the way I treated Georgia, mixed with the way I know Georgia is hurting because of her sister, steers my next text.

Me: Maybe you should ask your sister that... if you ever make the effort to spend time with her.

I shove my phone into my pocket and run back upstairs to see if Georgia's in her room. When I knock on her door, she doesn't answer. I twist the knob and since it's not locked, I open the door. What if she hit her head or something? I need to make sure she's okay.

When I enter the room, she's sleeping in her bed. Her face is splotchy from crying, and even in her sleep she looks sad. My phone buzzes in my pocket, but I ignore it, going over and sitting on the bed next to her.

When the mattress dips, she stirs awake. Her bloodshot eyes meet mine, and if I felt bad before, it's nothing compared to the way I feel now.

"Lexi said she bailed..."

Georgia blinks several times, then flinches. "I left my contacts in," she says, sitting up and swinging her legs around. She disappears into the bathroom and a few minutes later comes out with her glasses on.

"I thought you were out with your sister."

"Nope," is all she says, grabbing her laptop and sitting back on her bed.

"I got worried when I found out you weren't with her and you weren't answering your phone. I didn't know you were asleep."

"Well, now you know I'm okay, so you can go."

I sigh, momentarily closing my eyes. I fucked up and now she's pushing me away. I deserve it...

"I'm sorry about last night."

She looks up from her laptop. "What are you sorry for?"

"For pushing you away. I was upset and shouldn't have taken it out on you. We're friends and..." When I say the word friends, she flinches. I don't blame her. Before Fiona showed up, we were flirting and I was about to kiss her. But I can't go there. All we can be is friends. "I like hanging out with you," I finish.

"I don't need your pity, and I don't need you to hang out with me or babysit me or whatever it is you're doing."

"That's not why I'm hanging out with you," I argue. "I have fun with you. I just... I think we got swept up in the moment and I need you to know I'm not capable of anything more."

"Says every player." She rolls her eyes.

"Says every person who's been fucked over," I volley. "You've been in one short relationship, so you don't get it, but I was with

Victoria for over ten years. She was my best friend for years before that. I loved her, and she screwed me. We went from agreeing to spend the rest of our lives together, to her lying and cheating on me."

I release a harsh sigh and shake my head. "So, yeah, I sleep around now. Because being single gets lonely, but meaningless sex beats getting my heart smashed on again."

Georgia frowns. "I'm sorry. I shouldn't have said that, shouldn't have judged you. I spent years in school getting bullied and picked on because everyone assumed I was being stuck-up and thought I was too good to hang out. Guys thought I was playing hard to get... I hated the way they judged and labeled me without knowing the truth, and I shouldn't have done it to you."

"People are shitty. Me included." I shrug, and she grants me a small smile.

"You're not shitty. You're human."

Fuck, she's so damn forgiving. Whoever she ends up with is one lucky bastard.

"What do you say we go to lunch?" I suggest. "Neither of us has eaten."

"I meant what I said. You don't have to hang out with me."

"And I meant what I said. I want to. I like hanging out with you. I'm not hanging out with you because I pity you. I'm hanging out with you because I want to."

"You're sure?"

"Yes, now, c'mon. Get up, get ready, and let's go get something to eat. It's beautiful outside."

"Okay," she says. "I'll be ready in twenty minutes."

"I'll go change."

When I get to my room, I check my messages.

Lexi: What's the supposed to mean?

Lexi: Hello?

Lexi: My sister and I are just fine.

Lexi: <insert ten middle finger emojis>

Not wanting to cause shit, I text her back: **You're right, I shouldn't have texted that. Sorry.**

When she doesn't respond right away, I click out of the message, get dressed, and then shove my phone into my front pocket. When I step out of my room, Georgia is already dressed and ready to go.

"I was thinking we could go to the farmer's market," I tell her once we're in my car. "You mentioned finding some recipes to cook, so you could check for any fresh ingredients you need, and while we're there we can get lunch."

She smiles warmly at me. "That sounds great."

While I drive, she plugs her phone into my car and plays deejay. When her phone goes off with a text, it dings throughout the car and pops up on my screen as Lexi.

"She's sorry for bailing and wants to do a barbeque at her place tomorrow tonight," she says, rolling her eyes. I hate that what was once hurt is now turning to anger for her.

"You know, she does have a new baby... I don't think she's purposely bailing on you."

"I know," she says. "I'm not mad at her. I just miss her, and I guess in a way, I feel left behind. We had that perfect path pact, and I didn't think about what would happen if she found hers and I didn't find mine."

"You'll find yours," I tell her, reaching over and squeezing her thigh.

"Want to go to a barbeque tomorrow night?"

"Sure. Alec's been busy too, and I've only really seen him at work."

"Cool." She texts her sister back then turns up the music.

When we get to the farmer's market, we explore each of the booths. Georgia pulls up the recipes she found and buys several of the ingredients she'll need.

"I think I got everything," she says, popping a strawberry into her mouth. "I'm hungry. Where should we eat?"

I laugh that she's actually hungry. I swear for every item she bought, we ate two. Most women I'm around are so worried about their weight, they eat like rabbits. It's nice to be around a woman with an appetite.

"There's a Greek restaurant at the end." I point in the direction of where it's located.

"Mmm... I love gyros." She waggles her brows. "Let's do it."

We order our food, then find a table outside.

"Tell me something about you," I say, taking a bite of my chicken gyro.

"I love reading."

I snort. "No shit. Something else. Something I don't already know."

Georgia thinks for a moment. "I'm obsessed with *The Fast and the Furious* movies. I watch them at night when I can't sleep. I think I've seen each of them at least a dozen times."

"Those are the ones with that guy who died, right? Paul something or other..."

Her eyes bug out. "Paul Walker. And yes, those are them. Haven't you seen them?"

"Nope. Victoria wasn't really a movie person. She preferred all those reality shows..."

"Okay... but you haven't been with her in over a year. How have you not seen any of those movies?"

"I guess I'm not a sit-down-and-watch-a-movie-by-myself kind of guy."

"We're rectifying this tonight," she says, her tone dead serious. "I declare tonight a *Fast and the Furious* movie marathon night."

When we get to the condo, she puts away all of her farmer's market findings, while I get us set up in the living room at the coffee table. I was nervous that after the way I acted last night, things would be awkward between us, but I should've known they wouldn't be. Georgia isn't the type to hold a grudge.

"Today was nice," she says, sitting next to me. "Thank you."

"You don't have to thank me. Friends don't thank each other for hanging out with them. I had a good time too."

We watch the first movie, and then the second, and while we're on movie number three—technically it's number four because she insisted we skip number three—something about them needing to be watched out of order for it all to make sense—Georgia's stomach grumbles. "I think we missed dinner."

I glance at the time on my phone. "I think you're right."

We head into the kitchen to see what we have to make. I'm scouring through the cabinets, ready to settle on PB and J, when she says, "How about we make a flatbread? We can use some of the veggies I bought at the farmer's market."

"Sounds good to me." I close the cabinet.

She grabs a bunch of stuff from the pantry and fridge and gets to work making the dough. Apparently she found a recipe online and bought the stuff to make it but hasn't gotten around to it yet.

Once the dough is rolled out—that part was all me—and put on the wooden block, she starts slicing—and snacking on—the fresh mozzarella.

"What toppings do you like?" she asks, popping a slice into her mouth.

I laugh at the fact that she's eaten more of the cheese than she's put on the flatbread. "Anything." I steal some of the cheese from her and place it on top of the dough. "I'm not picky."

She chops up a tomato then takes a bite of one of the slices. "Oh my God, try this." She grabs another slice and brings it up to my lips. I open my mouth and she feeds me the tomato slice. When she doesn't retract her hand quickly enough, I playfully nip at the tips of her fingers, making her shriek with laughter.

"Not cool," she says with a laugh, placing the tomato slices on top. When she's done, she adds some basil then puts it into the oven and sets the timer. "Twenty minutes." She hops onto the counter. "What should we do while we wait?" She glances around like a bored kid, making me chuckle.

When she reaches for another piece of mozzarella, an idea comes to me.

"We could play the food game."

"What's that?" she asks, looking intrigued. The woman loves her food.

"You never played it as a kid?" I thought everyone did... When she shakes her head, I explain, "One person closes their eyes and the other feeds them a piece of food. The person being fed the food has to guess what it is. If they guess it correctly, it's their turn to feed the other person the food."

"What happens if they guess wrong?"

"They have to go again."

Her eyes light up. "This sounds like fun. I'll go first!"

"No way. I mentioned it. I go first."

She pouts playfully. "Fine. I'll close my eyes. I know food anyway, so I'll guess right."

She closes her eyes and I dash to the fridge to see what we have. I consider going with the hot sauce just to fuck with her, but instead go with something a *bit* more enjoyable.

"All right, open up." She opens her mouth and I slide the spoon between her lips.

Her face immediately scrunches up. "It's lemon juice." Her lips pucker and she coughs slightly. When she opens her eyes, she glares. "That was horrible."

"Hey, it could've been worse." I laugh. "I almost went with the hot sauce."

Her eyes widen. "I would've killed you." She jumps down. "Close your eyes. My turn."

I do as she says and a minute later, she's telling me to open up. I smell it before it enters my mouth. Cocoa powder. The spoonful is filled so high, I choke on the powder, my eyes opening in time to see plumes of it hitting her in the face. She coughs and splutters while cracking up laughing.

"Did you feed me the entire container?" I ask, spitting that shit out into the sink before grabbing a bottle of water and taking a large sip.

"Hey, cocoa powder is nicer than lemon juice!" She continues to laugh, and fuck if her laugh isn't the best thing I've heard in a long time. Her face is lit up and happy, and she looks so damn carefree. It's not often I see this side of her, but I fucking love it.

After going a few more rounds, where I make her eat mustard and honey, and she forces me to eat soy sauce and butter, the timer goes off for our flatbread.

Once she's drizzled some balsamic vinegar over it, we slice

and plate our food, then settle back onto the couch to continue our movie marathon. The flatbread is delicious and between the two of us, we devour the entire thing.

A few hours later, in the middle of the fourth—or is it the fifth?—movie, I hear the faint sound of snoring. I glance over at Georgia, who's snuggled up against my side, her face resting against my shoulder, and find her sleeping. Somewhere along the way, we ended up cuddled under a blanket together. I consider moving her to her room, to her own bed, but selfishly don't. I don't question myself—not wanting to have to consider the answer—as I shift us so we're both lying across the couch, with her head now tucked into the crook of my neck, and fall asleep to the sound of Georgia snoring.

Seven

GEORGIA

"What are you doing?" Chase asks, stepping into my bathroom. We've just gotten back from having breakfast and going for a walk on the pier and are hanging out until we have to head over to Lexi and Alec's place for the barbeque. "And why do you look like an alien who invaded Earth?"

I glance at him through the mirror and laugh. "I'm giving myself a facial. Want one?" It's meant as a joke, but I shouldn't be surprised when Chase shrugs and steps into the bathroom.

"Sure, will it make my face all smooth?"

"As a baby's butt," I joke.

"I've never felt a baby's butt," he says, taking the tube of the face mud. "What do I do?"

"First, wash your face with warm water."

He does as I say, then turns to me. "Now what?"

"Now, this..." I squirt a glob out and smear it across his

forehead, down the center of his nose, and along the tops of his cheeks. He has scruff along his cheeks and jaw, so I don't bother putting any there.

"Put it all over," he says, going cross-eyed as he tries to look down. "Maybe it'll make my beard soft too."

"Okay." I snort.

When I've covered his face completely, he looks in the mirror and smiles. "Take a picture with me."

"What?" I squeak. "No!"

"Yes," he says, pulling his arm around my neck and bringing me in front of him. He grabs his phone from the pocket of his sweats and snaps a picture. "This is totally Instagram worthy."

He types into his phone. "What's your name on there? I can't find you."

"I only have one for my business. I never really do anything worth posting..." And I don't exactly have many friends to follow or who would follow me.

"We need to change that. You're hanging out with me now. Everything we do is worth posting."

I shake my head and laugh. He's such a cocky ass. *And sweet, and sexy, and the perfect human bed*, I think to myself, remembering this morning when I woke up and was lying on the couch in the comfort of his arms, both of us wrapped up in a blanket like we were burritos. He opened his eyes and smiled and my heart damn near stopped in my chest. I've never fallen asleep with a man before, but it's something I definitely want to do again. Too bad it won't be with Chase since he's off-limits... The thought feels like lead settling in my belly. Do other guys cuddle the way Chase does? Are their arms as strong and comforting? I guess there's only one way to find out—actually get out and meet someone.

"It's as hard as cement," Chase says, poking at his face while he stretches his mouth open and closed, making the mud crack.

"That means it's ready to be washed off," I tell him through a laugh. Hanging out with Chase is never boring. I hope whoever I meet is fun like him. I can't remember laughing as much as I have since I've been hanging out with him the last few days.

"We should go swimming."

"I'm not sure the association will be happy with us rinsing our faces off in their pool."

Chase cracks up. "After we rinse off. We have a few hours before we have to go to your sister's for the barbeque." He grabs a couple of washcloths and dips them under the water, then hands one to me.

"Wow," he says, admiring his face once the mud mask is all off. "You're right. My face is smooth. Now, get a suit on, so we can go swimming."

I give him a two-finger salute and walk out of the bathroom. "Yes, sir!"

"That's what I like to hear," he says, following up his words with a hard slap to my ass.

"Ow!" I mock glare. "Keep your hands to yourself, or I'll slap you back."

"Don't tease me," he jokes with a wink.

After I'm in my bathing suit and cover-up, I meet Chase in the living room. He's sporting a pair of black board shorts and is shirtless, with a towel slung over his shoulder. I try to ignore how solid his body is, but it's so damn hard—pun not intended. Alec and Robert are the only two guys I've really paid attention to recently. And while Alec is like all muscular, and Robert was all... not, Chase is perfect. It's obvious he takes care of himself.

"Ready?" he asks, a smirk splayed across his lips.

Ugh, he totally caught me checking him out. I really need to stop doing that.

"Yep."

We walk down to the pool, and since this complex is mostly people in their twenties and thirties, there are a few people lying out, and a couple in the pool, but other than that, it's quiet.

We grab two available lounge chairs, and Chase throws his towel onto his, kicking his Nike slides off.

I take a deep breath and pull my cover-up over my head. I usually only wear my bikini when it's just Lexi and me at our parents' pool and we're lying out and tanning—well, I'm tanning, Lexi just burns. When we go to the beach or pool with other people, I tend to wear my one-piece or tankini. I don't know why. Maybe it's because I've never been comfortable with anyone paying attention to me, but now... it's time I made some changes. The other night at the club when I was dressed up, I felt good... sexy. And not because guys were checking me out, but because I felt pretty and feminine. I go jogging several times a week and have a nice body, so why cover it up all the time?

When my bikini-clad body is exposed, I glance down to make sure all the important parts are covered, and when I look back up, Chase is staring at me—and not like a friend.

"Is that new?" he asks, his voice gravelly. I know we're just friends, but I like that I have the ability to make his voice change. I've spent years hiding, and Robert barely paid attention to me. And with that thought, I vow to stop thinking about Robert. He's in the past and doesn't deserve a place in my present or future thoughts.

"No, I just don't usually wear it. Wanna swim laps?"

Chase clears his throat. "Yeah, sounds good."

Enjoying the fact that he's shocked at my bikini, I saunter past him, swaying my hips. I know I'm playing with fire, but the way Chase looks at me—even if he doesn't want to—makes me feel confident and sexy.

"So, it's like that, huh?" he calls after me.

I don't turn around, so when strong arms cage me in from behind, I shriek. "Chase!" I yell. "What are—" But before I can finish my sentence, he's hauling me over his shoulder, fireman style—pun intended—and running toward the pool. He leaps— yes, with my one-hundred-and-thirty-five-pound ass in his arms, he leaps—and drops us into the cool water.

When I pop up, pushing my wet hair out of my face, I lock eyes with him. "You're a dead man," I warn him.

"You'll have to catch me first," he taunts, taking off toward the deep end with me following after.

We spend the next couple hours swimming and messing around in the water. We swim laps and race, and then spend some time in the hot tub, until Chase reminds me if we're going to get to my sister's on time, we need to get out soon.

After I'm done showering and getting dressed, I check my emails, finding several from clients requesting work. Usually I don't have more than a couple, but as I scroll, finding one client who wants to know if I'm okay since I didn't respond within a few hours, I'm shocked by how behind I am. I never get this behind.

I keep scrolling and see I haven't checked my emails in a few days. I've been so busy with Chase I haven't had time to get work done.

I should probably feel guilty about that, but honestly, I don't. It felt good to get out and have a life. And the entire time—aside from that moment at the club—I didn't feel stressed. I make a mental note to do this more often. Maybe not with Chase, since eventually he'll want to go back to hooking up with women, but with myself. Lexi might be busy, but that doesn't mean I have to be holed up. It's time I find a life for myself.

"OH MY GOODNESS! LET ME SEE MY NIECE!" I SAY, snatching Abigail from Alec's arms. She's five months old and so freaking plump and adorable. I inhale her sweet scent and my heart skyrockets out of my chest.

"I missed you so much," I tell her, even though it's only been a little over a week since I've seen her. The one time I stopped by the gallery to see Lexi, Abigail was home with Alec since he was off work.

I sit us on the floor, so we can play with her toys. She smiles brightly and coos as she drops to her knees and makes like she's going to crawl away.

"Is she crawling?" I ask in amazement over how quickly she's growing up. One day she was this tiny little helpless baby and now she's giggling and cooing and moving all around.

"Not yet," Lexi says, sitting next to me. "We think she will be soon. She rocks on her knees, but doesn't actually go anywhere yet."

"She's so precious," I tell her, running my fingers through Abigail's soft baby hair.

"She is," Lexi agrees. "Can I talk to you for a second?"

I glance over at her serious face. "Yeah, sure."

"Outside?"

"Okay."

She tells Alec we'll be back, and then we head out to her backyard. The second the door opens, the smell of saltwater hits my senses. It's been a while since I've been to the beach. I should ask Chase if he wants to go soon. The thought immediately has me mentally berating myself. He probably has other friends he wants to hang out with. I can't monopolize all his time.

"What's up?" I ask, having a seat on one of her lounge chairs.

"Chase texted me yesterday."

"Okay."

"He implied maybe something was wrong... between us, I think. Afterward, he kind of took it back, but I think he only did that so he wouldn't get in the middle. Is everything okay between us?"

A part of me thinks it's really sweet that Chase texted Lexi, but another part of me really wishes he had left it alone. I didn't confide in him for him to tell Lexi.

"We're fine. I don't know what Chase said, but I was just having a bad moment, and—"

"Georgia, please don't lie to me, or play it off."

"Look, I was upset that you bailed a couple times. I hadn't seen you in a while and I missed you. It's stupid and I vented to Chase, but it's not your problem. I was honestly just having a bad moment."

Lexi's mouth twists into a frown. "I'm sorry," she says, taking my hands in hers. "I'm still adjusting to everything and—"

"You don't have to explain yourself. I'm happy for you. You found the love of your life, found your calling with the art gallery, and you have a beautiful baby..."

"Finish your sentence."

Tears fill my eyes, and I try and fail to blink them away. "And it's everything I want," I breathe.

"Oh, Georgia." Lexi pulls me into her arms and hugs me tightly. "You will have all of that. You already have the career of your dreams, and you're the reason why I even have the gallery. You just have to get out there so you can find someone to share your life with. It will happen."

Her words mimic my earlier thoughts. In order for it to happen, I have to get out and make it happen. I'm not going to meet anyone sitting in my room. The other night at the club was a little hard, but I think the more I go, the easier it'll get. I've just spent so many years staying away from huge gatherings, I've gotten used to being alone, or being with only my family.

"And as for us," she says, pulling back. "I'm sorry for not making more of an effort."

"You have a lot going on. Chase shouldn't have said anything. I should be understanding of your new life."

"No," she argues. "You're my sister, my best friend. Don't make excuses for me. I've been a shitty sister and that's going to change."

"It's okay. I promise."

We go back inside and a little while later our parents show up. Shortly after, our brother, Max, arrives with Ricco, introducing him as his boyfriend. It's been a long time coming. Everyone congratulates them and then Alec and my dad get started on the grill—the rest of the guys joining them outside.

"How's everything coming along for the opening?" Mom asks Lexi, referring to the art gallery that's scheduled to open soon.

"It's going good," Lexi says. "I met with the event coordinator and she's taking care of everything, thank goodness. I can handle the art, but everything else is out of my area of expertise. I hired a manager too, so that will help."

"If you need anything, please let me know," Mom tells her. "I'm so proud of you. You really have found your place in this world."

Lexi smiles. "Thank you. I think as soon as Abigail starts sleeping through the night, it will be a little easier."

"She's still waking up?" Mom asks.

"Only a couple times, and now it's more out of routine than to eat. The women in that moms' group I'm in said to let her cry it out, but I just can't do it."

"You have to do what's best for you and your daughter," Mom says. "I remember when Georgia was little and..." She trails off, realizing she was about to mention the time before she met Lexi's dad. She doesn't like to talk about those times. She was married to my biological father and from the little I know, he wasn't a good man. After she was with Tristan, he went after her. They fought and she ended up shooting him in self-defense.

"Anyway." She clears her throat. "People will give you their opinions, but at the end of the day, Alec and you are her parents and decide what's best."

"I agree," Alec says, walking in and sitting next to Lexi. "If we want to let Abigail lie with us at five in the morning, while she kicks the shit out of my ribs, then we can do that."

Everyone laughs, and Lexi groans. "I might've started a bad habit. I was just so tired and our bed is so comfortable."

"And Abigail agrees," Alec says with a wink.

"And how are you doing?" Mom asks, turning her attention to me.

"Good."

She raises a single brow, silently saying, *"You're going to have to give me more than that."*

"I'm okay, I promise," I insist. "Just working..."

"You've been doing more than that," Chase says, walking in with a tray of burgers. "We went to get manis and pedis the other day, and then lunch. We went dancing at Club Illusion the other night, went to a bonfire Friday night, went to the farmer's market yesterday... Made homemade flatbread and watched way too many of those Paul Walker movies. We even went swimming and did facials this morning. You should feel my skin... Smooth as a baby's ass." He rubs his hand down his face, and I giggle, remembering the facials we did this morning. He doesn't even know what a baby's bottom feels like...

At the same time, Lexi and Mom both whip their heads around to look at me. "You did all that?" Lexi asks. "I knew about the nails, but I didn't know you were out painting the damn town red."

"I'm the new Lexi," Chase says. "Only manlier and sexier, and way more fun." He winks at me, and I can't help but laugh.

"I'd hardly call it painting the town... I was missing you and Chase got me out of the house." I pray my face isn't showing any of the feelings I'm catching toward him. I have to keep reminding myself we're just friends, but it's hard when I already started developing feelings for him before he pulled the brakes.

Lexi gives me a speculative look, not taking her eyes off me for several long seconds. "We definitely need to have a sister day soon."

I force a smile, remembering when every day was a sister day. Now we have to plan one because everything is changing, and I need to accept that.

It's time to find my perfect path.

CHASE

"So, you want to tell me what's going on with you and Georgia?" Alec asks, jumping off the treadmill and walking over to where I'm lifting weights. He grabs a paper towel from the nearby dispenser and wipes down his face. When we're not putting out fires, we're usually either working out, eating, doing chores, or sleeping.

I set the weights down and walk over to the legs station. The gym here isn't big, but it has everything we need to get a good workout in while we're on shift.

"What do you mean?" I ask, playing dumb. I know damn well he's about to hit me the third degree. Alec's been friends with Georgia their entire life, and he's just as protective of her as he is of his wife.

"You know what I mean." He presses his hand against the leg weight so I can't open it. "You took her out to a club, to hang out at Carter's bonfire. Lexi's worried."

NIKKI ASH

"Lexi needs to focus on herself." I don't mean for the words to come out as harsh as they do, but it is what it is. The entire reason I was hanging out with Georgia to begin with was because of Lexi.

"Seriously? What's your problem with my wife?"

"I don't have a problem with your wife," I tell him, standing back up since I'm apparently not going to finish my workout. "My problem is the fact that Georgia was in tears because she misses her sister so much."

Alec's face falls. "We offered for her to move in with us."

"And you really believe Georgia would do that?" I've only known her for a short time and even I know that's not how she rolls. "I get it, you and Lexi finally got together. You're happy and in love and you have a baby, but maybe you need to remember who you guys were before. Lexi and Georgia were stuck at the hip. Now... well, shit's changed."

"And so, what? You swooped in and gave her your shoulder to cry on?" Alec accuses.

"We hung out... as *friends*. She's actually a lot of fun to be around when she's not holed up in her room."

"And that's all it is?" he questions. "Friends?"

"That's it." I raise a brow, daring him to argue.

"Yo, Chase, get your ass out here," Luke yells. "You have a visitor."

Grabbing my towel off the bench, I wrap it around my neck and walk out to see who's here for me, with Alec following after. When I get to the main area, Georgia, dressed in another pair of tiny shorts—this time cut-off—and a hoodie with the logo of her dad's MMA gym on the front, is standing in the middle of the room holding a metal pan of some sort in her hands. Her hair is up in a messy bun and she's sporting her sexy librarian glasses.

She's tan from us being in the sun yesterday, and her face is makeup free aside from her lips being glossy. Jesus, she looks fucking stunning... and I'm so screwed.

"Hey, what are you doing here?" I ask, stepping over to her.

"I brought this for you guys." She shrugs a shoulder and her mouth quirks up into a shy smile.

I take the pan, which upon closer inspection is the kind you use to cook and store food in, and set it on our table. It seats six people, so all the guys on shift can eat together. When I lift the foil, steam wafts out, along with the smell of meat and cheese.

"Holy shit," Carter says, coming over. "Is that lasagna?" He inhales and rubs his stomach. "That shit smells good."

"Yep," Georgia says. "I even made the sauce homemade with the tomatoes and veggies we bought at the farmer's market."

"That better be for everyone," Alec says, sidling up next to Georgia and throwing his arm over the back of her shoulders. My fingers tingle, wanting to push his arm off her and wrap my own around her. It's stupid. He's married to her sister, and we're only friends... But, even knowing all that, it doesn't change my reaction.

"Your sister can't cook, so it's been takeout or delivery every day," Alec adds.

"It's for everyone," she says softly, earning a kiss to her cheek from Alec. I damn near growl, wanting his hands and mouth off her.

"I hope it's good." She grabs a bag from the ground I didn't notice before and pulls out parmesan cheese and rolls. "These are homemade too," she boasts.

"Damn, Georgia, go big or go home, huh?" I joke, grabbing the plates and silverware and bringing them over.

"Eh... I think I'd much rather be at home," she says, scrunching up her nose. "It's safe there."

The guys all chuckle because she's fucking adorable, and my stomach knots. I have to remind myself she's not mine and we're better off as friends. Realistically, I know one day I'm going to have to let someone in, but I'm just not ready yet. And not with someone as sweet and innocent as Georgia. I come from a fucked up world and she was raised sheltered, always taken care of. We're too different and we'd never work. Then again, Victoria and I were from the same world and we didn't work either...

"Stay and eat with us," Scott says, pulling out a chair for Georgia. Alec has thankfully dropped his arm and is cutting the lasagna into pieces. Thomas grabs another chair and brings it to the table, so all seven of us can sit together.

"Are you sure?" Georgia asks. "I don't want to intrude."

"You're probably the most welcome person here," Luke jokes, taking a bite of his food. He chews and swallows and groans. "Damn, woman. Marry me right now."

Georgia snorts a laugh, and Alec glares, ever the protective pseudo brother.

"Is it good?" she asks.

"It's fucking delicious," Thomas says through a mouthful. "I'm going to need you to send me this recipe so I can have Hilary make it.

"No way." Luke shakes his head. "It's a secret recipe and my wife can only make it for me." He winks at Georgia and her face turns a light shade of pink.

"Why don't you take it down a notch," I growl at him, annoyed as fuck. Georgia and Alec both look at me. Alec's brow is raised and Georgia is frowning.

"I'm just saying, if you scare her off, she won't bring us any more food," I say, trying to play it off. All the guys are looking at me, so I dive into my food, ignoring all their stares.

When the food hits my tongue, the heavenly taste of meat and tomato and cheese hits my senses. Luke and Thomas were right. This lasagna is damn good.

"What do you think?" Georgia asks me.

"It's delicious. Even better than the flatbread we made last night." I smile at her, and she beams. In the background, Alec's glaring and Luke is smirking.

Just friends, I remind myself. That's all we can be.

When we're done eating, since it's Luke's day to do the dishes, I show Georgia around the station. Where we work out, sleep, shower. Our gaming room...

"So," she says slowly as I walk her over to her truck. "Seeing

79

Lexi and Alec and Abigail yesterday got me thinking about my future..."

My breath hitches wondering where she's going with this...

"I have my career, but I don't have anyone to share my life with," she continues, and I swear I stop breathing altogether. Is she about to ask me out? And why doesn't the thought have me wanting to run? I'm not ready. I should be thinking of a reason to bolt. Coming up with an excuse as to why I have to say no.

"I can't find anyone if I'm at home, so I want to get out... put myself out there. I want to one day get married and have babies, find a man I can cook for." She smiles softly, and I wait with bated breath for her to finish. Yes is at the tip of my tongue. It shouldn't be, but it is.

"I was wondering if..." She bites down on her bottom lip nervously. "Would you be my wingman?"

I'm about to blurt out yes, when it hits me... "Your wingman?" I ask, confused.

"Yeah. You like going to the clubs and picking up women, you know all the happening places in LA... And I don't really have any friends to go out with. I promise not to mess with your game." She laughs, and the melodic sound hits me like an arrow straight in the chest.

Jesus, I'm such a dumbass. She wants me to help her find a guy, not be her guy. It's probably for the best anyway. What the hell was I thinking?

"Yeah," I choke out, plastering a smile on my face. "I can be your wingman."

"Yay!" She jumps up and down and then throws her arms around my neck. "Thank you! I'm going to go shopping with my mom tomorrow. So tomorrow night, since you're off, want to go out?"

"Sounds good."

"Have a good night at work," she says, jumping into her truck.

"See ya." I wave as she drives away.

"So, just friends, huh?" Alec says, stepping up next to me as I watch her drive her monster truck away.

"Yep." I turn on my heel and walk back inside.

"You sure about that? Because when Luke mentioned—"

"Just friends," I bite out, cutting him off. "She even asked me to be her wingman."

"Her what?" Alec laughs.

"Her wingman. She wants to go out and find her Mr. Perfect, so she can marry said Mr. Perfect and move into a perfect house and have tons of perfect little babies running around." Yes, I'm aware of how bitter I sound.

Alec eyes me for a long moment then sighs. "I can't believe I'm even going to say this, but if you like her why don't you just tell her? It's obvious you do, and based on the way she blushed when you complimented her cooking, I would say the feeling is mutual."

Because it's not that easy... Because she's rich and comes from a great family and wants this perfect fucking life that I'm not capable of giving her. What do I even have to offer a woman like her? Not a damn thing.

"We're just friends," I tell him in a tone that says to drop it. "I'm going to take a shower."

Just as I'm walking toward the bathroom, the tone sounds through the station. I grab the receiver and take down the information from dispatch.

The six of us jump into the engine and take off to the location. And for the next couple hours, while we put out the fire, I push the thoughts of Georgia out of my mind and the fact that in twenty-four hours I'm supposed to help her find her perfect fucking guy.

Nine

GEORGIA

I can do this. I can do this. I can do this. Those are the four words I keep repeating to myself as Chase and I walk through the Z Lounge. According to Chase, it's a little more down to earth. Instead of a deejay, they have live music. But as we walk through the main area toward the bar, I'm not sure Chase's definition of down to earth is the same as mine because the music is thumping so loud it's vibrating the floor, and the bodies—lots of bodies—are grinding against one another to the beat.

Maybe this isn't the way for me to meet someone. Surely, a club—or in this case, a lounge—can't be the only way to meet the person you hope to spend your life with. There has to be other ways. Like online... I cringe at the thought. I created a profile on one of those dating websites once after Mason, Alec's stepdad—who is also my dad's best friend and, as I mentioned before, my godfather—said he got together with Alec's mom through chatting on a dating site. I don't know if the times have changed, but the number of creepy men was astounding and almost convinced me to switch teams. So, no, a dating site probably isn't the way to go. But I don't think this is either.

When we get to the bar, Chase orders himself a beer and me a lemon drop, then we go in search of a booth. They're all taken, but we find a table with two chairs open, so we have a seat. Making sure my new little black dress doesn't ride up and expose my goods, I scoot onto the seat carefully.

"So, what's the game plan?" Chase asks, taking a drink of his beer. His hazel eyes meet mine, and my belly clenches. He's so ruggedly handsome. He hasn't shaved in a while, so his scruff is now practically a full beard. Idly, I wonder what it would feel like between my legs. I read it once in a book and at the time didn't get it, but now, looking at Chase, I kind of do.

"I don't know!" I shout nervously over the music as I try to remove the image of Chase's face from between my legs. "You're an expert at this," I joke. "How do you get all the women you do?"

I expect Chase to laugh, but instead he frowns and takes another sip of his beer. Is it possible I offended him? I don't know why. He's always owned up to sleeping around. And I'm not judging him. Not now that I know why he does it. He was hurt. And one day he'll meet a woman who will help him heal. But until then, he doesn't want to be alone. And I get that. Because I'm so damn tired of being alone.

"Hey, are you mad at me? I was only joking."

"No," he says, putting his beer down. "But I don't go after women." He shrugs. "They come to me."

I swallow thickly. The women go after him... Of course they do. Because most women aren't afraid to go after what they want. I down the rest of my drink in one swallow and slam my glass down.

"Then that's what I'll do," I tell him, standing.

"What?" He looks at me like I'm crazy, and I probably am. But so was Lexi once upon a time, and unlike me, she found her perfect path. Now it's my turn.

"I'm going to go to the guys." I glance around and spot a cluster of men at the bar. "And I'll start by buying them a drink." Just like guys do when they want a woman.

"Whoa, wait," Chase says. "Maybe you should think about this first."

"Why? So I can second-guess myself and then freak out and bail? No way."

"No." He wraps his fingers around my forearms to stop me. "Because the women who approach me are looking to fuck. They're desperate."

"So, what do I do then?" Why does meeting someone have to be so damn difficult?

"Let the guy come to you."

"Okay..."

We return to the table, and Chase goes back to his beer while I look around. There are a lot of different people here. Couples dancing, women dancing with women. Men, who look similar to

Chase, nursing a beer. I look at one man in particular. He's sitting in a booth next to a woman. They're not talking, both just people watching like Chase and I are... and it hits me.

"How is anyone going to know I'm available?"

"Huh?" he asks, a V forming in the center of his brows.

"How is anyone going to know I'm available?" I repeat.

"I heard you. What do you mean?"

"Well, we've been sitting here for a little while and no women have approached you... It's probably because we're sitting together. They're assuming we're together. Maybe we should separate? Or I should come back when Lexi can join me." I clearly didn't think this whole thing through. If Lexi were here, guys would know I'm single.

"How about you stop focusing on meeting a guy and we dance?" Chase suggests, standing and taking my hand.

"But—" My argument is thwarted the second Chase pulls me into his arms and forces my hands to wrap around his neck. His hands slide down my sides and land on the small of my back. He bends and leans in so his face is close to mine. I can feel his warm breath against my ear, and it sends chills racing down my spine.

"You look beautiful tonight," he murmurs, pulling me in closer to him. My heart accelerates at his compliment. I should be focusing on finding a guy to get to know, but suddenly all I want to do is dance with Chase.

And that's exactly what we spend the next several songs doing. We're both sweaty—from the packed crowd, the hot lights, and the dancing—but I don't even consider leaving the dance floor—or Chase's arms—until he suggests we take a break and get a drink.

I follow him off the floor and over to the packed bar. "Do you want a lemon drop or water?" he asks.

"Water." I'm thirsty from all that dancing and alcohol isn't going to quench my thirst.

"Okay, be right back," he says, before cutting into the crowd.

I'm standing by myself for a few minutes, people watching, when a male voice speaks close to my ear. "Are you single?"

I twirl around and come face to face with a blond-haired, blue-eyed man. He's dressed in a white button-down collar shirt with his sleeves rolled up to his elbows and dark wash jeans. He's cute, and when his lip tugs up into a half smirk, he's even cuter.

I open my mouth to tell him I'm here with someone when I remember why I'm here... and that even though I was just dancing with Chase, I'm not here with him. "I am."

"Patrick," he says, extending his hand like a gentleman.

"Georgia," I say back, shaking his hand.

"Can I buy you a drink, Georgia?" he asks, his hand still holding mine.

"She already has a drink," a deep voice says before I can answer.

Patrick glances between Chase and me, and I can't see Chase because he's slightly behind me, but whatever he sees causes him to jump to conclusions, because the next thing I know, he's nodding and bowing out before I can explain.

"Hey!" I swivel around and slap Chase on the chest.

"What?" He hands me a bottled water.

"You totally just...cockblocked me!" Mind you, I don't have a cock, and I had no intention of having sex with that guy, but I don't know how else to describe what he just did.

"That guy looks like a douche," Chase says, shrugging and cracking open his water. He brings the bottle up to his lips and tips his head back, swallowing the entire bottle in one long guzzle.

"How would you know?" I ask, trying to sound annoyed but kind of distracted by the way his Adam's apple bobs up and down while he drinks.

"I could just tell."

"Well, my theory is correct. As soon as you were gone, he came over. Going out just the two of us obviously isn't the best idea."

Chase doesn't agree or disagree. "Want to dance some more?"

Well, tonight's apparently a bust anyway, and Chase is a good dancer... "Sure."

I WALK THROUGH THE ART GALLERY, AMAZED AND IN awe of the transformation. What was once a vacant, run-down building in the Arts district, is now filled with beautiful art from various artists, including Lexi. Lexi's plan is for the gallery to cater to all types of art, but every month a different theme and artist will be featured. A large portion of the proceeds will go toward raising money to help autistic children and adults, especially those who are low income or homeless.

I stop at a piece I haven't seen before and smile. On what looks like an eight by ten canvas, is a graffitied drawing of a woman standing with her back to the world, staring out at the ocean. She's holding her surfboard in one hand and her daughter's hand in the other. Seeing Lexi's art on display fills my heart with warmth. One day, someone will buy this painting and hang it up in their home or office. My sister's talent will finally be shared with the world—and not just in the form of graffiti on building walls.

"Lexi's sister," Aiden says, calling me over. "I painted this."

"Wow. It's beautiful."

Aiden is the reason this gallery came about. He's twenty-four years old and autistic. His stepdad used to hurt his mom and him and when he turned eighteen they kicked him out. He was homeless, living on the streets. Every day my sister would make sure he was taken care of the best she could, but she felt helpless. They became close and she wanted to save him. Now, he's living in an assisted living facility and works at the gallery.

"Thank you, Lexi's sister," he says, turning back to his painting. Lexi has various artists coming in to paint the gallery. Instead of it feeling stuffy like many do, she wants it to feel like you're immersed in the art.

"I called you last night," Lexi says, walking out with Abigail on her hip. The second she sees me, a bright smile lights her face, making my heart skip a beat.

"I was out with Chase." I take Abigail from Lexi and give her kisses. "I missed you, sweet girl." We move into her office and sit on her couch.

"You and Chase are close, huh?" Lexi asks, raising a brow.

"He was supposed to be my wingman." I roll my eyes. "Of course every guy just assumed we were together."

"And how about the women?"

"They were hot, but I don't swing that way." I wink playfully, making Lexi laugh.

"I meant for Chase."

"He didn't get hit on. We had a drink and danced. One guy actually did approach me, but Chase scared him off, saying he looked like a douche."

"Did he...?" Lexi's mouth twists contemplatively.

"Yeah, so now I'm not sure how I'm going to meet someone. I don't really have girlfriends, and you're busy being a mom to this cute little angel." I lift Abigail up and blow raspberries on her belly.

"I could have Mom watch her. It's been a while since I've been out."

"I wouldn't ask you to do that." I wave her off. "I'll eventually meet the right guy, when the time is right."

"You're not asking. It'll be fun. All these years I was waiting for you to finally go out and have a good time, and now that you're doing it, I'm at home." She pulls out her phone.

"Hey, Mom," she says. "Georgia is here and we were talking about going out one night this week..." She laughs. "Yes, that's why

I was calling... Okay, love you, bye."

She hangs up. "I think I just made her life," she jokes. "She's so excited to take Abigail." Lexi tends to keep her daughter close. I don't blame her, though. The way she found out she was pregnant and the months following were hard on her. I think she just feels so blessed to have her, she doesn't want to let her leave her sight.

"She's going to take her for the night since Alec is working." She grins. "This'll be fun. The Scott women are going to paint the town red!"

I crack up. "In case you forgot you're no longer a Scott."

"Pfft, semantics. I'll always be a Scott. I'm excited for tonight."

"Me too. I feel like I'm finally making strides to overcome my social anxiety. I didn't freak out at all last night when Chase and I were out."

"Maybe Chase has the right touch." She winks dramatically.

"Or maybe I'm just finally getting past my issues." I shrug, refusing to acknowledge that she may be right. I thought the same thing last night in bed before I pushed it to the side and fell asleep.

I hand her back Abigail. "Want to come over and we can get ready together?"

"Yes." Lexi beams. "This is so exciting. It's like my little Georgia is all grown up. I get to pick out your outfit and do your makeup."

"Sounds good." I stand and so does she. "I'll see you tonight. I'm making the guys dinner... this new fettucine recipe I found and want to try out. I'll save some for us."

"Yeah, I heard about your fabulous lasagna." Lexi side-eyes me.

"Alec said we should hire you to cook." She rolls her eyes. "He won't let me use the oven when he's not home. He said the guys at the station we're zoned to won't be as nice when the neighbors call."

"That's funny," I say with a laugh. "Hey, maybe I should open a restaurant," I joke.

"You made one meal," Lexi deadpans. "I would make a few more dishes before you put on your official chef hat."

I spend the rest of the morning making the dish, and once it's done, I have to admit, I'm a damn good cook. After putting some aside for Lexi and me for dinner, I put the remainder of the pasta into one container and the homemade biscuits I made into another one, and then head over to the station.

"Oh, shit," Carter says as I walk up to the entrance. "Is that food you're carrying?" He grabs the containers from me.

"It is, but before you get too excited, you better taste it to make sure it's good."

"Thought I was your taste tester," Chase says, walking out from nowhere. His hair is wet like he just showered, and he's in the middle of pulling his shirt over his head, so his hard body is still on display. The shirt comes down and I internally pout.

Or at least I think I do...

Chase smirks, as if he knows exactly what I'm thinking, and my cheeks heat up.

"You are the taste tester," I tell him, "but you have to be a good boy and share." I playfully pat him on his stomach and note just how hard his abs are.

The other guys hear us and join in, grabbing plates and silverware. I open the containers and distribute some onto each of their plates. Chase is the first to take a bite, and I swear his eyes roll to the back of his head.

"It's official, Georgia," he says. "You're an honorary member of station 115."

I laugh. "And what does an honorary member get?"

"The right to cook for us forever," he says with a smile, while shoving more food into his mouth.

"Wow, I'm so lucky," I say, sarcasm dripping in my words. "But you better enjoy it while you can, because tonight Lexi and I are going out. She's going to be my wing-woman, and when I meet the man of my dreams, I'll be too busy cooking for him to cook for you guys."

Carter, Thomas, and Luke laugh, but Alec and Chase don't.

"What do you mean you're going out tonight?" Chase asks, dropping his fork onto his plate.

"Mom's going to watch Abigail. We're going to hit the clubs. I'm hoping she'll be a better wing-woman than you."

Alec groans. "I think you guys should wait until tomorrow night. We can all go, make it a group thing."

"I agree," Chase adds.

"I'm down," Luke says.

"Me too," Carter agrees.

"Then it's settled," Alec says before I can even argue. "I'll let

Lexi know. Tomorrow night we'll all go out." What the hell just happened? I went from planning a girls' night out with my sister to it being turned into a group hang?

"Want some pasta?" Chase offers, like they didn't just railroad my plans.

"No." I pout. "I have some at home. But you enjoy. I need to go."

"You just got here," Chase notes. "Stay a while."

"I have work to do. Bye!" I give him a false smile, and after saying bye to the other guys, take off, annoyed as hell at the turn of events.

Ten

CHASE

"Did you see how pissed she was when she left?" Luke says with a shake of his head.

"Yeah, but oh well," I tell him. "Those women are crazy if they think we're going to let them go out without us."

"Yeah," Alec agrees with a sigh. I'd bet he's thinking about the shit that went down last year with Lexi. She was alone on the beach and was attacked. It was a fucked up situation and since then, he hasn't let her out of his sight other than to go to work. And I don't blame him. Underneath the thin layer of wealth and glamour, LA is a scary fucking place. I know that firsthand.

The rest of the shift flies by. We thankfully don't have any major fires—only one incident where a woman smelled gas, and after checking it out, we caught a leak—and at eight o'clock we change shifts. The guys all agree to meet at Boulevard, a new club that recently opened that Luke's brother is the bouncer at.

When I walk in the door, Georgia is standing in the kitchen in a racerback tank and yoga pants. She's dancing to whatever music is blasting in her headphones and shaking her peach of an ass while she blends something together.

I probably shouldn't do it, but I can't help myself as I quickly approach her and wrap my arms around her to scare her.

She shrieks, and her hand flings around to push me away. When she does this, the top to the blender flies off and pink explodes everywhere.

"Oh my God!" she squeals, quickly grabbing the top and shoving it back on the blender before shutting it off. "Chase!" She turns back around and slaps my chest. We're both covered in...

"What is this?" I swipe my finger across her cheek and pop it into my mouth. "Mm, strawberry shake?"

"I found a healthy recipe. I was making one before I go for a run. It's a protein shake."

"Well, it tastes delicious."

She glares. "I wouldn't know."

I swipe some more, this time off her neck, and push my finger past her lips. "Good, right?"

Her tongue darts out and swirls around the tip of my finger, and my eyes go straight to her mouth, imagining a different appendage of mine is in between her lips.

Her eyes go wide, as if just realizing what I did, and pulls her face back, her lips gliding off my finger and leaving it glistening wet.

MY KIND OF PERFECT

She clears her throat. "Yeah, it's good. I need to clean this up."

"I'll help," I croak, sounding like a horny fucking teenager. When she swivels around, I quickly adjust myself and think of old, smelly men, so my semi goes down.

We get the area cleaned up, and since there's still plenty of smoothie left, she pours us each some into a cup. The shake is delicious, but if I'm honest, the entire time I'm drinking it, I'm wishing I were licking it off her body.

Afterward, she invites me to join her on her jog. We spend the morning running to the pier, walking along the beach, and then run back.

"We should do this every day I'm off," I tell her when we get home.

"For sure. I'm going to shower. Alec and Lexi are coming over for dinner before we go out, and I'm making a new dish. I need to do some work stuff, but after, want to watch a movie?"

"Sounds perfect."

The more time I spend with her, the more time I *want* to spend with her. It's crazy that we spent months living together and I never bothered to get to know her.

It's because you were too busy fucking anything with a vagina to get over your ex-wife...

And now that I'm thinking about it, since the day Georgia and I started hanging out, I haven't even thought about hooking up with any women, nor have I dwelled on my divorce. For the first time it feels like I'm actually moving forward. I'm no longer bitter toward the way things ended, or the years I felt were wasted. With Georgia, I'm enjoying myself again. And not in the fake way I do when I stick my dick into some woman I don't know, but in a real way. Georgia and I laugh together, talk about shit. It's nice having someone to connect with.

I'm cleaning up my room, when my phone rings. "Hello," I answer without looking to see who's on the other end.

"Chase, I need you."

I close my eyes, listening to her slurred words. It's my mom, and she's drunk. Which makes no sense because the only time she ever gets drunk is... Shit! I pull the calendar up on my phone and the realization of what today is has sharp pains shooting through my chest. How could I forget?

"I'll be right there," I tell her before hanging up, grabbing my keys, and flying out the door. My mom and I aren't as close as I wish we were, but she's still my mom, and I love her and would do anything for her.

About fifteen minutes later, I arrive at my childhood home. It's located in a rougher part of LA, where the movies and television shows don't show because people would realize that the majority of LA isn't really all that glamorous.

Parking my vehicle in her driveway, I run up to the front door, and without knocking, go inside. I find my mom lying in her room with a bottle of vodka in her hands. The room is dark and smells like sex and alcohol. I gag a couple times, then open the windows, letting the light and air in.

Ignoring the fact that her sheets are probably full of sex as well, I edge onto the bed and pull her into my arms. There are only two days a year my mom gets drunk: the day my sister was born, and the day she died.

"Chase," she slurs. "You came."

"Of course I came," I tell her, cursing myself for forgetting the date. I always make it a point to visit my mom the night before and spend the night so she doesn't get like this. If I'm not here to stop her, she'll drink until she's sick and has to be hospitalized—it's happened more than once.

"I miss her so much," she cries. Her shoulders begin to shake, and when I push her hair out of her face, tears are racing down her cheeks. I don't bother to wipe them away, knowing they won't stop coming until she falls asleep.

Instead, I hold her close, telling her how much I love her, because that's all she really needs. To be comforted. The day we lost my sister, we also lost my father. My mom didn't take her death well, and my father couldn't handle taking care of my mom. He turned to the bottle and eventually his drunk ass left, leaving me to pick up the pieces. A few years later, he died from kidney failure.

"She would've been thirty-one today," Mom says. "My baby never got to live her life." I do the math in my head, and she's right. Audrina overdosed when I was seventeen and she was eighteen. It's one of the reasons why I decided on my career of choice. I first got my EMT license and then joined the fire academy. I wanted to

NIKKI ASH

save people, since I couldn't save my sister.

While my mom cries into my chest, I hold her, running my fingers through her hair and trying to calm her down. As long as I'm here, she won't drink, and since she's still awake, it seems I got here before she drank too much.

I don't know how long I hold her for, but when my phone vibrates for the millionth time in my pocket, I remember that I was so worried about my mom, I forgot to tell Georgia I was leaving.

Carefully, so I don't wake my mom, I pull my phone out. The time on the phone says it's four o'clock. I've been holding my mom for several hours. My heart breaks all over again for my mom. Some people rise up after a tragic event, others drown in it. If I weren't here to hold my mom up, she would drown.

The other three hundred and sixty-three days, she handles life. She works as a waitress at a local diner—the same one she's been working at since I was little—and pays her bills. She owns the home she lives in and refuses to move elsewhere. I've begged and pleaded, but she won't leave the home where Audrina grew up. Her room is the same way it was when she died, and she won't let anyone touch a thing. I've tried to get her to see someone, to get help, but she won't. I've spoken to a few people about it, and everyone says the same thing—unless she wants to get help, I can't make her. She's not an alcoholic, she doesn't do drugs, so there's nothing I can do.

Georgia: Hey, you left...Everything okay?

Georgia: I'm worried.

Alec: Yo, where you at?

Alec: Everyone's worried. I called the station and nobody's heard from you.

Gently, I set my mom down on the bed. She stirs but stays asleep. I type out a group text to Alec and Georgia.

Me: Sorry I left in a rush. I won't be able to make it tonight.

Alec knows I had a sister who died but doesn't know the specifics, and Georgia doesn't know anything about my family, so trying to explain it all in a text isn't exactly the best way to tell them. I hate that I won't be able to be with Georgia tonight, but my mom needs me. I'm all she has.

After a brief conversation through text with Georgia and Alec, who tell me if I need anything to let them know, I tell them to have a good time and then start cleaning up the house for my mom. The place is a disaster. My mom usually keeps the house clean. Everything in it is aged, but she's always made sure to take care of what she owns. Based on the dirty dishes and empty alcohol bottles all over, I would guess she started drinking last night, probably had whatever guy she's sleeping with over, and took her pain over losing my sister out on the place.

Just as I'm finishing up, Mom comes out of her room, her eyes glossy with new tears. "I'm so sorry," she says, enveloping me in a hug. "Every birthday, every anniversary of her death, I tell myself I won't do this…"

"It's okay, Mom," I tell her, hugging her back. "You're doing the best you can."

She glances around and sighs. "Thank you for cleaning up."

"How're you feeling?"

"I'm... okay. If you don't have any plans, would you like to go to the cemetery with me?"

"Of course. Why don't you go shower and get dressed, and then I'll drive us over."

"Thank you, Chase," she says, wiping a tear that's escaped, before heading back to her room.

The drive to the cemetery is quiet, and so is the walk over to where she was buried. But once we're there, Mom starts reminiscing about the past. We spend the next few hours talking about how smart and sweet Audrina was. The truth is, she had a bright future ahead of her. Until she met Danny. He was a bad boy, and she thought he was cool. She swore they loved each other and she would do anything for him, including drugs. Mom and Dad tried to get her away from him, but it only made her want him that much more. Everyone said it was just a phase and she would get through it... Unfortunately, she died before she could.

Tests revealed the drugs she took were laced with something that caused her heart to stop. She overdosed in the living room of Danny's house, and because he was too wasted, he didn't notice. And when he finally did, it was too late.

Once we're both cried out, we decide to grab something to eat. It's late, after midnight, so I take us to a diner, where we order breakfast for dinner, which was Audrina's favorite.

"How are you doing?" Mom asks.

I pop a piece of pancake into my mouth. "I'm good. Just working...chilling. The usual."

"Any new women?" she asks with a hint of a smile.

Mom used to be close to Victoria, considered her to be a daughter, and when she started doing drugs, she was right there, trying to get her help. She never wanted Victoria to end up like Audrina. But when she found out what Victoria did... let's just say blood is thicker than water.

Now, every time we talk, she asks me if I'm seeing anyone. She's mentioned on several occasions she would love to have a grandchild. Since I'm now her only living child, I'm the only one who can give her one.

"Nope," I tell her, refusing to think about Georgia and the fact that she's probably out right now, dancing with some guy who'll ask her for her number... Because she's gorgeous and any guy would be stupid not to.

Mom eyes me, and I can tell she's about to grill me, but my phone goes off. I glance at the text from Alec, reading it several times, refusing to believe what it says. The gods wouldn't do this... not today of all days.

"Chase," Mom prompts. "Everything okay?"

"No." I shoot out of my seat and pull a couple of twenties out of my pocket to pay for our food. I don't know how much it is, but it doesn't matter.

I'm out the door and in my car in seconds, heading to Los Angeles General Hospital. My mind is racing, and my only focus is getting there, so when my mom asks, "What's going on?" it hits me that she's in the car with me. I should've dropped her off at home, but I wasn't thinking.

"A friend of mine is in the hospital. Once we get there, I'll pay for a car to take you home. I wasn't thinking."

"Oh no," she says. "That's okay. What's wrong? Who is it?"

Shit, I don't want to tell her what's wrong. She doesn't even know Georgia, but I know she'll take it hard.

"It's Georgia..."

"Your roommate?" she questions. "I never hear you talk about her." I glance over at her and swallow down my emotions, thankful my mom is here with me right now.

"We've become close... friends," I choke out, hating that fucking word. "She was brought to the hospital because—"

Before I can finish my sentence, my phone dings with an incoming text from Alec letting me know her room number.

"Is she okay?" Mom asks.

"I don't know. Let me call you a cab..."

"No." She shakes her head. "This fancy phone you gave me for Mother's Day can do that. You go, and once you know what's going on, please let me know."

She pulls me into a hug. "I love you, Chase."

I look into her eyes. "You sure you'll be okay?" It's still Audrina's birthday, and the last thing I want to do is leave my mom alone.

"Don't you dare worry about me," she says. "I promise I'm okay now. Thank you for today. Now go."

We walk to the front of the hospital together, and then after hugging one more time, I take off inside. Since I'm in the system, they let me go through without asking questions. Every step toward her room has my heart thumping outside of my chest, and by the time I get there, I'm so worked up, it's hard to breathe.

With a quick knock, I walk in and find Tristan, Charlie, Lexi, and Alec all standing around a very still, very pale Georgia. If it weren't for the heart monitor beeping, I would think she's dead. Visions of my sister surface. Her ice cold body, blue lips, pale face. Her un-beating heart.

"What the fuck happened?" I growl, barely able to contain the anger that's radiating through my veins.

Everyone's eyes swing over to me, but Tristan is the one to speak. "She was drugged."

"Yeah, I got that from Alec's text. But what. The. Fuck. Happened?"

"She was talking to this guy..." Lexi starts, but her words are garbled from her crying and she can't finish her sentence. Alec wraps his arms around her and moves her to the couch.

"She was dancing with this guy, and she started to feel sick," Alec says. "He offered to take her home, but we told him no. She was complaining of feeling hot and lightheaded, and then she dropped to the ground and starting having a seizure. The guy took off in the chaos of us calling for an ambulance. They ran tests and found GHB in her system."

Fucking GHB? "She was roofied?" My hands fist at my sides, ready to punch something. "Where is this asshole?" I will kill him, consequences be damned. There's no way another fucking murderer is getting away.

"The cops checked the cameras and are asking around, but we only know his first name—Kenny," Alec says.

"You should've been watching her!" I bark.

"I was!" Alec yells back. "You don't think I feel like shit? Of course I do!"

"Hey," Tristan says. "Shit happens. I'm pissed too, and if I ever see that fucker, he's dead, but Alec and your friends were all there. He called nine-one-one, and she's alive because of it."

I walk over to her and take her hand in mine, needing to calm myself down. I know realistically it wasn't Alec's fault, but he's the only person I can blame until I find the guy who did this to her.

Someone pushes a chair toward me, and I take it, sitting next to her. I entwine our fingers together and drop my face to her knuckles, trying to inhale her scent. She smells faintly of the perfume she wears, but mostly all I can smell is the hospital, and flashbacks from when I came to this same hospital to see Audrina surface. I try like hell to push them back. Georgia is alive. She's going to be okay—unlike my sister, who will never take another breath again.

"Damn it, Georgia," I say under my breath. "I never should've let you go out without me." Tears prick my eyes, and I swallow down my emotions. I wasn't there to save my sister all those years ago, and I wasn't there tonight to keep this from happening to Georgia.

"It still could've happened," Alec points out. "Nobody but that asshole who drugged her is to blame."

"Maybe not, but I started this. I told her to get out of the house so she could meet someone. Now look at her. She's been drugged and almost died." If I had been there, I never would've let any of those dickheads near her.

"People take shit every day and are fine," Tristan says. "Georgia just so happened to have a bad reaction."

"None of this is your fault," Charlie says, resting her hand on my shoulder. I glance up and she smiles sadly. "For years Georgia was stuck in that shell of hers. We accepted it because it's just who she was, but you got her out of the house. She's been so happy every time we talk. We even went shopping together for a dress, something we've never done. She's been cooking and baking, and she speaks so highly of you..."

I hear what they're saying, but I should've been there with her, protecting her. She's too fucking naïve, they all are. Raised with silver spoons, they don't know the bad and ugly out there. But I do, because it's what killed my sister and then pushed my father away. It's what destroyed my wife. What keeps my mom living in that shitty fucking neighborhood.

The heart monitor picks up and then Georgia's eyes flutter open. She starts coughing and wincing, and Charlie runs out to get someone.

"Chase," she croaks, looking a mixture of in pain and confused. "I... don't... feel good."

I grab a garbage can by her bed and raise it up in time for her to dry heave.

"Why isn't she throwing up?" I ask.

"She had her stomach pumped," the nurse says, walking briskly into the room. "Hello, there, Georgia, I'm Nurse Kelly. We're giving you nausea medication, but you might still feel sick. That's normal. I'll up the dose for you. Your abdominal muscles will also be sore for a few days. That's normal as well. We're giving you fluids because you're dehydrated." She goes about checking her, and Georgia, who is too weak to even talk, simply closes her eyes and nods.

We spend the next few hours watching her sleep. Alec's parents, Mila and Mason, stop by, and Alec leaves to go grab Abigail since Max, Lexi and Georgia's brother, was keeping an eye on her. But her parents, sister, and I stay.

She eventually wakes up but is groggy, and the doctor says that's normal. When she's discharged with a prescription for nausea medication and instructions to rest and drink plenty of fluids, Charlie suggests Georgia goes home with them. But of course Georgia doesn't want to be fussed over...

"I'm off until Monday," I tell them. "I can stay with her at the condo. I'll make sure she's okay." There's no way I'm letting her out of my sight.

Georgia gives me a small, grateful smile. "Thank you."

The nurse gets her into a wheelchair—per hospital rules—and I wheel her out.

"I'll go grab the car," I tell Georgia. "Be right back."

I run to where I left my car and pull it around to the entrance.

"I'll be by to check on you," Lexi says while I help Georgia into the passenger seat. She gives her a hug. "I was so scared."

"I know," Georgia tells her. "I'm sorry."

"You have nothing to be sorry about," Lexi says. "I just... all I could imagine..."

"I know," Georgia says again, knowing what she's saying without actually saying it. She could've been attacked the way Lexi was. Shit could've had a way worse ending.

"Take care of my baby," Charlie says, hugging me. "I'll be by with soup later."

"Sounds good," I tell her.

The ride home is quiet, with Georgia leaning against the window with her eyes closed. I know she's not asleep, but I don't know if she's resting or just doesn't want to talk.

Without thought, I scoop up her hand and thread her fingers through mine, needing to feel the warmth of her flesh. She's alive. Her heart is still beating. She's going to be okay.

She rolls her head toward me and briefly opens her green eyes, and like an electrical current straight to my heart, it hits me: I'm in love with Georgia Scott.

GEORGIA

"All right, we got blankets, pillows, your favorite red flavored Gatorade, some crackers for you to munch on in case you're hungry..." Chase glances around, and even though I feel like shit, I can't help but smile. I never imagined Chase to be such a good nurturer, but he is.

"Anything else?" he asks, the middle of his brows dipping in concern.

"I'm good," I assure him. "And if you have something—"

"Don't even dare finish that sentence," he says, his gaze searing into me. "The only place I want to be is right here with you. We're going to spend the next forty-eight hours binge watching whatever the hell you want while you rest and heal." His tone leaves no room for argument, so I don't.

"I'm going to shower real quick," he says. "While I do that, figure out what you want to watch."

"Okay." I cuddle into the blankets and grab my laptop so I can check my work emails.

"Nope." He snags my laptop from me. "No work. You need to rest."

Before I can argue, he's gone, with the laptop.

Using the remote, I click through the different options of what to watch, but as I'm going from show to show, my mind begins to wander back to last night.

Dancing with Lexi.

Drinking.

Meeting Kenny.

Dancing with Kenny.

Drinking with Kenny.

I was so caught up in trying to find Mr. Perfect, I wasn't paying attention. And it nearly got me raped... or worse, killed.

How could I be so stupid not to see what his intentions were? All he wanted to do was drug me. The thought is both scary and depressing. I watch women meet men all the time. They flirt and laugh and it leads to more. Why can't that happen for me? Why does the one guy I actually like not like me back? And the guy I try to get to know, to push the other guy from my thoughts, have to be a crazy psycho?

I sigh and cuddle farther into my blanket. Maybe I just need to take a little break from trying to find the perfect guy... So far this love stuff isn't all it's cracked up to be. Maybe my perfect path isn't finding the perfect man, maybe it's just finding myself. I can focus on cooking and my work...

But even as the thoughts flow through my head, it saddens me. The way my heart feels full when I hold Abigail. The way it thumps against my chest when Chase looks at me and talks to me. I want more. It's too bad I can't figure out how to get it. And clearly going to the club isn't the way to go about it. Not if I want to remain alive...

"What's going through that beautiful head of yours?" Chase asks, stepping into my room. His hair is dripping wet from his shower, and since he's still in the middle of putting on his shirt, his chest and abs are on display. Why must he always do that? Is it too much to ask that he finishes getting dressed *before* he comes near me? It's like his goal in life is to tease me...

My gaze drags lower. He's wearing a pair of basketball shorts that are hanging off his hips and show off how fit he is. He finishes putting his shirt on, hiding the goods, and I mentally pout, already missing the view.

"Georgia." He chuckles, having obviously caught me staring. Oh well, if he's going to walk around half-naked, then he can't be shocked when I stare. "Before I walked in you looked like you were deep in thought."

"Just thinking about that stupid perfect path."

"You know there's no perfect path, right?" He walks over and sits on the bed next to me. "Life isn't perfect and no path you take will be either as long as you're out of that shell and in the real world." There's a hard edge to his voice I've never heard before.

"You have no idea what real life is like," he continues. "Women get drugged every day, raped, killed. Only the rich and privileged think there are perfect paths because they don't experience the shit us poor people do." *Us poor people do...*

"You make six figures a year as a firefighter, drive a BMW, and live in a nice condo," I point out. "You hardly have room to judge." I don't know a lot about his childhood, but even if he was poor, he's not anymore.

"I lost my sister when she was eighteen," he says, shocking the hell out of me. "She overdosed after she became addicted to drugs because her asshole dealer boyfriend got her hooked. I found her in his house dead. I was seventeen. That's where I was yesterday... at my mom's. It was my sister's birthday, and like every year, my mom was drowning herself in a bottle."

Oh my God, no wonder he's freaking out. I was drugged on the birthday of his sister who died from drugs. Without hesitation, I sit up and pull Chase into a tight hug. "I'm so sorry. I can't even imagine what you're going through." I wrap my arms around him tighter and he sinks against me.

"I was so fucking scared for you," he grumbles into my neck. "When Alec texted... fuck." He pulls back and his glassy eyes meet mine. "I was the one who suggested you get out..."

"This isn't your fault."

"I should've been there," he argues. "Alec was focusing on Lexi and—"

"No, you shouldn't have been because you were where you

were supposed to be, with your mom because she needed you."

"Next time you go to the club, I'll be going with you."

I scoff. "Trust me, that won't be happening. Me and clubs are done."

Before he can reply, there's a knock on the door. "I'll get it."

A minute later, my mom walks through my door with a sad smile on her face. "I wasn't sure if you would be awake, but I told Chase I would be by with soup..."

"You don't have to come up with an excuse to check on me," I tell her. "You're my mom."

"I know," she says with a watery laugh. "How are you feeling?"

"I'm okay. Sore and tired, but I'm alive."

"You are," she says, tears pricking her eyes. She sits on the edge of my bed and pulls me into her arms. "I was so scared, Georgia. You're my baby girl and if something happened to you..."

Chase walks in with a tray at that moment and my mom pulls back. "I'm sorry. I guess it just really hit me. We could've lost you."

"You didn't lose me, and nothing like that will ever happen again."

Chase sets the tray on my lap. There's a bowl of chicken noodle soup I recognize from my favorite deli, a glass of orange juice, and some crackers.

"Thank you," I tell both of them. "It smells delicious."

"I'll give you guys a few minutes," Chase says. "Holler if you need anything."

When he's gone, Mom waggles her brows at me. "He's sweet."

I groan. "And just a friend."

"Your choice?"

"No, his. He was hurt and isn't looking for anything more."

"He seemed awfully worried about you for someone who's *just* a friend. He yelled at Alec and wouldn't leave your side."

"He blames himself. It was his idea for me to get out."

"Yeah, I heard that, but I don't know." She shrugs. "I just got a vibe."

"A vibe, huh?" I laugh as I take a spoonful of my soup. "Well, your vibe is way off. We're just friends. He was my wingman, but now that I have no intention of ever going back to a club, I have no idea how I'm going to find a man."

My mom eyes me for a moment. I expected her to appreciate the fact that I'm planning to stay away from clubs, so I'm shocked when she frowns. "What happened was scary, but you can't let one bad experience keep you from doing what you want to do."

I set my spoon down. "I was drugged, Mom. I went out to a club a few times, hoping to find a guy, and I was drugged. I think I'll stay right here, in my house, where it's safe. Maybe I can try online dating or something," I half joke.

Mom doesn't laugh. "Do you remember last year when you were dating Robert?"

"Ughhh... How could I forget?" I groan.

"He wasn't a very nice man," she agrees.

"Hence why I broke up with him." I take a spoonful of soup.

"But afterward, instead of getting back out there, you went

months without dating," she points out.

"Who would want to date after that?"

"And now, you've had something bad happen to you, and you're saying you're not going to go back to a club..."

"So?" I set my spoon down and take a sip of my orange juice.

"When I was married to your father," she says, her voice a tad shaky. "Not Tristan... But your biological father, Justin... He was abusive."

Her words have me abandoning my food and drink. My mom doesn't talk about her past life, ever.

"And not only verbally," she continues. "He would hit me too. He would come home and attack me." She visibly shudders. "As you got older, it got worse. I was terrified that one day he would hurt you, so I came up with a plan to run away with you, to get away from him." A single tear slides down her cheek and she swipes it away. "I slowly put away money so we could disappear. But before we could, he caught me. We fought and I hit my head. When I woke up, I couldn't remember what happened, and he claimed you were dead."

"What?" I choke out in shock.

"I was devastated and ran. I had no clue you were really alive and he was hiding you to punish me."

I don't even know what to say. What horrible person would do that to a mother? And I share DNA with him? But now it makes sense... My memories of my bio dad locking me away in my room. The way he treated me.

"I never told you," I admit, "because you hated to talk about Justin, but I have these memories of him yelling at me and throwing me in my room because I was crying for you. I didn't know why you weren't there, but now it makes sense."

Mom's eyes widen and several tears leak from her lids. "You never told me."

"At first I thought they were nightmares, but as I got older, I realized they were memories... I didn't want to upset you."

"Oh, Georgia. I wish you had told me. I'm so sorry. I should've told you about my past... *our* past. It's just that..." She sighs. "It's so hard to talk about it."

"It's okay, Mom. So, what happened after you left Justin?"

"After I ran, thinking you were dead, I ended up here in Los Angeles," she says with a watery smile. "I met Tristan and Lexi, and I fell in love with her at first sight." She sniffles back her tears. "But it took me a little while to let Tristan in. I was scared that what happened to me before would happen again."

"Well, who can blame you?"

Mom shakes her head. "I was so focused on the bad that already happened, I almost missed out on the good." Mom moves the tray off my lap and sets it on the nightstand. Then she takes my hands in hers. "What happened with Robert sucks. He was a shitty guy and will probably end up alone, but what I'm concerned about is the fact that after him, you didn't date for months. And now you're saying you're never going to a club again. You can't allow the bad to keep you from the possibility of the good."

She's right. It's exactly what I do. I stay in my room, in my little bubble, where I'm safe. It might've stemmed from when I was little and my bio dad kept me in my room for damn near a year, but I'm a grownup now and it's time to stop letting my fears dictate what I want in life. I want to be free...free to love, free to live. Just be free to do what I want.

"You're right. I've worked myself up over the years, creating a mountain out of a molehill, and it's time I take control of my life. I know what I want, and right now, the only person standing in my way is me."

"HOW ARE YOU FEELING?" CHASE PLOPS DOWN ON THE bed next to me. He props his muscular forearm up against the side of his head and looks at me with his mesmerizing hazel eyes.

"Better," I tell him truthfully. "My mom and I had a really good talk, and I've come to a decision..." I twist my lips, unsure if I should tell Chase. He was really worried about me going to the club, and with his sister...

"Well, go on," he says through a laugh. "What's this decision?"

I take a deep breath, then in a rush, say, "I'm not going to give up finding the right guy... even if it means going to a club."

Chase blinks once. Then again. And then his mouth is on mine. He threads his fingers through the back of my hair and tugs me over to him. At first I'm in shock, wondering what the hell is happening right now. But then his tongue darts out, licking across the seam of my lips, and just like that, my mind goes blank, my body doing all the thinking for me.

I scoot closer, my body sighing into his, and he deepens the kiss. His lips mold with mine, our tongues tangling in one another. His hand leaves my hair and skates down the side of my body, until it lands on my hip. And then he's gripping my hip and rolling me onto my back. His legs push my thighs apart and he settles on top of me.

Our kiss is messy, desperate. Filled with all of our pent-up sexual tension. I run my fingers through his hair, and wrap my thighs around his waist, pulling him closer to me. When the hard bulge in his pants grinds against my center, I let out a needy groan, which spurs him on. He nips at my bottom lip, then sucks it into his mouth, before he breaks the kiss and moves to my neck. I tilt my head slightly, giving him better access, and he licks a trail along my sensitive flesh, taking his time and covering every inch.

I've only been kissed by a couple guys in my life, and none of them made me feel like this—as if my body is being wound up tightly in the best way. If he continues, I have no doubt I'll eventually snap. My lady parts are clenching in want. My nipples are hard, and as Chase works his way down my body, his fingers brush up against them, making me moan. How can such a simple touch elicit so much pleasure?

Needing to feel him, I pull his shirt over his head and toss it to the side. I run my nails along his hot flesh and laugh when a shiver visibly overtakes him.

"Fuck, Georgia," he murmurs, kissing his way along my collarbone. I'm wearing a tank top sans bra and he pulls the front down, exposing my breasts. As if asking for permission, he stops and glances up, his eyes shining with lust and desire.

The second I nod my permission, his lips wrap around my nipple. He sucks it into his mouth and bites down gently on the tip, causing my entire body to bow.

"Holy Jesus," I groan. "Do that again."

He chuckles at my demand, the rumbling vibrations shooting straight through me. My thighs tighten around him, and it makes him laugh harder.

I feel out of control. Every touch, every lick has me needing more.

As Chase is dragging my tank up and over my head, a door slams and then a few seconds later a feminine voice yells, "Hey, sis, I'm—Oh shit!"

Lexi.

"What hap—What the fuck?"

Alec.

"Oh God," I groan, at the same time Chase curses under his breath. "Give us a minute," I squeak, as Lexi's laughter rings out through the condo, no doubt remembering the time I walked in on her and Alec.

I scramble to right my tank top, mortified. What did we just do? Chase made it clear he doesn't want to settle down, and that's precisely what I'm looking for. I can't be another notch on his belt. It'll not only destroy me, but it'll ruin the friendship we've been building. A friendship I don't want to lose.

I try to push Chase off me, but he doesn't budge. "Move," I hiss in confusion. "And... put your shirt back on."

"Hey." He grabs my chin with his thumb and forefinger. "Breathe."

"What?" My chest is rising and falling in quick succession.

"I can see your brain is in overdrive. Don't second-guess what just happened."

"What *did* just happen?"

"You and me," he says, his lip quirking into a sexy grin.

I open my mouth to ask what he means by that, but before I can get the words out, Lexi yells, "We're still here and waiting!"

CHASE

Fuck. I've imagined how her pillow soft lips would feel against mine a million times. How her smooth skin would feel under my touch. I knew if I kissed her, if I touched her, I wouldn't be able to stop. And I was right. Her taste, her smell, her scents of pleasure, when I hadn't even pleasured her yet, are fucking addicting. And I'm fucked because I'll be damned if anyone but me will ever touch and taste her again. Fuck that, Georgia is mine. Fuck the risks, fuck my heart, just... fuck.

"We need to talk," Alec growls the second Georgia and I step into the living room. I raise a brow and he adds, "Alone."

"Stop," Georgia says softly, obviously embarrassed at having been caught. "Please."

Alec glares at me. He warned me to stay away, and he was right to do so... before I spent time with her. Hell, I don't blame him. This last year I've turned into an uncaring manwhore. But I wouldn't do that to Georgia. She's different.

"So, what..." Lexi says. "You two are together now?"

"No," Georgia rushes out, shaking her head quickly.

"Then what? You're just hooking up?" Lexi's glaring eyes meet mine, but I keep my mouth shut, letting Georgia and her sister have this conversation.

"What? No," Georgia argues. "It was just... a mistake."

And now I'm jumping in. "Like hell it was a mistake." Georgia's shocked gaze swings over to me. "Kissing you was *not* a mistake."

"I just meant we got carried away," Georgia backtracks. "Chase has been so nice to me and it was just... a moment."

"No, we didn't, and no, it wasn't," I argue again. I'm not going to let her play this off. Hell, I'm already thinking about the next time I can kiss her again. Unless...

"Wait, do you regret the kiss?" I never even considered she would regret kissing me.

"I—" she begins, her eyes darting toward Alec and Lexi, hoping one of them will save her.

"We just came by to check on Georgia," Lexi cuts in and stands, surprising me when she kisses Georgia's cheek then grabs Alec's hand and drags him to the front door. "We can see she's in good hands, so we'll go." She shoots me a wink. "See you guys later."

Alec grumbles his goodbye, but I don't miss the daggers he's shooting my way. He's protective as hell of Georgia, and as my best friend, he knows the way I've treated women this past year. We're definitely going to have a conversation soon.

Once they're gone, Georgia attempts to slip back into her room, but I catch her by her arm and stop her before she can run. "I meant what I said. I don't regret kissing you. It wasn't a mistake. I thoroughly enjoyed it, and if it's up to me, I'd like for it to happen again."

Georgia allows herself a small smile before she schools her features. "I enjoyed it too, but..." I raise a brow, waiting for her to make her argument so I can shoot it down.

"Well, c'mon, Chase," she finally says. "I'm a virgin... and you're..." She waves her hand at me. "You're not."

I crack up laughing. "No, I'm not. But so what?"

"So, as hot as you are, and as good of a kisser as you are, I can't be just another woman you stick your dick in."

Fuck, I love it when she says shit like that. It isn't often Georgia talks like that, but when she does, it's a goddamn turn-on.

I step closer to her and rest my hands on her hips. "What if I want you to be the only woman I stick my dick in?"

Her cheeks heat up, and I grin. Her innocence is so refreshing. "I would say you should reconsider because I'm not having sex until I fall in love." She raises a challenging brow at me, thinking her little confession is going to deter me, but what she doesn't realize is since we started hanging out, I haven't had sex at all, and surprisingly, I don't miss it. I would rather hang out with her and have a meaningful conversation than have meaningless sex.

"Before I got divorced, Victoria was the only woman I'd had sex with." Georgia's brows shoot up to her forehead. "This last year I was searching for an escape. I was hurt. I loved her and she cheated on me. She took something as sacred as our marriage and shit on it like it meant nothing to her."

I take her hands in mine, lacing our fingers together. I love how delicate and soft her hands are in contrast to my rough ones. "I can't take back how I've spent the last year, and honestly, I'm not sure I would want to. I handled shit the best I could, but that was all before you. And I know actions speak louder than words, so whatever I say right now isn't going to hold as much meaning as me showing you. But that's exactly what I would like to do... Show you that I have no desire to spend my time with any other woman but you."

Georgia releases a harsh breath. I expect for her to argue, to throw my past in my face, tell me there's no way I can be faithful, so I'm shocked when she simply says, "Okay, I'd like that... for you to show me."

I laugh softly. I should've known that once again Georgia is different. She's innocent and trusting and doesn't play games—just a few of the reasons why I'm attracted to her.

I pull her into my arms and hug her, giving her a kiss on the top of her head and inhaling her vanilla scent. "Thank you. You won't regret it."

She pulls back and smiles. "Does that mean no more clubs to look for the perfect guy?" Her green eyes twinkle with laughter.

"That definitely means no more clubs." Remembering she was in the hospital only a few short hours ago, I scoop her up into my arms bridal style and stalk into her room. I set her down on the middle of the bed and climb over her. We're in the same spot we were in before her sister barged in.

"No more clubs," I repeat, dipping my face down and pressing my lips to the curve of her neck. I nibble lightly and she giggles, so I do it again, loving the sound.

"WHAT THE HELL WAS THAT SHIT?" ALEC BARKS THE second I walk into the station. Everyone stops what they're doing and the place goes silent. After Alec and Lexi left, and Georgia agreed to give us a shot, we spent the rest of the weekend watching reruns of shows, eating takeout, and in between, making out like teenagers. We created our own little bubble, and it completely slipped my mind I would still have to deal with Alec.

"Georgia and I are dating," I say nonchalantly.

He gets in my face. "I warned you to stay away from her. You can have any woman you want. We might be best friends, but Georgia is family."

"And if we get married that'd make us family," I joke, but then the thought of Georgia and I getting married hits me, and instead of freaking out, I find myself smiling. Sure, it's way too soon for that, but that doesn't mean I can't still imagine it. Georgia, dressed in white, walking down the aisle...

"Holy shit," Alec hisses, "you're thinking about it."

"What?"

"You're actually thinking about what it would be like to marry Georgia."

"I really like her," I admit. Actually, I'm in love with her, but I can't say that yet. It's too soon. People will think I'm fucking nuts. "We've been hanging out a lot and we just click."

"If you hurt her, I'm going to have to beat your ass," Alec warns.

"Same," a voice says from behind me.

I turn around and find Mason and Tristan walking up.

"Just left breakfast with my girls," Tristan says, sizing me up as he walks over to us. I knew Georgia left early this morning to meet her mom and sister for breakfast. She was gone before I woke up and left me a note that she'd be by later with a new recipe for me to try. But I didn't realize her dad would also be there, or that we would be the topic of conversation. But I guess I should've expected that. I'm just not used to parents interfering. I mean, my mom cares, but she's not one to make a fuss. And Victoria's parents were barely around. Nobody ever cared or questioned anything we did.

"Breakfast's already over?"

"Nah," Tristan says, shaking his head. "They're still at the house, eating and gossiping. I overheard Lexi asking her sister about what she walked in on as I was walking out the door... Figured I must've misunderstood, because the last I heard, you promised to bring her home and take care of her." Tristan tilts his head to the side slightly. "Wasn't aware taking care of her meant almost sleeping with her."

I stifle a groan. "Nothing happened."

"Yeah, because Lexi and I showed up," Alec points out.

"Good job, Son," Mason says, patting him on the shoulder.

"Look, I get it," I tell them. "You guys are all protective of Georgia, but I'm not the bad guy here. I didn't plan for this to happen, but when she said she planned to go back to that club to find the perfect guy—"

"The fuck?" Mason hisses at the same time Tristan barks out, "Like hell."

"Exactly!" I throw my hands up in the air. "Anyway, she said that shit and it just happened. I kissed her, but nothing more than that happened." Not much anyway...

"So, you kissed her to stop her from going out?" Tristan eyes me accusingly.

"What? No. Don't twist my words." I hit Tristan with a pointed look. Georgia's father or not, I won't be accused of shit that isn't true. "I like her, and when she said that shit, it made me admit it."

"So what exactly are you two?" Mason asks.

"Dad!" Georgia yells. "I knew it!" She stomps up the station's driveway, and I can't help but smile. She's dressed in light blue skinny jeans that show off her sexy curves and a thin pink tank top. White Vans on her feet. Her hair is straightened, and she's wearing a little bit of makeup. Not a lot, but enough to make her emerald eyes pop and her lips look all silky and kissable. And I would totally kiss her, if it weren't for the scary way she's glaring at her dad as she stalks toward us.

"Georgia, honey, what are you doing here?" Tristan asks, his voice now soft. I've been around Georgia and Lexi long enough to know they have their dad wrapped around their fingers.

"The second the door closed, I knew where you were going!" She steps in front of me and turns around to face her dad. I can't see her facial expression since I'm now standing behind her, but I can see the way her arms cross over her chest and hear her humph in aggravation.

"Georgia, why don't you just let the men talk?" Mason says.

"Excuse me?" Georgia shrieks, making me snort out a laugh. Is he crazy? "This is *my* business, not any of yours."

"Well, it's kind of mine, too," I point out playfully, placing a reassuring hand on her hip and ignoring the way all three guys glare down at the gesture.

"Mine and *Chase's*," she corrects, glancing back at me with a soft smile. My stomach knots and it takes everything in me not to crush my mouth to hers right this second.

"You were drugged a few days ago," Tristan says, his eyes darting between Georgia and me. "You can't blame me for wanting to protect you."

"I get that," Georgia says. "And I appreciate your concern, but maybe next time talk to me."

Tristan nods and Georgia hugs him and then Mason. Lastly, she hugs Alec. "Thank you for looking out for me."

"I don't care if we work together, or that he's my friend," he says to her, making sure I can hear. "If he hurts you—"

"Then I get hurt," she says. "I won't allow it to affect your friendship. I know Chase's past, but I believe him when he says I'm his future." Fuck, and there she goes again, squeezing the hell out of my heart.

Alec looks like he wants to argue but instead nods. "All right." He hugs her again. "I need to get going on my chores." He hugs his stepdad and shakes Tristan's hand before disappearing inside.

"I've got my eye on you," Mason says, moving his pointer and middle finger back and forth between him and me. "Treat my goddaughter right."

"Uncle Mason," Georgia groans.

Mason pops his palms up in surrender.

"Let's do dinner soon," Tristan says, extending his hand out for me to take. "I've gotten to know a little about you as my daughter's roommate, but I'd like to get to know you now as her..."

"Friend," Georgia says before I can answer. "We're friends, Dad." *Like hell we're just friends*, I think but don't say out loud. She probably doesn't want her dad to give her a hard time, but we'll definitely be clearing that shit up when we're alone and I'm not at work. Georgia and I are more than friends. We might be in the early stages of this relationship, but she's mine.

"Let me know when you want to get together and I'm there," I tell him, shaking his hand.

Once he's gone, Georgia sighs. "I'm so sorry."

"You don't have anything to be sorry about." I tug on the front of her tank so she's forced to come closer. "You have a lot of people who care about you."

"I do," she says. "I better get going..."

"Yeah." I cup the side of her face and she looks up at me. "But first, I need to do this..." I dip down and capture her bottom lip with my own, then her top. She moans into my mouth, parting her lips slightly, and I push my tongue inside, quickly tasting her, before pulling back.

When I open my eyes, hers are still closed. I press one more soft kiss to her perfect mouth and then her eyes flutter open. "I really like kissing you," she admits.

"I really like kissing you too." I tuck a wayward strand of her hair behind her ear. I need to get inside, but fuck it's hard to let go of her.

"I better go," she says.

"Yeah," I reluctantly agree. "I'll see you later with dinner, right?" I couldn't give a fuck about the food. I just want an excuse to see her.

"Definitely."

After I watch her get into her massive truck and take off, I head into the station. The guys are all standing around bullshitting, but when they see me, like the assholes they are, they start hooting and hollering.

"So, it's true?" Luke asks. "Is Mr. Manwhore officially a one-woman man?"

I can see Alec standing in the corner, staring at me and waiting for my reply. I look over at him and our eyes meet. "Yeah, as far as I'm concerned, I'm off the market."

The guys all cheer and laugh—everyone except Alec—but I don't take it personal. Just like I told Georgia, actions speak louder than words. Once Alec sees through my actions how serious I am about Georgia, he'll come around.

GEORGIA

Chase: I have to stay late for a meeting. When I get home I was thinking we could do something.

Me: Sounds good.

"Who are you texting with?" Lexi asks, a sly smirk on her lips. "Your boyfriend?" She scoops a bit of oatmeal up and feeds it to Abigail, who opens her mouth like a cute little birdy.

I was surprised to find Lexi, with Abigail on her hip and breakfast in her hand, standing on my doorstep first thing this morning. But since I'm always down for spending time with my sister and niece, it was a pleasant surprise.

"He's not my boyfriend," I correct her, popping a piece of blueberry muffin into my mouth. "We're just... talking... hanging out," I say, hoping I come across nonchalant. The truth is, I don't know what we are, and I don't want to get hurt thinking we're more while Chase is assuming we're less.

"Really? Does he know that?" She swipes up on her phone and types something quickly, then turns it around.

I stare at her screen to see what she's showing me, but I'm not sure what I'm looking at. "Is that his profile pic?" I look at a smiling Chase, dressed in his work uniform. His arms are crossed over his chest and his muscular forearms are bulging slightly. He's so damn sexy without even trying.

"Georgia, focus," Lexi says. "Yes, it's his profile picture and yours." I realize then, my picture is next to his. "He updated his status this morning, putting that he's in a relationship with you." Her eyes go wide. "Nothing says more serious than making it Facebook official."

I crack up laughing. "Does anyone even go on Facebook anymore?"

Lexi groans. "I don't know. Who cares. The point is he did, and when he did, he publicly announced that he's in a relationship with you. Didn't you get the notification?"

"I don't even have the app on my phone. I only go on it to see the photos Grandma and Grandpa post while they're traveling."

Lexi rolls her eyes and feeds Abigail another bite of her food. "Well, everyone saw this. Mom... Dad... All your guys' friends and family."

My heart pitter-patters at the thought. When I was dating Robert, I could barely get him to take me to a work function. Yet, Chase just announced to the entire Facebook population that he's in a relationship with me.

"I see that look on your face." She points an oatmeal-covered spoon at me. "You've totally fallen for him."

I nod, not even wanting to deny it. "I have, Lex. I mean, it's too soon, but..."

"Time doesn't determine anything. Look how quickly Alec and I got married once we finally gave in to our feelings."

They were married within three months, but... "You guys were in love with each other for years and just wouldn't admit it. Up until recently, I couldn't stand Chase, and I don't think he even noticed me."

Lexi snorts. "Oh, trust me, he noticed you. Alec is super pissed about all this. Apparently Chase wanted to ask you out a long time ago and Alec told him you were off-limits."

"What?" I shriek, shocked as hell.

"Yep. He didn't want to take a chance of you getting hurt by Chase. They got into it yesterday." She wipes Abigail's mouth with a wet-wipe, then hands her her sippy cup, helping her take a sip of water from it.

"I don't want Alec and him to be on bad terms. I'm a big girl and can make my own decisions."

"That's what I told him," Lexi agrees. "Plus, if Chase hurts you, I'll kick his ass."

She lifts Abigail from her mini high chair I keep here for when they come over and hands her to me. Abigail grins and giggles as I place kisses all over her cheeks. The sound wraps around my heart like the most beautiful rose covered vines.

I'm still giving her kisses when the door opens and Chase walks inside. His eyes meet mine, and those same vines tighten, forcing my heart to clench in my chest.

"Hey," he says, a small smile splaying across his face.

"Hey," I say back.

"Oh Lord." Lexi groans. "I'm getting out of here before I end up pregnant by just being in the same room as you two."

Chase snorts a laugh, but otherwise ignores her, coming over and giving Abigail a kiss to her cheek and then giving me a kiss to mine. "I'm going to jump in the shower," he says. My eyes stay trained on his body—on his ass—as he saunters down the hall and disappears into the bathroom.

"Oh em gee," Lexi says once he's gone. "You're totally going to F.U.C.K. him."

I bark out a laugh. "You know she doesn't know the word yet, right? And you could just say sex and it wouldn't be a bad word."

"Don't you change the subject." She wags her finger at me. "What happened to waiting until you're in love?"

I swallow thickly. "We're not going to have sex. We're just getting to know each other." But even as I say the words, I know if Chase wanted to, I totally would. I want him that badly.

"I gotta go," she says. "Have fun being in denial and call me afterward so we can talk deets. Bye!" She grabs her diaper bag and her daughter and flits out of the condo, slamming the door behind her.

I clean up the dining room table and kitchen, then head to my room so I can get changed and be ready to go when Chase gets out of the shower.

As I'm walking down the hall, Chase steps out of the steamy bathroom in nothing but a towel hanging low on his hips. He halts in place to let me pass by, but I'm flustered at seeing him half naked and dripping wet, and I stumble over my own two feet. He reaches out to catch me, and I would be thankful that he's the reason I'm not going to land face first on the wood floor, except when I go to grab a hold of him, my hands slide down his slick chest and abs and tug on his towel. The material drops to the ground, leaving him naked as the day he was born.

"Shit," he says, grasping my shoulders. "That was close."

Before I can stop myself, my eyes descend to where the towel was... to where it no longer is, and catch a glimpse of his dick.

He clears his throat and bends to scoop up his towel. My gaze goes back up to his face and he's sporting a knowing smirk.

Embarrassed, I scurry to my room and close the door, leaning against it once I do. Holy shit, I just saw my first dick... and it was Chase's. I didn't stare at it long enough to catch too many details, but the area above it was neatly trimmed and it was dangling between his legs. I drop to the ground and my head bangs slightly against the door. I close my eyes, trying to calm my erratic heart and start counting.

I've lost track of what number I'm on for the millionth time when there's a knock on my door. "Georgia, you ever going to come out?"

"I thought I would just die of embarrassment in here."

Chase laughs. "You have nothing to be embarrassed about. I'm the one who should be embarrassed. You saw my dick when it wasn't at its best."

"What?" I say through a confused laugh.

"Can I come in?"

I get to my feet and stand, slowly pulling the door open.

"There she is," he says, thankfully now fully dressed. I mean, I also enjoyed him without any clothes on, but... "You're blushing again," he points out. "Are you imagining me still naked?" He hits me with a cocky smirk.

"Oh God. Kill me now."

"Eh, then I wouldn't be able to do this." He entwines his fingers through my hair and crashes his mouth down on mine. I gasp and his tongue delves past my parted lips. It takes me a second to catch up, but once I do, I kiss him back. My belly flip-flops and butterflies soar in my chest. Nobody has ever made me feel the way Chase does with a single kiss.

He pulls back slightly, ending the kiss, and his hands palm the sides of my face. "That's much better," he says, his tongue swiping across his bottom lip like he's trying to savor my taste. "I've been dying to do that since I got home. Working twenty-four-hour shifts sucks." He presses his lips to mine for another brief kiss, and I sigh into him, not wanting it to end.

"You kissed me last night when I brought you dinner," I point out, playfully rolling my eyes, but deep down secretly loving that he's implying he missed me while he was gone.

"And then I had to go sixteen hours without doing it." His hazel eyes lock with mine. "A couple friends of mine are barbequing at the beach. I think Alec and Lexi might swing by later. Wanna go?"

"Sure, just let me change into my swimsuit and then I'll be ready to go."

After stopping by the store to pick up some drinks and snacks, we head over to Venice Beach. It's a beautiful day, but hot, so I'm thankful I snagged Lexi's umbrella she left at the condo when she moved out. I strip out of my cover-up and shorts, leaving me in only my pink and black striped bikini, while Chase digs a hole and sets up the umbrella. Once he's done, I lay a blanket under it. He introduces me to a couple of his friends I haven't met yet, but most of them I already know from the fire station, and then we settle on the blanket in the shade. He removes his shirt and I notice, unlike his friends, he doesn't have a single tattoo on him.

"What?" he asks, when he catches me checking him out.

"You don't have any tattoos."

"Neither do you." He takes my hand in his and absently plays around with my fingers.

"I want one."

"Yeah? What would you get?" His fingers trail over my palm and up the inside of my wrist. I've noticed that when we're together he likes to touch me. His hands are always on me in some way. And when I'm talking, he always pays full attention to me. I like that.

"I don't know. Something meaningful since it'll be on my body forever."

"That's why I haven't gotten one. Growing up everyone in my neighborhood was covered in them. Usually shitty ones done in dirty basements." He cringes. "I told myself I wouldn't get one until I had a damn good reason to. Guess I just never had one."

"That makes sense."

His phone dings with a notification, which reminds me... "Lexi showed me something earlier... on Facebook."

He doesn't even look at his phone, instead focusing on me. "Oh yeah? What did she show you?" The way one side of his mouth is quirked up tells me he knows exactly what she showed me.

"Your relationship status."

Chase's grin widens. "That I'm in a relationship with you."

"Is that what we are? In a relationship?"

"Damn right, we are." He pulls my face close to his, and his mouth connects with my own. "You're mine," he growls against my lips. "And I'm yours." He closes his mouth over mine in a searing kiss that matches the tone of his words.

I'm his.

And he's mine.

I like the sound of that.

"Get a room!" someone shouts, forcing us to break apart.

"Go on a date with me tonight," he says, tucking a stray hair behind my ear. He's still holding me, refusing to let go, and my mind is all over the place.

"Why?" I blurt out.

His brows furl. "I thought we just covered this... we're in a relationship. That means you're my girlfriend and I'm your boyfriend." His face breaks out into a sexy boyish grin and I laugh, realizing he has me so all over the place I didn't finish my question out loud.

"Not why are you asking me out... Why did you change your mind about wanting a girlfriend?"

"You did," he says, kissing the corner of my mouth. "I couldn't see myself putting my heart back out there again, risking someone hurting me, until you."

I swallow thickly at the seriousness of his words. "Thank you," I tell him, not caring that we're having this conversation on the blanket at the beach, surrounded by his friends. "I'll be careful with it."

"I know you will. Now, how about that date?"

"A date sounds perfect."

CHASE

"Screw the date. Let's stay home." I'm only half serious. The half that's staring at Georgia, dressed in a sexy beige off the shoulder dress that stops mid-thigh and shows off every one of her perfect curves.

Georgia's eyes go wide, not picking up on my joke. "Why? What happened?"

I cut across the room and pull her into my arms. "You look too damn good. That's what happened." I kiss the corner of her mouth, not wanting to mess up the shiny lip gloss shit she's wearing. Later, I tell myself. Later, I'll mess that shit up.

"You're so cheesy."

"I'm dead serious." I glide my hands down her hips. Touching Georgia has become my favorite pastime, an addiction of sorts. She's soft and smooth and everything about her is so damn perfect.

"Let's go, silly!" she says with a giggle. She steps around me and I have the pleasure of watching her ass sway from side to side, her heels clicking across the wood floor, as she walks over to the front door.

"You coming?"

I quirk a brow, letting her comment settle in for a moment. Of course, she doesn't catch on because she's too damn innocent.

"Yeah," I say with a laugh. "I'm coming."

Twenty minutes later we arrive at Salvatore's, a small Italian restaurant on the beach that's reservations only. The hostess shows us to our table, which is outside, then leaves us with our menus. There are four chairs, and knowing I'm going to want to touch Georgia, I sit in the one diagonal from her instead of across.

"I've never been here," she muses, glancing out at the water. It's early fall, so there's a slight chill to the air. Not enough to be considered cold, but enough to make it nice out.

"A friend of mine owns the place." It's how I was able to get a last-minute reservation. "We grew up in south LA together."

Georgia smiles. "Does your mom still live there?"

"Yeah, she won't move away from there. It's the last place my sister lived."

Her smile fades. "I'm so sorry about your sister. I can't even begin to fathom what it would feel like to lose my sister."

Not wanting the night to take a sour turn, I shake my head. "Let's talk about something else."

"Don't do that," she says, taking my hand in hers. "I don't just want the good, the fun... I want all of you. The ugly, the scary, the shitty. I want it all."

Fuck, this woman. I raise her hand and kiss the tops of her knuckles. "Thank you."

We spend our date going from topic to topic. We talk about our pasts, our families, what we want for our futures. We laugh and joke and it's obvious the chemistry between us is there. The entire time we eat and drink and converse, we touch each other. I learn I'm not the only handsy one in this relationship, and I love that she can't keep her hands off of me.

It's honestly one of the best dates I've ever been on, and I know it's because it's with Georgia and what we're doing here is real. I spent the last year faking it, thinking it was the way to go about getting over the shit that happened with my ex-wife. But all I was doing was hiding behind a bunch of fake as fuck hookups. I don't regret it because they led me to this moment, but looking back I could've handled it better.

After we share a slice of cheesecake for dessert, I suggest we go for a walk on the beach.

"Actually," Georgia says, swiping her tongue across the seam of her lips. "I'd rather finish this date at home." Her green orbs burn into mine, and she doesn't have to tell me twice.

"Check, please!" I yell jokingly, making her laugh.

The second we're through the door of the condo, Georgia's arms go around my neck and I lift her off her feet, carrying her to her room. I drop her onto the bed and then take a moment to look at her. The way her hair is splayed out across her pillow as she looks up at me with her trusting emerald eyes and her perfect, pink, kissable lips. "You're so beautiful."

Her mouth curls into a shy smile. "Come kiss me."

"I will, but first I want to explore." Once my mouth touches hers, it'll be damn hard to stop.

After kicking my shoes off, I remove her heels, then kiss the instep of each of her feet. I trail kisses up her smooth, tanned legs, nip playfully at her hips through the material of her dress, and then settle over her.

I kiss my way along her neck, until I get to her pillow soft lips. Our mouths finally connect and my body sighs against hers. I could stay like this, kissing her, touching her for hours, maybe even days.

"Touch me, please," she murmurs against my lips. Her words are so soft, so shaky, I almost don't hear them.

"Where?" I ask, knowing our levels of experience are way the hell different and not wanting to take this anywhere she isn't ready for.

I open my eyes to wait for her to answer and hers pop open as well. For a moment, we just stare at each other. She licks her slightly swollen lips, which was caused from our kissing, and then says, "Anywhere... Everywhere."

Her legs tighten around me and I stifle a chuckle. She's turned on and is craving a release. "It would be my pleasure." I sit up and rake my gaze down her body. "Turn over."

Her eyes widen slightly, but then she does as I asked, flipping onto her belly and exposing the zipper that starts at the top of her dress and continues to just above her ass.

I pull the zipper slowly down, exposing her flesh. "It's like unwrapping a birthday present," I muse. Georgia shakes her head but doesn't say a word.

When the zipper hits the bottom, I pull the dress apart. Her skin is smooth and flawless, a couple freckles peppering her shoulders. I lay a kiss to each of her shoulder blades before I unclasp her bra. Her skin smells sweet. The same scent she always wears. It's a smell I'm finding myself craving all the time.

"Lift up," I tell her, leaning over her and kissing the shell of her ear.

She does so, and I pull her dress and bra down her body, leaving her in only a nude thong. Unable to help myself, I take a playful bite out of her ass cheek, making her yelp.

"Sorry, it just looks so damn delicious."

Before she can come up with a comeback, I massage the globes of her ass, causing her to release a moan. "Be right back," I tell her.

I hop off the bed and find her lotion in the bathroom. When I return, she's still in the same position. I squirt some into my hands and then begin to massage her shoulders. They're tight, telling me she's nervous. She's never exposed herself to a man like she's doing right now, and I don't take that shit lightly. I have no doubt when she asked me to touch her, she was expecting me to get her off, but I want more with Georgia and I need her to understand that. I want to make her feel good, and not just sexually.

As I massage her back and shoulders, the tension in her body slowly, little by little, bleeds away. When I work my way down to her ass, she tightens up momentarily, but then quickly relaxes.

Spreading her legs slightly, so I can kneel on the bed, I massage the globes of her perfect ass. She's toned and tight all over from jogging daily. She loves to eat, but she also loves to work out.

I dip my head and give the area I bit earlier, a kiss. She squirms slightly and when I look up, I catch her glancing back at me with lust-filled eyes.

Shocking the shit out of me, she spreads her legs wider, making it clear what she wants. But I'm not going to let her get away with keeping her mouth closed. She does that too often. But not with us. I want her thoughts, her words. "What is it you want?"

"I already told you. For you to touch me... everywhere."

I smirk. "Where exactly?"

She glares. When I quirk a brow, refusing to let it go, she releases a harsh breath then whispers, "My... pussy... please."

I chuckle softly. "So polite."

Gripping her thighs, I spread them farther, then run my fingers along the crack of her ass and then between her folds. I dip a single finger inside and find she's soaked.

"Turn over."

She does, exposing her perky tits, toned stomach, and neatly trimmed pussy. There are so many places I want to touch, kiss, lick, fucking worship, but before I can do any of that, I want to get her off. She's back to being wound tight, and I prefer it when she's relaxed.

And I know just the way to make that happen. Since she's a virgin and has never been properly taken care of, I focus on her clit. Using her juices, I massage soft circles across her swollen, needy flesh. Her eyes go wide, and her hips buck. The act making me realize something...

"Have you ever given yourself an orgasm?" Her cheeks tinge pink, giving me my answer. "Oh, baby. Be prepared to have your mind blown."

I drop down between her legs and lick up her center, inhaling her sweet musk. While I slowly lick her clit, I reach up and tweak her nipple.

"Chase," she breathes. "I'm... I think I'm going to—" Her words are cut off by a loud, guttural moan. Her knees tighten around my face, and her entire ass lifts off the bed. Her legs tremble as she rides out her orgasm. I don't stop stroking her clit until she drags her fingers through my hair and tugs on the ends, silently pleading for me to stop.

"Holy shit," she says, her smile lazy and sated. "That was so good." She giggles, and I laugh at how adorable she is. A few weeks ago, she was stuck in her little cocoon of safety... But now...

"What?" she asks, nibbling the corner of her mouth nervously.

"You remind me of a butterfly." I crawl over her and pull her blanket up to cover her naked body. Then I lie on my side, next to her. She turns over onto her side, so we're facing each other.

"A butterfly?"

NIKKI ASH

"Yeah, like you've completed the final stage of metamorphosis and have shed your cocoon." I tuck a stray tendril of hair behind her ear and lean in to kiss her mouth. "You've been transformed from a caterpillar into a butterfly."

The corners of her lips tug into a huge smile. "Like I'm free." A single tear skates down her cheek and I catch it with the pad of my thumb. "It's because of you," she says. "You help me spread my wings and fly."

"No, my beautiful butterfly. That was all you."

Georgia throws the blanket off her and climbs on top of me, forcing me onto my back. "It's my turn," she says with a mischievous grin.

"Your turn for—" Before I can finish my question, she's sliding down my body, taking my shorts and briefs with her. Once she's slid them off my legs, she throws them onto the floor then settles herself between my legs.

"I've never done this before, but I'm a quick learner," she says. "I know the women—"

"Whoa." I put my hand up to stop her. "Who's in this room with us?" Her brows furrow in confusion. "Us," I answer for her. "No other men or women. Just us. I don't give a fuck what any other woman did, nor do I want to compare what we do to anyone from my past."

Her eyes go wide. "I just don't want you to be disappointed."

I look her dead in the eyes, needing her to know how serious what I say next is. "Nothing you do could ever disappoint me." I

152

have a feeling some shit went down with that dumbass Robert while they were dating, but I'm not going to go there. Just like I don't want any other women in this room with us, I don't want that fucking loser in here either.

"Okay." She sits up on her knees. "But like how you gave me that orgasm... It's because you're experienced. You know what a woman wants and how to get her off. I'm not going to ignore that fact."

When I open my mouth to argue, she raises her hand. "I'm not jealous, Chase. And I'm not going to hold your past over your head. But I shared a wall with you for months, so I know the women you've been with know how to please you."

Fuck, now I'm seriously wishing I never would've brought a single woman over to this place. It's one of the reasons why when I carried Georgia inside, I brought her to her room and not mine. Nobody's been in this room, in this bed, but her.

"I've never done this before," she says. "And I want it to be good for you, like it was for me."

"Whatever you do will be good because it's you."

She snorts. "How romantic. I've read enough romance novels to know the gist of how it's done, but there's so much to it. I want you to tell me if I do something you like or don't like. Okay?"

I nod once, agreeing, because I can tell she needs me to.

She smiles softly, then turns her attention to my flaccid dick. She takes my shaft in her hand and kisses the crown. And that's all it takes for my dick to get excited. It immediately perks up, and she smiles down at it before glancing back up at me.

"In my books, some guys like to be deep throated and some prefer to be licked and teased... What's your preference?"

Holy. Fucking. Shit. She did not just go there... "Georgia, if you do either of those things, both my dick and I will be happy. Just put your mouth on me and do whatever you want, babe," I choke out.

She looks like she wants to argue, but thankfully nods, then does as I suggested... puts her warm, wet, perfect mouth on my dick. She tongues the head, then licks my shaft. And then she parts her lips and takes me all the way into her mouth, and I damn near shoot my load down her throat.

I watch with rapt attention as she owns the hell out of the blow job, giving it everything she's got. When I'm ready to blow, I warn her and she pops off, finishing me off with her hand.

Ropes of cum shoot out, some of it landing on my thighs, and the rest on her tits. She glances down at the cum on her chest and swipes a bit up.

She isn't going to do what I think she is... She pops her finger into her mouth and sucks, her brows dipping in contemplation.

"I was wondering what it tastes like," she explains. "Some girls spit and some swallow... It doesn't taste horrible, but I'm not sure I would want to swallow that."

She scrunches her face up, and I crack up laughing. "I don't give a fuck if you spit or swallow."

I can honestly say I've never had a sexual experience like this before. And I fucking love it. Because it's real. It's honest. This isn't just a one-night stand. This is us learning about each other. Being in a relationship with one another. I never thought I would want any of that again. Until Georgia.

GEORGIA

I wake up to the feel of a hand gliding down my side. Remembering I fell asleep in Chase's arms last night, I don't bother opening my eyes. He reaches around and slides his hand under the material of my panties and cups my mound. I move my top leg over and hook it around his leg, eager for him to make me feel good again. He gave me multiple orgasms last night and I'm addicted.

Chase chuckles and kisses my neck, parting my folds and inserting a finger inside me, then another one. I moan, feeling full, and wondering if it's possible to take my virginity like this.

He moves me to my back, and while fingering me, takes a nipple into his mouth. I don't remember falling asleep topless, but I'm definitely considering never wearing a shirt again in bed if that means giving him easy access.

"This orgasm is going to feel different," he murmurs, lifting his face to kiss me. I consider warning him that Robert once tried to finger me, but it went nowhere. But then, his fingers move inside of me, eliciting pleasure I've never experienced, and any thoughts of Robert are gone. As Chase expertly strokes my insides, working me into a frenzy, I remember what he said last night: nobody belongs in this room but us. He was right. It's just me and him in this room, in this relationship.

He curls his fingers inside me, his thumb massaging my clit, and within seconds my orgasm is ripping through me. His mouth crashes against mine, swallowing my moans of pleasure. We kiss for several minutes, until his alarm goes off, reminding us both that he needs to get ready for his shift.

When he breaks the kiss and climbs off the bed, I pout. "Wait, what about you?" I nod toward the obvious hard-on he's sporting. "Come back here so I can... do you."

"Do me?" He laughs. "You sure you graduated from college?"

When I glare, he laughs harder. "I have to get ready for work." He leans over me and kisses me again. "But now I have something to look forward to when I come home."

He walks toward the bathroom and stops. "I can't wait to come home, so you can *do me*."

I chuck a pillow at him and miss, causing him to bark out another laugh.

After he leaves for work, I go for a jog around the neighborhood, make myself breakfast, and then get started on my work for the day. My mom sends a group text to Lexi and me, asking to do lunch one day this week, and we both respond that any day works.

Which reminds me that I haven't eaten since breakfast.

I'm heading toward the kitchen, when there's a knock on the door. I open it to find a beautiful woman—in a fake, plastic, Barbie sort of way—standing in the doorway.

"Can I help you?"

When she eyes me up and down like I'm the gum on the bottom of her stiletto, I know she's here for Chase. This isn't the first woman to stop by, but I have to say, it's been a while. It used to happen a lot when he would bring a different woman home every night. It slowed down after he agreed to take things to their place, and it's only happened a couple times since Alec and Lexi moved out and I moved into the master bedroom—telling Chase he could go back to his extracurricular activities here, since we were no longer sharing walls and a bathroom.

"I'm looking for Chase. I left something here the other night."

The other night... That's a lie. Chase hasn't brought anyone home in a long time. But I'm not going to point that out. "He's not here, so whatever you left, you'll have to come back for another time."

I'm about to swing the door shut, when she places her hand on it. "I'll only be a second."

I sigh. "What is it you left?" Maybe I can find it for her and then send her on her slutty stiletto way.

She smirks. "My dildo."

It takes everything in me to keep a straight face. "Your dildo?" I heard her the first time, but I'm hoping she made a mistake.

"I'm sure you know how kinky Chase is..." She winks. "If I could just grab it, that'd be great. It's expensive and my favorite."

A lump forms in my throat. Too many times I heard the noises through the too-thin walls, so I know how sexually active Chase is, but it's hard to hear about it from the mouth of one of the women he's been with, knowing I'm not active at all.

"You'll have to ask Chase for it."

"I would, but I lost his number."

Or he didn't give it to you...

Grabbing my phone from my back pocket, I call him.

"Hey, butterfly," he says when he answers.

My heart pitter-patters in my chest at his nickname for me, and for a moment I forget why I'm calling. Until the woman clears her throat at the same time Chase says, "Georgia? Everything okay?"

"Yeah. There's a woman here for you, named..."

"Charleigh," she says.

"Charleigh left her dildo in your room and would like it back because it's expensive and her favorite."

"Fuck," he curses. "Georgia..."

"Do you want me to go into your room to get it, or give her your number?"

"Do not give her my number," he says quickly. "I never gave it to her."

I didn't think so...

"Fuck, umm... fuck!" he hisses. "Can I talk to her?"

"Okay," I tell him, handing her the phone, while mentally patting myself on the back for remaining calm, cool, and collected.

She says hello in the most obnoxious, nasally way, and I have to force myself not to roll my eyes.

"But, Chase, it was a hundred dollars," she whines. "How about if we meet up and—" He must cut her off because she stops talking and glares at me. "Okay, fine," she says with a huff before handing me back the phone. "He said I can go in his room and get it."

"Go for it." I open the door and let her in.

I hear Chase's voice, so I put the phone back up to my ear, realizing he didn't hang up. "Hello?"

"I'm so sorry. I told her she can grab what she left. Fuck, I'm—"

"It's okay," I say, not wanting to argue in front of Ms. Dildo. Not that there's anything to fight over. Chase has a past. I knew that.

A moment later she comes sauntering out of his room, holding a bright blue huge-ass dildo. She doesn't say a word, just glares, and then she's out the door.

"Georgia," Chase says. "You there?"

"Yeah, she just left..."

"I hate that I'm at work. Can we talk when I get home?"

"Chase, stop," I tell him, trying to shake the image of him shoving that huge dildo inside her. "It's okay. There's nothing to talk about." And then, because I'm awkward as fuck and can't stop talking, I add, "But maybe if you're holding anyone else's sex toys hostage, you could give them back. Maybe put out an ad for them to come get them..." It's meant as a joke, but it totally falls flat, making me sound jealous and petty. "I'm just kidding. I have some work to do. I'll see you later."

He says okay, sounding sad as hell, and then we hang up.

Since cooking has become something I really enjoy doing, I look up my bookmarked recipes I haven't made yet and get to work making a creamy mushroom chicken pasta.

While I'm cooking, I can't stop replaying what happened in my head. When I think about what exactly is bothering me, I come to the conclusion that it's not because he's been with other women, but because he hasn't been with me. And since my plan was to wait until I'm in love, he'll be waiting some time. I don't believe he would cheat on me, especially not after having been cheated on himself, but that doesn't mean he's not going to be left feeling unsatisfied.

When I finish making the food, there's way too much, and it's then I realize I doubled the recipe, making enough for the guys at the station, like I often do. I consider whether to bring them the food. I don't want to distract Chase at his workplace. I also don't want things to be awkward, but maybe showing up there with food will be like a little peace offering. *It's okay you shoved monster-size dildos into your one-night stands...* Oh geez, I seriously need to lay off the jokes, even if they're only in my head.

When I arrive, I see Alec first. He smiles and walks over to me, taking the pan of food from me. "We were about to do a run to the store to pick up food for dinner," he says, kissing my cheek. "Chase didn't say you were coming by."

"Shoot! I forgot to tell him." My mind was just so scattered. "I should've asked him first if I could come by."

Alec eyes me. "You don't have to call or ask before coming here, Georgia." Maybe not before, but doesn't that change once you're in a relationship with one of the guys who work here?

"Damn right she doesn't," Chase says, pulling me into a searing kiss that makes my legs feel like Jell-O. "Fuck, I missed you," he murmurs against my lips as he lifts and carries me toward the station.

I faintly hear Alec grumbling something about getting a room, but I'm too distracted by Chase's mouth on mine.

I assume he's just carrying me to the kitchen, so I'm confused when he keeps walking through the station and out another door.

When we finally stop, he pushes me against a wall. I don't know where we are, but my only focus is on Chase. The way he kisses me like he can't get enough of me. The way he makes me feel special and wanted and beautiful.

"Does this mean you forgive me?" he asks.

"There's nothing to forgive." And that's the truth. I refuse to be that insecure woman who gets mad every time her man's past gets brought up. He's thirty years old. Of course he has a past.

Gently, he releases my legs so I drop to the ground. His fingers slide up my bare thigh toward the apex of my legs, but before he makes it up the inside of my shorts, I cover his hand with my own.

"You gave me three orgasms last night and then one this

morning. It's your turn..."

Chase's face contorts into a look of confusion. "This isn't a tit for tat..."

"I know, but I want to make sure you're taken care of." It's the least I can do since he's going without sex because of me.

He steps back and tilts his head slightly to the side. We're both quiet for a beat before he speaks. "This is about that woman..."

"It's not about her, but yes, her coming by and me seeing that giant dildo reminded me how different our sexual experiences are."

"I don't give a fuck about that."

"You say that now, but you haven't gone a long time without sex yet."

"A night of being with you the way we were last night means more to me than a thousand nights of meaningless sex." He cages me into his arms and kisses me softly. "I'm falling for you, and I don't give a fuck how long it takes before we have sex. Days, weeks, months, years. I. Don't. Care. I just want to be with you. Understood?"

Warmth spreads through my chest. "Yes."

"Good. Now let's go eat before the guys take all the food. I'm starved."

After we eat, Chase walks me out to my truck, where we make out like teenagers for several minutes before he reluctantly lets me go, only because the tone goes off and he rushes to get the information so they know where they have to go.

Instead of going home, I head to Lexi's, calling her on the way to make sure she's up for company. Since Alec is at work, she'll be alone with Abigail and it'll be the perfect time to have a sisterly talk. But first, I'll go by the coffee shop and get us a couple coffees.

"LIKE, HOW BIG?" LEXI ASKS.

"Big."

"Show me with your hands."

I spread my hands apart and her eyes go wide.

"Holy shit, I don't care how much I love Alec, you won't find me sticking a fake dick the size of an eggplant inside my cooch."

"It's not about the size of the dildo..." I tell her with a laugh.

"Okay, then what is it about?"

"I don't think I want to wait anymore."

She raises a brow. "You are not changing your mind about waiting until you're in love because Chase screwed some dumb skank with a giant squash."

I'm in the middle of taking a sip of my drink, so it all comes out, all over me and the table. Abigail giggles, thinking I'm a riot.

"Things have changed," I tell her, wiping down the table. "I'm going to be twenty-two next month and Chase is thirty. We're both grown adults."

"You're right," she says. "Just make sure you're doing it for the right reasons. Because you like him and want to be with him, and not because you think you have to keep up with the parade of women he had coming in and out of his room."

CHASE

I walk through the door of the condo, both mentally and physically drained. My eyes are barely able to stay open, but I force them to long enough to find Georgia, who is still asleep and cuddled into her blankets. I peel my clothes off me and then drag myself into her bed, wrapping myself around her body like a human burrito.

She squirms slightly, adjusting to my intrusion, and then turns over so she's snuggled into my chest.

"You smell weird," she says, her voice gravelly from sleep. "Like soap and... something else."

"We were putting out a fire all morning." I hold her tighter, thankful she's alive and safe. I love my job, but days like today suck. "It was out of our zone, but station 116 called for backup."

"Everyone okay?" she asks, her arms encircling my torso.

"The fire started in an apartment on the seventh floor. Everyone got out, except for two. A four-year-old and the babysitter. Parents were out and came home to find their child dead."

Georgia gasps. "I'm so sorry, Chase." She pulls me down to her and kisses the corner of my mouth.

"The babysitter made it... Admitted to smoking and leaving it lit."

"Oh no." She holds me tighter. "That's horrible."

"I'm so damn tired," I tell her, hearing the slur in my words. "I know I said we'd talk when I got home but—"

"Shh," Georgia murmurs. "There's nothing to talk about, Chase. We're good. Just go to sleep."

My eyes meet hers and my heart clenches in my chest, recognizing how different being with Georgia is. I just had a shitty night, the entire time questioning why this world is so fucked up and God is so cruel, but the moment I'm in her arms it's as though everything, even just for a brief moment, is perfect. I know it's only an illusion, and everything on the outside is still there, but maybe that's how it should be when you're with the person you love—as if the entire world, every shitty part of it, fades away while you're together.

I WAKE UP TO FIND GEORGIA SITTING NEXT TO ME, typing away on her laptop. When she feels me shift, she stops typing and glances down at me.

"Hey," she says softly.

"Hey." I drag myself up and lean against her headboard. "What time is it?"

"Five."

Shit, I slept the day away. Then I remember why and my stomach sinks. Losing someone in a fire always sucks, but a child... Fuck.

Georgia closes her laptop and sets it on the nightstand, then takes my hand in hers. "I wish there was something I could do or say..."

"You're doing it." I lean over and kiss her. "Why don't we get out of here? Go grab something to eat."

"You sure?"

"Yeah." It will do me some good to get out and be distracted. Especially since I'll be back at work at eight o'clock tomorrow and will need to be in my right mind.

"All right," she agrees.

After we're both showered and dressed, we head out. We're in my vehicle, trying to decide where to go, when my phone rings over Bluetooth, alerting me that my mom is calling.

"Hey, Mom," I say, answering.

"Hey, baby. What are you up to?"

"Nothing. About to grab something to eat. You?"

"I wanted to see if you'd like to go to dinner... You know since it's your birthday."

Georgia gasps. "Today is your birthday?"

Shit, is it? "What's today?"

"Chase, don't tell me you forgot your own birthday," Mom chides. "Is that why you ignored all my calls this morning?"

"I was sleeping. Was up all night putting out a fire."

"It's your birthday?" Georgia repeats, glaring at me.

"Who's with you?" Mom asks.

Georgia's eyes go wide, as if now realizing my mom can hear her.

"My girlfriend," I tell my mom, grinning at Georgia.

"What?" she shrieks. "You have a girlfriend? And she didn't know it's your birthday?"

Georgia's back to glaring at me. "He didn't tell me," she says. "Would you like to join us, Ms. Matthews?"

"Oh, please call me Sharon, and I would love to meet you. Have anywhere in mind?"

"Well, since it's Chase's birthday we should go somewhere nice."

I hold my breath, knowing it's going to be somewhere expensive. Georgia is from a different world than my mom and me.

"Oh! How about Zavarelli's in Venice since you love Italian. Have you guys ever been?"

When Mom doesn't say anything, I do. "I don't think either of us has been, but I do love Italian."

"Perfect!" Georgia beams, completely oblivious to the tension in the car and over the phone.

Mom clears her throat. "Okay, I'll, umm, see you guys soon."

I know she was planning to pay since she always does for my birthday, but I have no doubt this restaurant will be out of her budget.

When we arrive, my suspicions are confirmed. The place is expensive. While we wait for my mom to arrive, Georgia puts our name down for a table and I glance at the menu. Shit, over fifty dollars a plate. There's no way my mom is going to be okay eating here.

"Hey, Georgia, if there's a wait we can go somewhere else."

She frowns. "It's only a few minutes, but if you don't want to eat here..."

"It's not that," I tell her, pulling her into my arms. "But my mom always insists on paying for my birthday dinner. Growing up we didn't have shit for money, but every year for my sister's and my birthday, my parents would take us out to dinner." It was literally the only time we ever went out to dinner.

Georgia's brows furrow in confusion. "You only went out to dinner twice a year?" She's not judging. She's curious. Because she wasn't raised like I was, where eating out was a luxury people in my neighborhood couldn't afford.

"Yeah, it became a tradition. And she's going to want to pay tonight, but..."

Georgia nods in understanding, her face falling. Damn it, I didn't mean to upset her. "I'm sorry. I didn't even think."

"No, don't be sorry. You didn't know and you were trying to be nice."

My phone dings with a message from Mom: **I'm sorry, I can't make it after all. Rain check?**

I try to hide the text from Georgia, but she sees it before I can. "How far do you live from here?" she asks.

"About thirty minutes. Why?"

"Tell your mom we'll be there in forty-five minutes." She takes my hand and speed walks to my car. I do as she says and then pocket my phone.

After a quick trip to the grocery store, I pull up to my childhood home, hoping my mom had enough time to pick up. She'll be embarrassed if we walk in on the place in less than perfect condition.

Georgia and I grab the bags of groceries she bought—without letting me see—and walk up to the front door. Before I can knock, Mom swings the door open. "I just got your text. What are you doing here?"

"The restaurant didn't have any availability," Georgia lies. "So, I thought we could make dinner here." She holds up the bags. "I'm learning how to cook and have been dying to make Margherita pizza. We could all make it and hang out... I also brought a cake."

Mom's gaze flits between Georgia and me and then her eyes light up. "That sounds perfect." Georgia walks inside, heading straight to the kitchen, while my mom and I hang back for a second.

She pulls me into a hug. "Happy Birthday. I'm so glad you're here."

"C'mon, you two," Georgia yells. "If I have to make it all myself, I'll be eating it all myself."

Mom laughs. "I've only known her for a minute, but I can already tell she's different..." *Than Victoria,* she means but doesn't voice.

"She definitely is," I agree.

When I step farther into the house, noticing how clean it is, she says, "Since the day you came over... that night..." Of the anniversary of my sister's death. "I've been making some changes."

"Really?"

"I saw how scared you were for that girl at the hospital and I didn't want you to feel that way toward me."

I take a look around again with new eyes and see just how clean the place is. "That's good, Mom," I tell her.

"I've also broken up with my boyfriend," she admits proudly. "He wasn't any good. I'm taking some time for myself."

"Good," I tell her again, kissing her temple. "I'm proud of you."

The night is spent with delicious food and great conversation. My mom and Georgia hit it off, despite how different they are, and I know it's because of Georgia. Because even though she's worth millions, she doesn't act like it. She's real and sweet and doesn't have a judgmental bone in her body, and fuck if tonight didn't make me fall even more in love with her.

"You know," she says, when we get home. "I saw in a movie once that the man gets birthday sex." She waggles her brows playfully.

I halt in my place. "Butterfly..." Is she saying what I think she's saying?

She saddles up next to me. "I like you and you like me..." Actually, I'm in love with her, but we won't go there right now. "And we're both adults. I don't see why we have to wait."

"Because you said you didn't want to have sex until you're in love," I remind her.

"So, my plans changed." She shrugs shyly.

I'm all about letting a woman make her own decisions, but the fact that she's saying this right after that chick showed up to get her fake dick tells me she might not be thinking clearly.

"There's no rush," I tell her, taking her into my arms and placing her on the bed. "We have our entire lives to be together." Before she can argue, I connect my mouth with hers, silencing her.

GEORGIA

"He won't have sex with me."

Mom snorts and Lexi laughs.

"I'm being serious. Because I told him I want to wait until I'm in love, he won't have sex with me." It's been almost three weeks since Chase's birthday dinner and he meant what he said about it not being a rush. That night, while he refused to let me give him birthday sex, he did get a birthday blowjob... But that was it. He won't take things any further. We make out, give each other orgasms, but he always stops before we have sex.

I even tried to get him drunk the night of Lexi's and my birthday outing, but he wasn't having it. He did give me some amazing orgasms that night, before we fell asleep in each other's arms.

"I think that's romantic," Mom says.

Lexi and I both roll our eyes at the same time.

"Well, it's going to happen," I tell them. "And tonight."

"Tonight?" Lexi confirms.

"Yep. For one, I'm in love with him, and two, I'm ready."

"You're in love with him?" Mom asks, covering her heart with her hand.

"I am, and I want to take this next step with him. Even if we don't work out down the road, I won't regret being with him."

"Then it seems like you're ready," Mom says. "Are you on birth control?"

"Yep. And we've both been tested, so we know we're clean. I want it to be special... Chase has to work late, so I'm planning to cook him dinner when he gets home. I want to buy some lingerie."

Lexi laughs. "Alec never appreciates the lingerie. He just wants to rip it off."

"Same thing with Tristan," Mom adds.

"Mom!" We both groan at the same time.

"What?" she says. "It's girl talk. I can't help that your father is who I'm having sex with." She shrugs. "So, you want to buy lingerie? There's only one place to go: Agent Provocateur."

Chase: On my way home. Want me to pick up dinner?

Me: Nope, dinner is made. ;)

I SHAKE OUT MY HANDS, TRYING TO GET RID OF MY

nerves. I'm not nervous about having sex with Chase. I'm ready. I've talked to my mom and sister about what to expect and researched as well. I know it seems like overkill, but I want to be prepared. What I'm nervous about is Chase turning me down. I'm putting myself out there and I'll be devastated if he tells me he doesn't want to have sex with me yet.

I considered serving dinner first then giving him me for dessert, but then I wondered if we would be too full and it would make us both feel gross—well, specifically me since I bought a skimpy piece of lingerie and want to look sexy in it. After eating a meal, I'll probably look pregnant with a food baby.

So, instead, I'm serving dessert first: me on a platter, er, well, in the bed. Since I'm already dressed in the lingerie, with my hair done—I went with natural waves—and just a bit of makeup on, I climb onto the bed and position myself in the center, ignoring how stupid, instead of sexy, I feel. The lights are dimmed and I lit a couple of candles on each side of the bed for ambiance.

The door opens and closes and then I hear Chase's footsteps getting louder, the closer he gets. "Butterfly," he calls out as he opens the door. He stops in his place, taking me in, and I wait with bated breath for his reaction.

When he doesn't say anything for several long seconds, I curse myself. Maybe the candles were too much...

But then his hazel eyes lock with mine and I see the lust filled in them. He kicks his shoes off and then walks over to the bed, sitting on the edge. "Was expecting dinner, not dessert," he says, always on the same page as me. "This is a pleasant surprise."

He pulls his shirt off, exposing his six-pack abs he works hard for, and then crawls onto the bed so he's kneeling in front of me. He spreads my legs slightly so he can fit between them and drags his hands up my bare thighs. "You look gorgeous," he says, dropping his hands to either side of my head and kissing me. "I'm the luckiest fucking guy in the world to have you to come home to."

He kisses me again, this time slipping his tongue between my parted lips. Before things get hot and heavy, I have something I need to tell him, so I pull back slightly.

"I'm ready," I tell him, needing him to know this isn't just me getting sexy. "I know it's only a short time since we've been together, but you've quickly become to mean so much to me." I cradle his face with my hands, needing the connection. "I've fallen in love with you, Chase, and I know without a doubt I'm ready to have sex with you."

The most beautiful smile spreads across his lips. "It's about damn time you caught up to me," he says, shocking the hell out of me. "I've known I was in love with you since the night I saw you in the hospital."

I gasp. The night of the hospital? That was several weeks ago... "You've loved me since then?"

"Yeah, but I didn't want to scare you off." He shrugs. "I love you, butterfly, so damn much."

"I love you too."

Our mouths unite, and our tongues meet, swirling against each other. Chase uses one hand to hold himself up, and the other explores my body. When we break apart, coming up for air, he peppers soft, open-mouthed kisses along my jaw and neck. His face dips and his lips cover my nipple, sucking on it through the silky material.

"Did you buy this for me?" he asks, running his palm downward and landing on my hip.

"Yes," I breathe.

He smiles softly. "Then I won't rip it off your body."

He sits up and gently peels the straps off my shoulders, pulling them down my arms and exposing my breasts. He takes one into his mouth, swirling his tongue around the hardened nipple. I squirm, like I always do, wanting more.

I reach down and unbutton his jeans, and then Chase pulls them down the rest of the way, removing his socks and briefs, leaving him naked.

My gaze goes to his hardened length, excited to finally have it inside me. I wouldn't admit it to Lexi, since she lost her virginity when she was younger, but I'm glad I waited until now. Until I'm old enough to understand my body and Chase's. Until it was with someone I love.

Chase tugs my negligée off the rest of my body, leaving me in only the tiny G-string that barely covers anything.

He situates himself between my parted legs and then kisses the top of my mound through the thin material. I sit up on my elbows, so I can watch as Chase drags the material off my legs and drops it off the side of the bed.

The second the flat of his tongue laves up my center, my eyes roll upward and I drop onto my back. He plunges two fingers inside of me, filling me completely, and the pleasure intensifies. Every time he does this, I feel so full, I can't imagine how good it'll feel once his dick is inside me. I squirm at the thought, just as my orgasm hits me like a tidal wave, waves of pleasure washing through me.

I've barely come down from my high, when Chase is on me. His mouth crushes mine, as his body connects with my own. He parts my thighs with his and then he enters me. I try to stay relaxed, but it's hard when it hurts so badly.

"Breathe, butterfly," he murmurs against my mouth.

I do as he says, and then he pushes past the barrier of my virginity.

"You okay?"

"Yeah," I tell him, dragging my fingers through his hair. "Keep going."

With his arms caging me in, and our bodies flush against one another, Chase slowly and gently and deeply makes love to me. He tells me how good I feel, how much he loves me, and when he finds his release, draining every drop into me, I've never felt so cherished in my life.

GEORGIA

Beep. Beep. Beep. Beep.

I pry my eyes open as Chase's alarm goes off, reaching over and hitting end so the noise will stop. Once it's quiet again, I glance over and find Chase passed out on the other side of the bed. He's lying on his back, naked, with one of his arms over his head, and the blanket covering the bottom half of him. My thighs clench in memory of both times we made love last night. The second time with him making sure I came as well.

My heart swells at how selfless and caring he is. I don't know why his ex-wife cheated on him, but I can't imagine wanting anyone but him for the rest of my life. Her loss is definitely my gain.

"Either stop staring, or get over here and ride me," he says, his voice raspy from sleep.

When I laugh at his grumpy playfulness, he smirks, wrenching open one eyelid. "I wasn't kidding." He throws the blanket off him and exposes his hard as steel dick.

I crawl over to him, ignoring the soreness between my legs, and climb onto his body. My hands go to his shoulders and his find my hips. We work together to guide his shaft into me, both of us moaning once he's completely seated in me.

"I could live like this," he says, reaching up and brushing my hair out of my face. "Inside you... It's my new favorite spot in the world."

He grips the back of my mane and pulls my face down to his. His tongue traces my bottom lip, then my top, before it slips past my parted lips—teasing, caressing. His skilled mouth devours mine, as he starts to move inside of me. I had assumed since I was on top I would be in control, but Chase's actions, as he fucks me from the bottom, deeply, steadily, say otherwise.

The way we move has my climax building quickly, and too soon, my entire body is trembling in pleasure as the most mind-blowing orgasm grips me.

"Fuck," he groans. "Your pussy is so damn tight." His eyes squeeze closed, and his dick swells inside of me. A second later, warm seed is filling me. As if coming drained him of all strength, he releases his hold on me and sighs deeply.

"Yep," he says softly. "I could definitely live right here inside of you. The outside world be damned."

After we've showered together, where he gives me one more orgasm, telling me it's to tide me over for the next twenty-four hours while he's on shift, he heads to work.

After meeting Lexi for breakfast, where I gush about how amazing being with Chase is, and we share stories about our guys, I go home and spend the next several hours working. When I'm all caught up, I lie on the couch, wishing Chase were here, and binge watch an old show.

As my eyes are closing, a text comes in from Chase: **I have to cover for a guy tomorrow morning, so I won't be home until later, but I want to take you out. Be ready for 5:00.**

Butterflies swarm my belly.

Me: Will do.

At five o'clock on the dot the next day, there's a knock on the door. I groan, seriously hoping it's not another one of Chase's sex toy skanks.

Reluctantly, I get up and open the door, mentally preparing myself. Only it's Chase on the other side, dressed in a pair of black dress pants and a royal blue button-down shirt with the sleeves rolled up to his elbows.

Before I can ask him why he's knocking on his own door, he pulls a bouquet of multicolored flowers out from behind his back, and my heart flutters. "For me?" I ask dumbly. I've never been given flowers before.

Chase chuckles. "For you."

"Thank you. They're beautiful." I take them from him and bring them into the kitchen. They're already in a pretty vase, so I just add water then set them on the center of the table.

"You look beautiful," he says, his eyes traveling down the length of my body. I'm dressed in a floral print dress that stops several inches above my knee and ties in the front, exposing a bit of cleavage. I've paired it with my black Saint Laurent peep toe heels.

"Thank you. Do you keep clothes at work?"

Chase's expression turns nervous. "I, um, well, I used to leave from work sometimes and go out..." Ah, during his playboy days.

He clears his throat. "You ready to go? We have reservations at six and you know how traffic is around here."

Flowers... reservations... "Are you trying to romance me?"

Chase throws his head back with a laugh. "Yeah." He closes the distance between us. "That's what boyfriends do, butterfly. We romance our girlfriends."

Not all boyfriends do that, I think but don't voice out loud.

"Okay, but just so you know, I'm already a sure thing, so if it's to get in my pants, it's unnecessary."

Chase chokes on his laughter. "Good to know." He kisses the corner of my mouth. "But it's not to get in your pants. It's to remain in your heart." My heart stammers in my chest. I didn't know love could feel like this, and I'm so thankful I didn't give up on finding it. If I had, I wouldn't be here with Chase.

We arrive at Cove 54 a few minutes before our reservation and are brought to our table right away. After the waitress reads off the drink specials, since it's a bit of a special occasion, I order an

Apple Pie martini. Chase orders a Coke.

When the waitress walks away, Chase raises a brow. "An Apple Pie martini?"

"What? It sounds good, and we are on a date... I figured I would adult."

He laughs. "Okay, *adult*. How was your day?"

"Good. Yesterday, I met my mom and Lex for breakfast. It was nice. I got a lot of work done. Went for a jog..."

The waitress sets our drinks down and I take a sip. It's delicious. Fruity and sweet. We order our meals, and once she's excused herself I ask Chase how work was.

"It's been unseasonably dry, so the amount of fires have been higher than usual. Hopefully it rains soon."

We spend our meal flitting from one subject to the next. I love how well we click and how our conversations are comfortable and flow easily. I don't have to think about what to say, it all just comes naturally.

When dinner is over, Chase declines dessert, telling me he knows a place that has the best homemade ice cream sandwiches. When he was little and he and his sister would get good grades, his mom would take them here. It was a bit of a drive, but worth it.

It's within walking distance from the restaurant, so with his hand in mine, we walk there. There's a bit of a line, but it moves quickly.

"One chocolate chip cookie dough ice cream sandwich," he tells the woman.

"We're sharing?"

"Trust me, they're huge."

After he pays, she hands him the dessert. He's right. It's more than big enough for two people. The cookie is gigantic and is bent in half like a taco, with the ice cream in the middle.

"It's not a sandwich. It's a taco!"

"Yeah, a delicious taco."

We walk away from the ice cream place until we arrive at a more secluded spot. There's a small pond with benches surrounding the area. Instead of sitting on the bench, Chase and I sit on the grass near the water.

"How are we supposed to eat this monster-sized ice cream taco?"

"Like this." He lifts the taco and brings it to my lips, so I can take a bite. It's sweet and cold and delicious.

"Mmm... So good." I go to take another bite, but he pulls it back over his head, reminding me of when he stole my laptop and did the same thing.

"Uh-uh, you have to share," he says with a smirk.

Unlike last time, he's on the ground with me, and within reach. Before he realizes what I'm doing, I climb into his lap, straddling his thighs. Out of shock, he falls back slightly, just barely holding on to the ice cream.

I reach for the ice cream and pluck it out of his hand. "You share," I tell him, taking a big bite.

He laughs, then his arms go around my waist. He lifts his upper body up, colliding with my own, and his mouth crashes against mine. His tongue delves between my lips, swirling against mine. "Mmm... you taste delicious," he murmurs against my mouth.

My center grinds against his pelvis, and I feel the hard bulge in his pants. I glance around and it's dark, not a person in sight. It would be so easy... too easy...

I drop the ice cream into the grass and Chase groans, as if he knows what I'm about to do. "Baby, someone might see," he starts, but I shut him up with my mouth.

I quickly undo his zipper and pull his dick out of its confines. Since I'm in a dress, I simply pull my panties to the side and then guide myself onto Chase. To anyone walking by, it would look like I'm just sitting in his lap.

"Fuck, butterfly," he grunts, when I lift up slightly and then slam down. Without any foreplay, I'm tight around him, to the point it's almost painful.

His mouth latches onto my neck, sucking and licking my sensitive flesh. His fingers pinch my nipple, tweaking and pulling on the erect nub through the thin material of my dress and bra. His other hand finds its way under my dress and lands on my clit, massaging gentle circles across it. Soon, I'm soaking wet, sliding up and down his shaft. And then I'm coming. Hard. His mouth connects with mine, muffling my sounds of pleasure, as he chases and finds his own orgasm.

When we've both come down from our highs, out of breath and spent, he chuckles softly, his eyes meeting mine. "You never cease to amaze me," he says softly, kissing me hard on the mouth. "It's the most beautiful thing, to watch you spread your wings and fly."

GEORGIA

Me: You guys up for some lunch?

I've been working all morning on designing a new website for a huge internet-based company and when I finally came up for air, I realized I hadn't eaten all day and I'm starving...and missing Chase. He's been busy at the station the last several days because one of the guys on another shift moved and they need to hire someone to replace him. Since they're short a man, he and a few other guys have been covering the guy's shift, which means, aside from the couple nights he slips into my bed and makes love to me before disappearing before I wake up, we've barely seen each other.

Chase: Made by you? Always. We're just getting back from a house call, so we're all starved.

I find a recipe I have all the ingredients for, and once I'm done making it, I package it up in a container and drive over to the station. I park my truck and grab the dish, and am walking up the drive, when I hear something. I stop and listen. Crying.

I glance around but don't see anyone. Setting the food down on a bench in the garage, I walk slowly toward where the crying is coming from, until I find a stroller with a baby in it near the front door. I rush over to it and look around for the owner of the baby. Who in the hell would leave a crying baby here?

Unable to handle the sound of the baby crying, I pick her up to try to soothe her. Luckily, it's fall in October and in the seventies. Even with the temperature on the cooler side, she's still warm. Her face is red and splotchy from crying and when she looks up at me with her beautiful, tear-filled hazel eyes, my heart is physically removed from my chest.

"Shh, it's okay, pretty girl." I hold her close, hoping to slow her crying down, and thankfully it works.

"Mamamamma," she stammers through her cries.

I wipe the tears from under her eyes. "I don't know where she is," I tell her. "But we'll figure it out."

"Georgia," Alec says, walking around the corner. "What are you— Is that a baby? What are you doing with a baby?"

"I found her here," I tell him, holding her close to my chest. Most likely exhausted from all the crying, she lays her head on my shoulder and snuggles into me.

"Let's bring her inside and see if there's a note or something in her stroller," Alec suggests.

He grabs the stroller and I follow him in, rubbing the baby's back. Her cries have finally stopped and she's quiet, twirling a piece of my hair with her finger.

We walk inside and the guys all swing their heads my way, each sporting a different look of confusion.

"That's not Abigail, is it?" Luke asks.

"No," I tell him. This baby is bigger, probably several months older than my niece. "I found her at the front door."

"What the fuck?" Thomas says. "Nobody rang the doorbell."

Chase walks in, taking in the sight in front of him, and says, "What's going on?"

"I heard a baby crying, so I went to check it out and found her in a stroller by the front door."

"What the hell?" Chase says.

"Maybe she thought she could leave the baby because of the SafePlace sign," I point out.

"It's for the youth, not for parents abandoning their children," Chase says in disgust.

"Well, she obviously cared enough to leave her somewhere safe," I tell him, sitting in a chair. "It's better than harming her or leaving her somewhere she could be hurt."

"I found a note," Alec says. His eyes meet Chase's and something about the expression on his face has my belly doing a flip-flop. "It's addressed to you."

"Me?" Chase walks over and takes the envelope from Alec. He takes one look at it and curses under his breath.

He rips it open and unfolds the note inside. While he reads it, everyone is quiet, but when the little girl in my arms lifts her head to look at me, and her hazel eyes meet mine, I already know what the note says.

"She's mine," Chase murmurs. "According to my fucking bitch of an ex-wife she's mine." His eyes meet mine before they land on the baby. "Her name is Hazel."

I find myself holding her tighter now that I know she's Chase's daughter. I don't want to judge Victoria, but that doesn't stop me from wondering how she could do this to him.

"Her birth certificate lists a Raymond Forrester as the dad," Alec says, "and based on this, she was born January first, making her ten months old."

"That's the guy she was cheating on me with," Chase says. "She was pregnant while we were still married and didn't say a damn word."

"What does the letter say?" I ask.

"She wanted her to be Raymond's but when she was born and had my hazel eyes she knew she wasn't. She didn't want to lose him, so she lied. Hazel had a herniated belly button and when they brought her in to have the surgery they asked for the parent with her matching blood type to donate blood in case there's an emergency since she has a rare blood type. Neither parent matched and he threatened to leave her, saying he won't raise another man's baby." Chase tosses the letter to me. "She chose him over her daughter."

I shake my head and place the letter on the table. I don't need to read it. All I want to do right now is hold this precious little girl.

"So, what do we do?" I ask.

Chase's hard expression softens. "Fuck, I love you."

"What?" I ask, confused.

"You said 'we'."

"Of course I did..." Because we're a *we* and I'll be by his side every step of the way.

"Mamamama," Hazel murmurs, taking my face in her hands. "Mama."

My eyes meet Chase's and he shakes his head. "I can't believe she did this."

"Do you want to hold her?" I ask, standing.

His eyes go wide. "I..."

"You hold Abigail all the time," Alec jumps in. "You got this."

I notice everyone else has left the room, obviously wanting to give Chase some privacy and space. "Hazel," I say, stepping over to Chase. "This is your daddy."

Slowly, I hand her off to Chase, but as we're making the exchange, she grasps ahold of my shirt. "Mamamamama," she screams, her eyes filling with tears.

"You found her, so she feels safe with you," Alec says.

I glance at Chase, who looks completely heartbroken. "Hey, she'll get to know you," I tell him. "She's just scared."

"And she knows how good you are," he says, cupping the side

of my face. "I don't blame her for wanting to remain close to you. I feel the same way." He kisses the corner of my mouth.

"I think we should call DCFS," Alec suggests. "Make sure you do it the right way so she can't take her away from you since you're not legally the father yet."

"I agree." Chase pulls out his phone. "But first, I'm hiring an attorney."

He calls several attorneys, including the ones my dad and Alec's mom recommends, but at the end of each call, instead of hiring them, he keeps thanking them and hanging up.

"What's going on?" I ask him, concerned. After rocking Hazel, she fell asleep, so I laid her down on the couch, creating a barrier so she's safe. Since Carter was in the room watching TV, he said he'd keep an eye on her.

When Chase doesn't answer right away, I take his hand in mine. "Don't shut me out. What's wrong with all these attorneys?"

He sighs. "I can't afford them. LA is expensive as hell. I have some money in savings, but it won't be enough if we run into any problems, and then I'll have to switch attorneys. I have a couple credit cards, but I need to buy her stuff..." He sounds so damn defeated, and my heart aches for him.

"Who do you want to hire?"

He eyes the list he's made. "The guy Mia recommended sounded good. He's a little older, but handled her divorce."

"Then hire him," I tell him.

"Georgia, I can't let you—"

"Yes, you can, and you will. We're in this together. I have more money than I'll ever spend in my lifetime. Money I received from a man who hurt my mom and neglected me." Tears fill my eyes, but I force them back. "There's *nothing* I would rather spend that money on than to help a father get custody of his little girl."

Three hours later, Chase has hired attorney Ben Schneider. Ben has filed for emergency custody based on Victoria's note and has an appointment scheduled for Chase to take a court-appointed paternity test tomorrow, as well as a court date scheduled for next week.

Hazel has woken up, and after looking through her bag and finding some baby food but no bottles, and speaking to Abigail's pediatrician who assures me at this point it's okay to feed her regular soft food, I heat up some sweet potatoes I brought that was part of the lunch for the guys and feed them to her. I also shred some of the chicken and feed her that as well. She eats while sitting in my lap, the entire time banging on the table and giggling at Chase and Alec, who make faces at her.

"Chief said I can use the personal days and vacation time I've accumulated to take some time off and get Hazel situated," Chase says a little while later.

"Good. We can go by the store and order her stuff and have it delivered. While we're there, we can get anything else she needs like clothes and diapers and wipes..." I start making a mental list of everything she'll need.

"What about a car seat?" he asks.

"It's attached to her stroller."

After installing her car seat into my truck, since she doesn't want to leave my side, Chase and I head home to drop off his car and then go to the baby store.

I place Hazel into the shopping cart and she looks around curiously while I wheel it through the store. Noticing that Chase is completely out of his element, I take over, grabbing everything we might need. On occasion I ask him for his opinion and he gives it to me, but for the most part, he lets me do my thing. I'm not a mom, obviously, but I was there with Lexi while she was buying everything for Abigail, and my cousin Micaela also has two babies—RJ, who's two and a half, and Dustin, who's six months old.

While we're walking through the clothing section, Hazel reaches out and grabs a onesie, making us both laugh.

"Do you want this, pretty girl?" I ask, finding her size and handing it to her.

Her face lights up as she brings it to her mouth, munching on the fabric. "I think she likes it," Chase says with a soft smile aimed at his daughter.

After ordering a complete nursery and paying extra for next day delivery, we check out with the cashier and then head home. We're both exhausted, so we go through a Starbucks drive-thru to get caffeinated, and once we're home, I play with Hazel while Chase brings everything in and then sets up the portable crib-slash-play pen, so she has somewhere to sleep tonight.

"Where should we put it?" he asks.

"Either my room or yours…"

"About that," he says, gripping the curves of my hips. "I know we have an extra room, but I was thinking, what if we kept the spare room as is and cleaned out my room for her nursery?"

I tilt my head to the side, pretending like I have no idea where he's going with this, and he laughs.

"Fine, I'll spell it out for you." He tugs me closer, glancing over at Hazel, who's on a blanket on the floor, happily banging on her new toys.

"Will you officially move in with me?" His brows dip. "Or I guess, can I officially move in with you?"

I laugh at his silliness. "Yes, I would love for you to move in with me." I wink saucily, making him chuckle.

"So, we put her crib thing in my room?" he asks.

"I think since this is a new place and we're pretty much strangers to her, we should put it in our room."

"I agree," he says with a grin.

Once it's set up, we feed her and then give her a bath. By eight o'clock, she's half-yawning, half-whining, telling us it's time for her to go to bed.

"You want to try to put her to bed?" I ask Chase, handing him Hazel. In the last few hours she's really warmed up to him.

He's hesitant at first but nods in agreement, taking her from me. I hold my breath, praying she won't cry, and release it when she lays her head down on his shoulder.

I watch as he rocks her to sleep, and when he's not looking, I pull out my phone and take a picture. It's the first one of him and his daughter. Tomorrow, I'll print and frame it.

Since neither of us is ready to go to bed yet, after Chase lays her down in her temporary bed, while I click on the baby monitor, we tiptoe out to the living room, both of us dropping onto the couch in exhaustion.

"I couldn't have done this today without you," Chase says, pulling me into his lap. I straddle his thighs and run my fingers through his hair. "I was so damn shocked and scared...I didn't know which way was up."

"Yes, you could've. And you would've. Because you're an amazing man and her father, and I can already tell you love her."

"I do," he admits. "I'm so damn mad at Victoria, but I'm also so grateful that she gave me that precious little girl." He shakes his head. "It's so fucked up."

"You can't change what happened, but you can control how you handle it, and you're handling it." I kiss the corner of his mouth. "And I must admit, watching you rock her to sleep was the sexiest thing I've ever seen."

GEORGIA

"What are we doing with this dresser?" Chase asks.

I glance at it. It's Lexi's old bedroom set. It's in perfect condition, but we don't need it, and I doubt she'll want it. "Let's put it out front and call one of those donation places to pick it up."

Hazel cries from her crib, letting us know she's awake. "I'll grab her," Chase says.

I step over to the dresser and pull the top drawer out. It's filled with Chase's shirts. I pull them out and place them on the bed, then open the next drawer. Each one is filled with clothes. I'll need to make room in my dresser for all of this stuff.

"Hey, butterfly, do you remember how much—" Chase's words are cut off when I open the bottom drawer, finding what looks like an entire sex toy shop in there, and gasp in shock.

"Shit," he says. "I was supposed to clean that out, and then

Hazel..." He thrusts the baby at me then slams the drawer shut. "This was before you... way before you."

I'm speechless. There must've been fifty different types of toys in there.

Chase hauls ass out of the room and then back in with a bag. But before he opens the drawer, he glances at me. "Hazel's hungry."

He's trying to dismiss me so I won't see all the toys. Too late for that. I nod and take her out to the kitchen, setting her in her high chair, and then go about preparing some mashed up veggies and meat, all while trying to rid my brain of the sight of all those toys. I have questions... so many damn questions.

A few minutes later, he passes by us with the bag in his hand, opening and closing the front door. He must be throwing it out in the dumpster. When he comes back in, we work in silence to rid his room of the furniture, and just as we're finishing, the furniture company with Hazel's stuff arrives. The day flies by, and by the time everything is set up and Hazel is in her own room asleep, we're both drained. Normally parents have months to prepare for a baby, not hours.

I'm showering the day off, when Chase steps into the shower to join me. His arms encircle me from behind, and he presses a soft kiss to my shoulder, making me sigh under his touch.

"I'm sorry," he murmurs into my ear.

"You have nothing to be sorry for."

"I said I didn't want anyone else in our relationship, in the bedroom, but by not getting rid of that shit, I brought them in."

"Can I ask you a question?" It's something I've been thinking about all day.

"You can always ask me anything." He spins me around so we're facing each other and backs me against the wall.

"Did you use those same toys on different women?"

He shakes his head. "Most of what you saw was still new. Only a couple toys had been used and I was planning to throw them away, but I forgot. I wasn't about to drop a dildo into our garbage can."

"So you keep a stash of toys for when women come over?"

"*Came* over," he corrects. "Past tense, because the only woman I've been with in several months is you. But yeah." He averts his eyes, looking slightly uncomfortable. "I kept them for when women came over."

I nod even though he can't see it since he's not looking at me. "I better get out in case Hazel wakes up." She's actually a very good sleeper, and independent. She rarely cries or fusses. I'm afraid to think it's because she was neglected.

He sighs but moves his hand so I can get out. After drying off and getting dressed, I go to bed, feigning sleep when Chase comes in a few minutes later. I feel the bed dip, but he doesn't try to hold me like he usually does. I want to roll over and say something, but I'm upset and don't know how to deal with it. He probably thinks I'm mad about the toys, but I'm not. I can't change what he did before us nor would I want to. I love Chase the way he is. What I'm upset about it is the fact that we've been sleeping together for a while now and he hasn't once tried or mentioned using a single toy.

Me: Can we meet without kids?

Lexi: Sure! Alec is off today so he can stay with Abigail. Where?

I TYPE OUT THE ADDRESS OF THE LOCATION AND TELL her to meet me in an hour.

"I'm meeting with my sister," I tell Chase, who's lying on the floor, playing with Hazel.

"Everything okay?" he asks. We haven't talked since I found the toys yesterday, and we need to. But first there's something I need to do.

"Yeah, I won't be gone long."

I bend at the knees and give Hazel a kiss. She glances up at me and grins her adorable toothless grin. "I can pick up lunch on my way back."

"Sounds good."

I'm about to stand, when Chase grips the back of my neck and tugs me into him for a kiss that feels like so much more than just a kiss. It's a plea, an apology, a declaration.

"I love you," he murmurs against my lips.

"I love you too."

"A SEX SHOP?" LEXI LAUGHS. "YOU KINKY LITTLE BITCH!"

I roll my eyes. "I found an entire drawer of sex toys in Chase's room when we were moving his stuff from his room to mine."

Lexi's eyes go wide. "Damn, so Chase is the kinky one."

"Nobody's kinky," I groan. "I read an article on sex toys and a lot of them help heighten the pleasure."

"Hmm...Maybe I'll pick out a few things to surprise Alec with." Lexi waggles her brows.

We enter the store and the woman at the desk, who is dressed in sexy lingerie and wearing blood red lipstick, smiles. "My name is Jenn. Let me know if you need any help."

I pull out my phone and open the list I've made. "I need to buy this stuff," I tell her, turning the phone around so she can see it.

"Right this way." She stops in front of a wall of dildos. "Do you know which size you'd like?"

I think about the article I read. It said to get one around the same size as your significant other's. "Around eight inches."

Lexi snorts, then laughs. "Oh my God. Is that the size of Chase's dick?"

"Can you act like a mature adult about this, please?" I brought her here because I was scared to death to come alone, but now I'm rethinking that.

"Sorry. I'll take one too. But make mine eight *and a half* inches." She winks, and the woman laughs.

"Mine was a guess. I didn't actually measure him."

After we both pick out our choice of dildos, we move on to the next item.

"Oh, shit," Lexi says. "Butt plugs? You're totally going to let him in the back door, aren't you? Now, that's love."

Jenn shakes with laughter. "This one is a customer favorite." She hands me the silver teardrop-shaped toy. It's kind of heavy and has a pretty blue jewel at the front of it. "You'll need lube too." She plucks a bottle off the shelf. "Never allow anyone in the back door without proper preparation."

I read that in the article as well.

"I want one with a yellow jewel," Lexi says, grabbing it off the wall, along with a bottle of lube. "And I'm going to need to read this article you read."

We go from area to area, getting all the items on my list, and a few others Jenn suggests, and once we're done we both check out—Lexi having bought everything I did.

"This was fun," she says once we're outside in the parking lot. Then her face goes serious. "You're doing all this because you want to, though, right? Not because you feel like you have to, to keep Chase."

"Chase hasn't once asked me to use toys."

"So you're doing this because you think he wants to?"

I've thought a lot about this since that sexy toy slut came by to pick up her dildo. "I'm doing it because I want to. Because he obviously has the toys for a reason, and I've heard the way those women would scream in pleasure. Every time he touches me, he brings me pleasure. I think he hasn't brought up the toys because he sees me as this delicate little flower, and I don't want to be that person. I'm *not* that person." At least not anymore...

"He thinks I'm mad because he used those toys with women before me, but I'm hurt he doesn't want to use them with me. Up until now, we've been open and honest with each other. I don't know why he's shutting me out regarding this matter, but I'm going to force him to talk to me. Then hopefully, get him to use them with me."

Lexi nods thoughtfully. "You're a different person with him. And not in a bad way. I never would've thought he would be the guy for you, but after seeing you two together, I can see that you're both crazy in love with each other. You're good for each other."

After a few more minutes of talking, we hug goodbye, with the promise to meet later this week to get Abigail and Hazel together—and to discuss which toys are the best—Lexi's suggestion, not mine.

I stop by the deli to pick up lunch, then head home. Chase is sitting on the couch, watching a baseball game on TV. When I walk in, he pauses it. "Hazel just went down for her afternoon nap."

I set the food on the table, then head back to our room to hide the bag of toys in my drawer for later. We eat lunch, steering clear of any sex toy talk, focusing on Hazel and what the lawyer said, and once she's awake, since it's nice out, we take her for a walk to the park.

"No, pretty girl. Don't eat the sand," I tell her, removing her hand from her mouth.

Her cute little face scrunches up at the word no, making Chase and me laugh.

"How about the swings?" Chase suggests, lifting her up and flying her through the air like she's a plane to take her mind off the sand. He's so good with her, and I love to watch them both. The way she's accepted him so completely... it's as if she knows he's her dad. I don't have any other babies to compare her to, since I've never lived with one, but I thought the transition would be rougher. Instead, she shocked us by warming up to both of us.

Chase sets her in the swing and buckles her in. Her mouth immediately goes to the plastic piece in the front, and I half-gag, while Chase places a blanket in the front.

"She's like a puppy," he says with a laugh. "Chewing on everything."

"She's probably teething." We've been busy reading about babies every chance we get, since neither of us had any notice we'd be getting one, and we both want to know what to expect.

"I talked to your mom earlier," Chase says nonchalantly.

"Oh really?" They've spoken a few times since Hazel's come into our life. My mom is supportive, hell, both my parents are, and have offered to help in any way they can.

"Your parents are going to take Hazel tonight." His eyes meet mine. "So we can talk."

I swallow thickly, not liking this. What could he want to talk about that requires Hazel to be elsewhere? Is he planning to break up with me?

"She's only just become familiar with us. Don't you think it's too soon for her to spend the night somewhere else?"

"We'll pick her up tonight. We're dropping her off around four." He said we, so maybe he's not breaking up with me.

"Okay."

We hang out a little longer at the park, until Hazel whines she's hungry. While I take a shower and get ready, Chase feeds her. Then while he gets ready, I put together a diaper bag for my mom. Hazel's been around my parents, so when she sees them, she doesn't cry.

"Have a good time," Mom says with a smile. "We'll be here."

"Thank you for watching her," Chase tells her, kissing her cheek.

"Anytime."

"Where are we going?" I ask, once we're back in Chase's car.

"Home."

Home...Well, okay, then.

CHASE

I have to fix this. Georgia and me. I couldn't fix my marriage, and now I know it was a blessing in disguise, but I can fix us. I'm determined to make this right. I have to. Georgia is different than Victoria. Our relationship is different. The love I feel for her is different. And I'm not going to lose her over sex toys.

Grabbing a bottle of wine I know Georgia likes, I pour us each a glass, then sit on the couch across from her. I'm not really a wine drinker, and she only drinks it on occasion, but it's the only alcohol we have here, and I'm thinking alcohol might be needed for the conversation we're about to have.

"Thanks," she says, accepting the glass from me and taking a sip.

"I'd like to talk to you about what you found in my drawer," I begin. "I want to explain."

Georgia nods, sipping more of her drink.

I take a deep breath, praying that opening up and being honest with Georgia doesn't mean losing her. "As I told you before, Victoria was the first woman I was with sexually. We were young and we both learned a lot about ourselves and each other through exploration. When she started using drugs, and I had her go to rehab, I resorted to porn and my hand." I shrug sheepishly, hoping Georgia understands it was my way of satisfying myself while my wife was gone and that I'm not some weird porn freak.

"Watching the porn, I came across videos with sex toys..." I clear my throat. "I was curious and bought a few so Victoria and I could try them out once she got out. The drugs had kind of messed with our sex lives, the intimacy between us put on the backburner because she was too busy getting high. Only when she got out and I mentioned them, she freaked out on me, telling me I was sick and accusing me of cheating on her."

Georgia's eyes go wide, but I focus on finishing my story before I chicken out. "I never brought it up again. Sex between us went from hot and heavy to almost nonexistent and the intimacy between us was gone. We still had sex occasionally, but it was more due to marital obligation on her part. And then she started cheating on me. I didn't know it at the time, but looking back, it makes sense. She would only have sex with me once in a while to keep me from bitching."

I blow out a harsh breath and down the wine, setting the glass on the table. "When we got divorced, I started having one-night stands. One night a woman I was with busted out some sex toys.

At first, by using them, I felt like I was sticking it to Victoria. Like a fuck you." I laugh humorlessly. "But I quickly learned toys can heighten the sexual experience. I picked some up at the store and would try them out with women who didn't mind."

I lock eyes with her so she knows how serious what I say next is. "I don't require toys in bed. I just want you, however I can have you. I was just having fun. I was a twenty-nine-year-old man who had only been with one woman. But the truth is, Georgia"—I set her drink on the table and take her hands in mine—"had I known what was on the other side of your door, I wouldn't have been with a single one of those women. I'm not trying to romance you," I say with a playful smirk to lighten the mood. "I'm just being honest. So please don't read too much into those toys, and please don't walk away thinking I'm some weird, kinky porn freak."

Georgia barks out a laugh. "I don't think you're weird or a freak, and even if you were, I'm okay with both." She stands and pulls my hand. "Come with me."

I follow her into our room and she pulls a bag out of her drawer, handing it to me. It's black, and there's only one store I know of that uses black bags.

I open it up and peek inside it, finding all types of sex toys. "Georgia..." I shake my head. Of course, instead of running, she would try to please me. But that's not what I want.

"Before you give me some speech about how you don't need toys, yes, I bought these after seeing them in your drawer, but I didn't just buy them for you. I bought them for us. I love our sex life, and if these toys can make it even better then I'm up for trying them out."

Fuck, how the hell did I get so damn lucky to find this woman?

"And you swear you're not doing this because you think I need it?" I set the bag down and glide my hands down her side to her hips.

"I'm doing it because I want to. I promise."

I tug her close to me, until our bodies are flush against each other. "And if we do anything you don't like or you're not comfortable with, you'll tell me?"

"Yes," she breathes.

I move us to the bed, lifting her into my lap, and grab the bag of toys, dumping it out. There's so much shit here. I would've loved to see her buying all this, picking out what she wanted. I can tell by the stuff she bought, she put thought into it.

"I read an article about sex toys," she says, her cheeks tingeing an adorable shade of pink.

"Don't be embarrassed." I kiss her lips, loving how soft and warm they are. "You reading up on it, going to the store to buy this stuff, is not only fucking sexy but it means the world to me. You didn't make accusations, you didn't judge, and it made me fall in love with you that much more."

She smiles softly. "Lexi went with me and bought everything I bought. I'm sure Alec will be thanking you later."

I chuckle, elated that we're able to talk like this.

"So, while you were reading, did any of this stuff stand out to you? Anything you want to try first? We have a few hours before we have to pick up Hazel."

Georgia bites her bottom lip, looking over the items she purchased. "I don't know. I'm curious about all of them. It seemed like a lot of the women in the comments on the article like the butt plug and anal beads..." Her fingers run along the small bottle of lube. "They seemed to like anal in general. But a few said it hurts." She lifts a dildo. "I'm not sure how I would feel about using this instead of you. I like the feel of you inside me."

She glances up at me and shrugs shyly. "I'm okay with trying anything. You know more about this stuff than I do. I trust you to make sure whatever we do is good for the both of us."

Fuck. This. Woman. The way she opens herself up and puts her trust in me is so damn refreshing.

"Take your clothes off and lie on your stomach," I tell her, grabbing the blue jeweled butt plug and the anal vibrator and taking them with me. In the bathroom, I open both packages and wash the items with hot, soapy water, then dry them both off.

When I come back, she's lying just how I told her to, with her slim back and pert ass on display. Her head is resting sideways against her pillow, and her arms are above her head. I set the items on the bed, out of the way and then strip out of my clothes, leaving me in only my boxers.

I climb onto the bed and straddle the backs of her thighs. Squirting some oil in my palms, I begin at her shoulders, massaging her tissue. She moans and sighs, her body instantly relaxing. I work my way down her back, massaging any knots I can find. Once I get to her ass, I rub some more oil into my palms and then massage the globes, teasing at the crack. She tenses up slightly, assuming I'm going to take her ass, but I keep moving down, massaging her thighs and calves, and then giving her cute feet attention.

Once I've massaged every inch of her, and she's loose and comfortable, I work my way back up her body, stopping at her ass. I give it extra care, opening her cheeks and oiling it up, before I insert a single finger into her tight hole.

She tenses up, but quickly relaxes, spreading her thighs a little to allow me better access. I push my finger in and out of her, adding another one and then deepening my thrusts little by little, until she's writhing against the bed, moaning softly.

"This might burn a little at first," I warn her, as I push the butt plug in. It's on the smaller size, so her hole opens up easily and sucks it right in. When I know it's in there good, I roll her over onto her back.

"How does it feel?"

"I don't know," she breathes. "I can't really feel it so much. I felt it more when you were using your fingers."

"You'll feel it soon." I pull my boxers off then spread her legs, dropping on top of her with my palms landing on either side of her head.

I cover her mouth with mine. The kiss starts off slow and gentle, but soon we're ravenous, our tongues moving frantically against each other. I reach between our bodies and dip my fingers between her thighs, finding her soaking wet. Needing to feel her warmth, I guide myself into her until I'm balls deep in her tight pussy.

She breaks our kiss, her head going back with a moan. "I feel it," she says. "I feel..."

"Full," I finish for her. Between my dick in her pussy and the butt plug in her ass, she feels full. I know this because I can feel the hardness of the butt plug through her inside walls.

"Fuck me, Chase, please," she begs, tugging on my hair and pulling my face down to hers. I waste no time, drawing out slowly and then thrusting my hips forward, sinking inside of her again. And again. Her mouth moves to my neck, sucking on my flesh, while I bury myself to the hilt in her warmth over and over again until we're both groaning out our releases.

She sighs in contentment when I pull out, but I'm not done with her yet. "Don't move," I tell her, making her eyes go wide. I grab my boxers and wipe my dick off so I don't get cum all over the sheets, and then I slide down the bed.

"Chase, what are you doing?" She tries to close her thighs, but I push them open, watching as my seed drips out of her pussy. One day that seed will plant inside her and make a baby. The thought of her round with my baby growing inside her has my dick swelling.

I reach onto the floor and scoop up her shirt, tucking it under her ass, and then I lift her legs slightly, exposing the butt plug. I spread her cheeks and pull it out slowly. She moans, and I know what I'm about to do she'll love.

Grabbing the anal vibrator, I slick it up with a bit of oil then push it between her ass cheeks. Georgia groans as her hole sucks the object into her. I give her a moment to get comfortable and then I press the button on the end, making it vibrate. Her eyes go wide and she squirms.

"Feel good?"

She nods.

"It's about to get better." I drop to the side of her, taking one of her breasts into my mouth. I suck on her erect nipple, making her moan. At the same time, my fingers find her clit. I massage the swollen nub in gentle circles, working her up into a frenzy. The closer her orgasm, the tighter she squeezes her thighs, the louder her breathing gets. And the more turned on I am. I've been with more than my fair share of women, but not a single one of them compare to Georgia and the way she makes me feel.

I continue to stroke her clit, while the vibrator works her ass over. Until it all becomes too much and she falls off the edge, her entire body loosening as she comes. She screams my name in ecstasy, trembling all over. Her pussy gushes, covering my fingers with her juices, and I pull the vibrator out of her ass, making her moan loudly.

"Holy shit," she says, once she's come down from her high. "That was incredible." Her half-lidded eyes meet mine. "Which toy is next?"

I laugh, pulling her to me for a hard kiss. "No toys," I murmur against her lips, dragging her onto my lap. "Just me and you, butterfly."

CHASE

One Month Later

"Congratulations, Daddy!" Georgia says, throwing her arms around me. "How does it feel?"

Surreal, amazing, like my heart has been removed from the cavity of my chest and placed into my daughter's hands. "Really good," I tell her. "Thank you for..." Fuck, there's so much to thank Georgia for. I don't even know where to start.

"You don't ever have to thank me," she says, tears in her eyes. "I'm just so happy Hazel is finally legally yours."

Legally mine. Because Victoria signed over her rights. After the paternity test confirmed I'm Hazel's father, I petitioned the court for full custody. I wasn't sure if Victoria would fight me, maybe come to her senses that she's giving up her daughter. But she never did. A week after she was served, she signed the papers.

I didn't actually see her do it. She sent the notarized papers in the mail like the coward she is, along with a note apologizing for being a shitty person and saying she's going to rehab.

Georgia, like the too good person she is, suggested maybe I should go visit her and see if she's okay. It's a big decision to give up your child. I told her Victoria's not my problem and as far as I'm concerned she's dead to me.

"Let's go get our little girl," I tell her, throwing my arm around her shoulders and walking out the door. Hazel might not legally be Georgia's, but she's the best damn thing in Hazel's life.

When we arrive at the condo, all of our friends and family are there. There's a huge banner across the back wall that reads, "Congratulations," as well as an assortment of food and drinks spread out along the counters and table. Pink and yellow streamers and balloons are decorating the entire area.

"Congratulations," Alec says, giving me a hug. "Is paternity leave over yet? You ready to come back to work?" he asks, making everyone laugh. I took time off to get to know Hazel and to also deal with her custody, but I'm definitely ready to get back to work. Georgia has offered to keep her while I'm at work since she works from home, so it'll work out well.

"Yeah, I'll be back at work Monday."

"Dada!" Hazel yells to get my attention. I glance over at my mom, who's holding her, and smile.

When Hazel wiggles for her to set her down, Mom does so. Hazel steadies herself on her feet and then with a huge smile, takes one step and then another, until she's over to me.

"Finally!" Georgia laughs. "I got it on video!" Every time she's taken a few steps, neither of us has had our phones on us. She's been determined to catch it on video.

"You're such a good walker," Georgia says to Hazel, tickling her belly. "Pretty soon you'll be running circles around your daddy."

"Dada!" Hazel says, pointing at me. Fuck, I'm a dad. To the most precious little girl in the world.

Georgia beams. "Yep! That's your daddy."

"*Dow! Dow!*" Hazel says, wiggling her tiny butt to get down.

"I can't believe she's going to be one soon," I say to Georgia as we watch Hazel walk like a cute little drunk person over to Lexi, who scoops her up into her arms for a hug.

"It'll be a Harry Potter party," she says with a laugh. We showed her a dozen different baby shows, but she had no desire to watch any of them. It wasn't until we were watching a Harry Potter marathon on TV one night that she stopped and watched like her eyes were transfixed to the television. We thought it was a one-time thing, but every time we put it on, she'll sit and watch the movies for hours.

"Did someone say Harry Potter?" Mason asks.

"It's Hazel's favorite," Georgia tells him with an eye roll.

"I knew that little girl was special," he says. "Harry Potter is the shit." He clasps my shoulder. "Congratulations, Chase."

"Thank you."

After everyone leaves—Charlie refusing to leave until the

condo is cleaned up—and it's only Georgia, Hazel, and me, we settle onto the couch to watch a Harry Potter movie for the millionth time. Hazel snuggles up between Georgia and me and, within minutes, is snoring softly.

"I'm exhausted," Georgia says with a tired, happy smile on her face. "Today was a good day."

"It was." I lean over and kiss her. "Why don't you go take a bath and I'll put her to bed."

Her eyes sparkle. "Only if you join me." She winks, and my dick swells in my pants at the thought of fucking her inside the spa tub.

"Deal."

I lay Hazel down in bed, kissing her good night and turning the monitor on, then go in search for Georgia, finding her exactly where she said she would be—in the tub with bubbles filled halfway up her torso.

The lights are dimmed a bit and she's leaning against the edge with her head dipped back, her eyes closed. I take a second to take her in. The last few months she's come to mean so much to me. Every bump in the road, every obstacle, she's been there at my side. The positive in my negative. The light in my dark. The beautiful in my ugly. The fucking perfect in my way too imperfect world.

"Are you going to join me or just stare at me all night?" She lifts her head and her gorgeous green eyes meet mine.

I strip out of my clothes and, when she moves forward so I

can situate myself behind her, her perky tits splash in the water slightly. The water is hot and she fits perfectly between my thighs. She backs up, her soft body using my front to get comfortable, and her head lulls to the side, resting on my shoulder.

"If I could, I would freeze this moment," she says softly.

"In the bathtub?" I joke. Absentmindedly, I run my fingers along the underside of her breasts. She's soft to the touch, and I know if I were to taste her she would be sweet. Fucking perfect.

She laughs and it sounds lazy and content. "Maybe not exactly right here. I just mean in general." She takes my hand in hers and guides it to the top of her breast, indicating she wants me to massage her breast.

"I never imagined my life like this... With you and Hazel. I'm just so happy," she says with a sigh. "And it's because of you. Because you pulled me out of my room, refusing to let me hide."

I pinch her nipple between my finger and thumb and she moans softly. "I don't know what our future holds," she continues, "but right here, right now, it feels like I've finally found my perfect path."

I don't exactly believe in her perfect path shit, but I get what she's saying. Because with her in my arms, and my daughter under the same roof as us, things do feel pretty damn perfect.

I dip my head slightly and press a kiss to her bare shoulder and then her neck. I drag my hand across her stomach and find the apex of her thighs. "Spread your legs for me, butterfly," I murmur.

She does as I ask, and I push two fingers into her center,

pumping in and out of her. Even in the water, I can still feel how wet she is. I use her juices to create friction on her clit. Sucking on the sensitive spot on her neck, I quickly bring her to a climax. Her entire body trembles in pleasure, her moans filling the quiet room. I love that I'm the only one who's done this to her. Has made her happy, made her feel like she's found that perfect path.

As she turns around and straddles my thighs, guiding her warm, wet pussy around my rock-hard dick, I capture her mouth with my own. My fingers dig into her hips, helping her ride me. As our mouths tangle, our tongues dueling with each other, my mind goes to what she said a few minutes ago about wanting to freeze time.

If I could, I would freeze this moment—me inside her, her wrapped around me. After my divorce, I couldn't imagine ever settling down again. Giving my heart and soul to another woman. But with Georgia, I can see it all. The lazy Sundays, the family dinners, the laughs and smiles and the love. So much fucking love. And with those thoughts, I know it's not about freezing time, but about having what we have all the time. Every day for the rest of our lives.

And I know just the way to make that happen...

"OOH, OOH, OOH," HAZEL SAYS, TRYING TO MIMIC THE noise the monkeys make. It's Sunday and our last day together before I go back to work tomorrow morning, so Georgia suggested we take a family trip to the zoo. Which gave me an idea...

"That's right," Georgia says, kneeling next to Hazel. "Can you say monkey?"

"*Key-key*," Hazel says, butchering the hell out of the word before she pushes off the fence and toddles down the sidewalk toward the next exhibit.

Georgia runs after her, scooping her up and peppering kisses all over her face.

"I love seeing Georgia so happy," Charlie whispers to me. "Thank you."

After Georgia mentioned the zoo, and an idea formed, I invited her family to join us, as well as my mom. I also invited Mason and Mila and Alec's sister since they're considered family. I wanted to invite Kaden and Ashley, Georgia's grandparents, but they're already in Breckenridge for the holidays, along with Tristan's younger sisters, Emma and Morgan, and their families. We'll be joining them next week for Christmas. Micaela, her cousin and best friend, is also here with her husband Ryan, and their two kids.

"You don't have to thank me," I tell Charlie, watching Hazel throw her head back in a laugh as Georgia lifts her up and moves her kisses to her belly, tickling her. "I'm the lucky one."

We go from exhibit to exhibit, then stop for lunch, before continuing on. The entire time, I'm half here, half in my own mind. I have a plan, but the closer I get to it, the more nervous I get. What if it's too soon? What if she thinks I'm crazy? What if we end up like my last marriage?

But the second we step foot into the butterfly exhibit and Georgia beams at me, with my daughter in her arms, as hundreds, if not thousands of butterflies flutter around us, I know I have nothing to be nervous or scared about. Because this is Georgia, and everything about her and us is different.

I glance at Lexi and our eyes meet. I nod slightly, so she understands, and her face breaks into a knowing grin.

"This is so beautiful," Georgia says, spinning Hazel in a circle as the butterflies fly all around us. "Hazel, do you see the butterflies?"

"*Bu-fy!*" Hazel squeals, trying and failing to capture one.

"Yes, butterfly," Georgia says, kissing her on the cheek.

I watch my two girls interact, until Georgia glances over at me and smiles oddly. "You okay?"

Her question snaps me out of my trance, reminding what I'm about to do. "I'm prefect," I tell her, stepping closer. I give Hazel a kiss on her cheek, then turn my attention back to Georgia. "These last couple months with you and my daughter have been the best of my life."

Her lips curl into a smile that has the ability to light up the darkest of rooms.

"Remember when you said you wanted to freeze this moment in time because you're so happy? I felt that deep, because every moment I spend with you and Hazel are moments I want to freeze."

I pull the ring out of my pocket that I've been carrying around, waiting for the perfect moment. It's not in a box because it would be too bulky and obvious.

Georgia's eyes home in on it and widen. "Chase," she breathes.

"It's impossible to freeze time, but I don't think it's actually about freezing time but wanting those special moments to last."

She nods but doesn't say anything. Hazel, oblivious to what's happening, looks around at the butterflies, giggling and pointing.

"We can't freeze the moments, but we can spend the rest of our lives creating them, so many of them it'll feel like they're frozen in time." I drop to one knee and Georgia gasps, tears filling her eyes. "Marry me and spend the rest of our lives creating memories that are worth freezing. But not just with me as my wife," I add, "but as Hazel's mom."

Her becoming Hazel's stepmom isn't enough. She loves her as much as I do, and I want us to be a family. I want her to adopt Hazel and raise her as her own.

I extend my hand so she can see the ring. It's a simple platinum band with a circle diamond in the center with butterflies made out of tiny diamonds hugging both sides. When I saw it, I knew it was the ring for Georgia.

"Yes," she says, tears trickling down her cheeks. "Yes, I will marry you."

I slip the ring onto her finger and then stand. Cradling her face in my palms, I tip her head up slightly and kiss her soft and sweet.

Hazel screeches, wanting our attention, and Georgia and

I both chuckle into each other's mouth. "I love you," I murmur against her lips.

"And I love you."

"I DON'T WANT TO WAIT," I TELL HER LATER THAT NIGHT, after Hazel is in bed and we've finished making love.

We're both sweating and still catching our breaths, so it throws her off. "Wait for what?"

"To get married." I roll over onto my side and grip the curve of her hip. "For you to adopt Hazel. For us to add to our little family." We haven't talked about having our own children, but that hasn't stopped me from thinking about it.

Georgia's eyes widen. "So let's not." She kisses the corner of my mouth. "Let's elope. Go to Vegas and get married."

"Your parents and sister would kill us."

She shrugs. "So, we'll invite them."

"You don't want a big wedding?"

She shakes her head. "I just want to marry you."

"Then let's do it. Let's elope."

GEORGIA

One Month Later

"I can't believe you're doing this," Lexi says for the millionth time. "Who are you and what have you done with my sister?"

I laugh softly, trying not to jostle my arm.

"It's just like her tattoo," Chase says. "She's been transformed from a caterpillar into a butterfly." He winks my way and grins. I glance down at the work in progress on the inside of my wrist. A single butterfly. When the tattoo artist asked if I wanted it to be colored in, I told him no. The shades of gray represent the me before Chase and the butterfly is who I've metamorphosed into because of him.

My thoughts go back to earlier when we said our vows in a little chapel on the Vegas Strip in front of our family.

"I, Chase Matthews, promise to love and cherish you, to protect you

for the rest of our lives. I promise to stand by your side, to always support you, to be the person who cheers you on when you spread your wings, and like the beautiful butterfly you are, fly..."

After we said our I dos, Chase surprised me with the papers for me to legally adopt Hazel. I knew I'd be signing them, but I didn't know he had them rushed to be ready in time for me to sign the day of our wedding. Afterward, we went to a nice restaurant with everyone and celebrated. The babies were all getting tired, and we were about to call it a night, when my mom and dad offered to watch my cousin Micaela's little ones and Abigail, and Chase's mom offered to keep Hazel for the night, so we could continue the celebration.

We were walking past a tattoo shop and I told Chase I wanted to get a tattoo to commemorate the occasion. I told him he didn't need to get one as well. I knew his stance on tattoos—that he didn't want to permanently mark his body until he found the right one. But he shocked me when he said he would like nothing more than to get one with me.

Chase, not giving a shit how girly some might think it is, insisted on getting a butterfly as well, only his is a bit darker, and with Hazel's and my name etched in the wings, and it's on his left pectoral muscle over his heart.

"All right," the tattoo artist says, wiping my wrist. "Check it out."

I glance down at the gray shaded beautiful butterfly and smile. "It's perfect."

I show it to Chase, who nods in agreement. "Perfect."

"Where to next?" Micaela asks once we're paid up and standing outside. "I'm for once not pregnant. I vote we get drunk." Her husband laughs.

"You guys can go," Chase says, wrapping his arms around me. "I'm taking my wife back to our hotel room and not coming out until tomorrow morning." I tilt my face up to look at him and he waggles his brows suggestively.

"I'm down for hitting a club," Lexi says. She pulls me into a tight hug. "Enjoy your wedding night. Congratulations. I love you and I'm so proud of you." She chokes up on the last word and hugs me tighter.

"I love you more, Lex."

We break apart—both of us wiping the tears from our eyes—and everyone else hugs and congratulates Chase and me, before we go our separate ways.

When we arrive back at the room, I tell Chase I'd like to freshen up, and of course he insists we shower together. The entire time we're washing up, we can't keep our hands and mouths off each other. I think we both want to have sex in the shower, but at the same time, we also want to make love for the first time as husband and wife in the bed. When we get out, I brush my teeth and am about to take my birth control pill when Chase plucks it out of my hand.

"What if you stopped taking this?"

"My pill?" I'm confused. If I don't take it, I'll... "You want to have another baby?"

"Only if you do." He smiles shyly. "You and Lexi are close in age and get along well. And my sister and I were too, until..." He swallows thickly. "Until the drugs, we were best friends."

I encircle my arms around his waist. "I wish I could've met her."

"I wish you could've too." He kisses the top of my head. "What do you think?"

I back up and he holds up the packet of pills. Doing the math in my head, I figure out that if we were to get pregnant now, Hazel and the baby would be just under two years apart. That's if I get pregnant right away. I've been on the pill for years, so it could take months...

"Okay," I tell him. "No more pill. Whatever happens, happens."

"Hell yes." Chase's lips curve into a sexy smirk. "Let's get started now."

He lifts me over his shoulder, fireman style, and stalks over to the huge bed, dropping me onto the center of the mattress.

"Wait! I didn't get to put on my sexy bridal lingerie." I picked it out especially for tonight. It even matches my wedding dress.

"You can show me after," Chase growls. "Right now, I need to be inside my wife." His mouth crashes against mine and all thoughts of my lingerie disappear as I get lost in my husband.

CHASE

Four Months Later

"I'm pregnant." Georgia lifts the stick with the bold word **PREGNANT** written out. "Oh my God! I'm pregnant." Her eyes light up and a huge grin splays across her face.

"You're pregnant." I pull her into my arms, both shocked and elated. Neither of us thought she'd get pregnant so quickly, so when she missed her period a couple weeks ago, she was in denial. Until the morning sickness started and we agreed it was time to take a test.

"Mama! Dada!" Hazel yells from her crib, letting us know she's awake from her nap.

Georgia wraps the stick up in toilet paper and drops it into the garbage, then washes her hands. When we walk into Hazel's room, she's bouncing up and down with the most adorable smile.

"Up, please," she says, the word please coming out like *peeze*. I lift her out of her crib and place her on her changing table so I can change her diaper.

"I can't believe by the end of this year, we're going to have another little one," Georgia says, kissing Hazel's forehead. "I think we should look for our own place."

My head jerks up. "To buy?"

"Well, yeah." She shrugs. "Maybe in the same neighborhood as my parents or near Lexi..."

My brain starts calculating how much a house in one of those areas will cost. I spent the majority of my savings on Georgia's ring, and I still need to pay her back for the attorney.

"Hey," she says, picking up Hazel and setting her down. "If you want to stay here, we can. It was just a thought."

I watch as Hazel runs over to the corner of her room and drops into her oversized stuffed chair. It has her name stitched across the back and is pink, like most of the other stuff in her room. She grabs a book and opens it, mumbling to herself like she can actually read it.

"Chase, talk to me." I look back at Georgia, who's frowning. I consider lying to her, telling her I want to stay here, but the truth is, I would love to get a bigger place, buy a home we can call ours. The problem is, I can't afford anything like that—even with me up for a promotion at work, I still wouldn't be able to afford a down payment on a house where she's talking about.

But she can. Because my wife is wealthy as fuck. And despite her financial advisor suggesting I sign a prenuptial agreement, she refused, saying she won't go into a marriage with the idea that it will one day end. We haven't discussed money, both of us too busy focusing on Hazel and being newlyweds, but it's something we should've talked about.

"I only have a little bit of money in savings," I admit, making her frown. "And I know you're rich and can afford a million houses, but I want us to be equals in this marriage. I don't want to buy a house I can't afford."

Her face contorts into confusion. "So, because *you* can't afford it, *we* can't buy a house? How does that make us equals?" She crosses her arms over her chest. "The last time I checked, we're in this marriage together, and what's mine is yours and vice-versa."

I swallow thickly, having no response.

"You're right," I admit after a beat. "My words were based on male chauvinistic pride. I'm sorry."

Georgia nods. "I don't care about the cost of the house. I just want a place to call our own. With a backyard where our kids can run around and play. Maybe a porch swing where we can sit and grow old together. We have the money to live where we want and I want our children to grow up in a nice, safe neighborhood."

She's saying everything I've always dreamed about and I can't allow my pride to keep us from having what we both want. "I want all of that too." I tug on the bottom of her shirt, forcing her closer to me. "Let's do it. Let's buy a house."

"Thank you!" She squeals. "I can't wait!"

We spend the rest of the day playing with Hazel, and once she goes to bed, we check out listings for homes in the neighborhoods where her family lives. We find a few and email the agents, asking to set up a time to see them.

As we're turning off everything, preparing to go to bed, I get a text from an unknown number that has me stopping in my place.

Unknown: Hey Chase, it's Victoria. This is my new number. Can we please talk?

Can we talk? Has this bitch lost her mind?

Me: There's nothing to talk about. Don't contact me again. You're getting blocked.

I put her name into my phone, so I have her number then block her.

"Everything okay?" Georgia lays her head on my chest and drops her arm over my torso like she does every night.

"Yeah," I tell her robotically. Then I change my mind and go with the truth. "Actually, no." She sits up, concerned. "Victoria texted, wanting to talk. I blocked her."

Georgia's mouth turns down. "Chase...maybe you should hear her out. Before everything you guys were friends."

Fuck, can she be any more innocent and naïve?

"We're not those people anymore and her choosing to abandon our daughter proved that. I want nothing to do with her."

I can tell by the look on her face she doesn't agree, but she still nods and lies back down. "If you change your mind, I'll support your decision," she says, making me fall even more in love with her.

"CHASE...CHASE, WAKE UP." I WRENCH MY EYES OPEN AND glance around. It's dark in the room, so it's late...or early. "Chase."

My vision clears and I see Georgia sitting up in bed with tears in her eyes. I immediately shoot up on alert. "What's wrong? Is Hazel okay?"

"Hazel's okay," she says softly, "but when I woke up to use the bathroom, I was bleeding." Bleeding...Fuck. "I think I'm losing the baby."

"It could be anything," I assure her, knowing nothing about how pregnancy works but trying to remain positive. "Let's get you to the hospital." I turn on my phone and call Charlie to come over and watch Hazel.

Georgia's quiet the entire drive and stays that way once we're checked in with the emergency room. Since she's only a few weeks along, it's not considered top priority, so we have to wait our turn. The entire time, I pray to God she's okay, that bleeding is normal. But when she flinches and I ask her what's wrong, and she says she has bad cramping, I know no amount of praying is going to save our baby.

Four hours later, we're told Georgia is in the middle of losing our baby. She was only six weeks along and it's apparently common for miscarriages to occur before the twelve-week mark. The doctor discharges her, warning her the next few days she'll bleed a lot, her body naturally releasing the fetus, and suggests she follow up with her doctor.

On our way home, I text Charlie to let her know, and she texts back she'll take Hazel to her house so Georgia can rest.

When we walk inside, Georgia goes straight to Hazel's room. "Where is she?"

"I had your mom take her to her house so you can have some time."

Georgia frowns. "I appreciate that, but I'd like for her to come home."

I step over to her. "Don't you think maybe you need a little bit of time to mourn? You just lost a baby. I know we only found out yesterday, but it still fucking hurts."

"I know, but losing the baby makes me appreciate what we have that much more." Tears fill her eyes. "I just really wanted to hug our daughter." She wraps her arms around her torso and I pull her into my arms, once again falling deeper in love with my wife.

"We'll go get her later. We don't want her to see either of us upset."

"You're right. You should probably get to work. You're already late."

"I called out. I'm not going anywhere. Get into bed and I'll run out and grab us some breakfast." There's no way I'm leaving her side right now. I have no experience with this sort of thing, but it feels like she's still numb, and I'm worried when the numbness wears off, she'll release every emotion she's keeping locked away right now.

"Can you also get me pads, please? I forgot I don't have any."

"Of course."

She climbs into bed and I kiss her forehead. "I'll be back soon."

On my way to the store, I get a call from Alec. "Hey, man."

"How's Georgia doing?" Lexi's mom must've told them.

"She's hanging in there. I'm going to get us breakfast right now."

There's a moment of silence before Alec speaks. "So, um, this is a bad time, but...Victoria is here and she's refusing to leave until she can speak to you."

Fuck. She can't be serious showing up at my goddamn workplace.

"I'll swing by there."

"Sorry," he says. "I tried to get her to leave, but she's being stubborn, and the only other option I'd have would be to call the cops, but I wasn't sure you would want that."

"I'll handle it. Thanks."

When I pull up, I see the Mercedes I bought her parked in the drive. I'm hoping I can get her to leave quickly so I can get back to Georgia. When I step inside, I find her waiting at the table. Her long black hair is up in a tight ponytail and she's wearing a face full of makeup. When she sees me, she stands, exposing her body. She's wearing a tiny yellow tank top, distressed jeans, and a pair of

NIKKI ASH

heels. She looks good. Clean. Sober. Good for her. But if she thinks she's going to waltz in here and make demands, she's about to be disappointed.

"This is my workplace," I tell her. "You don't come here. Ever. Well, unless it's to drop off my daughter." She flinches at my words, but I don't have it in me to feel bad.

"You didn't leave me a choice," she says softly, very unlike her. "I don't know where you live and you blocked me."

Not wanting a scene to be made in the station, I nod for her to walk outside with me.

"When someone blocks you that means they don't want to speak to you," I point out once we're standing in the back. Since the fire station is a home that was remodeled, it has a backyard. We put a swing set out here so the kids can play on it when we hold family barbeques.

Victoria steps closer to me, and I immediately see the look in her eyes. Seduction. Not over my dead body. "I'm married." I lift my left hand to show her my ring. Her eyes bulge out of their sockets. "And my wife legally adopted Hazel."

She splutters, shaking her head, at a complete loss for words.

"You didn't really think you'd come here months after abandoning my daughter and I would get back together with you and we'd be some sort of happy family?"

She clears her throat. "I messed up. Please, Chase. I just want to see my little girl."

I don't even have it in me to laugh at her audacity. Georgia is home, waiting for me to bring her food and pads because she just lost our baby while this bitch is begging to see the baby she left on a doorstop.

"I gotta go."

"Wait, please." She places her perfectly manicured hand on my arm. "Can I at least see a picture of her?"

"No, you don't deserve to see anything or hear anything regarding her. You don't even deserve to breathe the same air as her."

"Chase. C'mon, please," she whines, her tone grating my last nerve. "I was in a bad place. I'm better. I was scared to live without Raymond, but he's gone now, and you're...married," she chokes out. "All I have left is Hazel."

"Wrong," I bark out. "You signed the papers giving her up, which means you have no rights to her."

A single tear slides down her cheek. "I made a mistake."

"You've made a lot of mistakes," I agree. "But as far as Hazel goes, the best decision you ever made was giving her up." My phone vibrates in my pocket and I pull it out. It's Georgia asking if I can please get her pain medication. Because she's suffering from a miscarriage and is in pain, while piece of shit women like my ex-wife can get pregnant and carry a baby without a care in the world. Sometimes the world really is fucked up.

"I have to go." I put my hand on her shoulder to quickly guide her out. "Don't come back here. You made your decisions and now you have to live with them."

I don't bother to say bye to any of the guys, just focusing on getting Victoria into her car. "Chase, I'm begging you," she pleads as I open her car door.

"Get in the car, Victoria," I bark out. Thankfully, she listens. "Focus on staying clean, go to meetings, spend time with your parents, get a job, a hobby. But do not come around here again."

I slam the door closed and stalk away, refusing to even give her a second glance. She isn't worth my time or energy and my wife needs me.

GEORGIA

"Park! Park!" Hazel yells as the park comes into view. It's been a little over a week since I miscarried and the only things keeping me together are Chase and Hazel. I saw the doctor and she assured me there's nothing wrong with me. She even said Chase and I are more than welcome to start trying again after my next cycle, but I think we're going to wait a little bit, so we can both move past the pain.

"Yes, that's the park," I tell her, pushing her stroller down the sidewalk. Chase is at work today, so we're meeting Lexi and Abigail to play and have a picnic.

We pull up and I unbuckle Hazel. The second I put her down, she takes off running toward the jungle gym. I glance around, looking for Lexi, but she isn't here yet, which doesn't surprise me. With her gallery opening a few months ago, she's been crazy busy working out all the kinks.

I follow Hazel around, keeping my distance, since she's going through this stage where she wants to be independent, but close enough that if something happens I'm right here.

There are a few other people at the park today, and Hazel makes a friend with a little girl who's playing in the sand with her sand toys. She runs to the stroller to grab her own sand toys and plops down next to the girl to play.

I smile over at the mom, wondering if maybe I should befriend her, but before I can go over and introduce myself, a woman steps in front of me.

She has jet-black hair and bright blue eyes. Her makeup is on the heavy side and she's dressed like she's going out to a club instead of to a park.

At first, I think she's just walking by, so I move to the right so I can see Hazel again, but she steps with me. "Can I help you?" I ask, moving slightly again so my daughter stays in my line of sight.

"I'm hoping so," she says. "My name is Victoria and that little girl is my daughter." She glances back at Hazel, and my hackles rise. Maybe it's the fact that I just lost a baby, or that she has the nerve to call her her daughter, but her attitude doesn't sit right with me.

"Actually, she's my daughter," I point out. "Just like Chase is my husband." Chase had told me she came by the fire station, begging him to take her back, for them to be a family again.

She clears her throat. "I'm sorry," she says softly. "That came out wrong. Can we please start again?"

"Or we don't have to start at all. Did you follow me here?" I look around to make sure there are still other people around.

"I did, but only because Chase won't talk to me. He blocked me and—"

"Can you blame him?" I ask, cutting her off. "You hid your pregnancy from him, tried to raise her as someone else's daughter, and only when he found out and you were going to lose him, did you tell Chase, by dropping her off at the fire station, where I found her bawling her eyes out all alone."

Victoria's face falls. "I was on drugs. I can't change what I did, but that's not who I am. I've been clean for almost six months now."

"And now that you're clean and your man won't take you back, you want Chase and Hazel?" I might hate confrontation and avoid it at all costs, but until now I never had any reason to fight. Chase and Hazel, they're my reasons to fight.

"No, I thought if I could get him back, he would let me see my—Hazel." Her eyes drop slightly. "I messed up...bad. But I miss her so much. And I know you adopted her...I'm just asking to see her, spend some time with her." Her tear-filled eyes meet mine. "I love her so much."

Just as I'm about to tell her this is between her and Chase, Hazel comes running over. "Mama!" she yells through tears. "Sand. Ouchy." She rubs her eyes, and I lift her into my arms. I carry her over to the table and grab a washcloth from the diaper bag, pouring some water onto it.

"Ouchy," she repeats.

"Don't touch it," I tell her, padding her eyes gently with the washcloth.

"Ouchy."

"I know, pretty girl." I sit her on top of the picnic table and wipe her eyes one more time. She looks up at me and blinks slowly, a small watery smile creeping up on her face.

"Better?"

"Yes. I hungry!" The word comes out like *ungry*.

"Aunt Lexi will be here soon with Abigail and then we'll eat lunch."

"Okay." Her beautiful smile widens and then her eyes go past me...to Victoria. I wait with bated breath for her to remember her. It's only been six months since she dropped her off, and she spent the first ten months of her life with her. Her top lip curls up into a shy smile and her hands lift for me to pick her up. I expect Victoria to say something, to tell Hazel who she is, but she doesn't.

"She's so beautiful," she chokes out. "Is she okay?" She's referring to the herniated belly button that was still healing when we found her.

"She's perfect."

Victoria nods. "I know right now isn't a good time to talk, not in front of her, but could we please talk? Mother to mother?"

Her words are like a knife straight through my heart. She's Hazel's biological mother. She gave birth to her. Her blood runs through her veins. I'm only her mother legally. And the baby that was growing in me...I lost.

But she doesn't know that, so when she says that, she's referring to the both of us being Hazel's mother. And in a weird way I respect her for saying that. Do I think she deserves the title of Mom? No. But she could've easily disregarded me as Hazel's mother as well.

"Hazel goes down for a nap at two o'clock. If you want to give me your phone number, I can call you."

She sighs in relief. "Thank you."

After giving me her number, she reluctantly leaves just as Lexi is walking up with Aiden and Abigail. "Who was that?" she asks, obviously having seen me talking to her.

"Chase's ex-wife."

Her brows shoot up to her forehead. "Hazel's..."

"Biological mom, yeah."

"What the hell did she want?"

"To see Hazel."

Lexi curses under her breath.

"Hey, Aiden, how are you?" I ask, changing the subject.

"Hi, Lexi's sister," he says back. "I'm hungry. Lexi brought me tacos." He holds up his bag.

"Tacos sound good."

"They are good," he says back. "Lexi, where do I sit?"

"On the blanket," she says, setting Abigail down so she can lay the blanket on the grass. I grab the cooler, and we sit on the blanket with the girls, getting their food ready, while Aiden eats his tacos and tells me about the gallery and all the painting he's doing.

"I have a new friend," he says. "Her name is Melanie and she paints."

Lexi grins and whispers, "She's his special friend."

"That's nice," I tell him, ignoring Lexi. "Does she paint at the gallery?"

"Yes, and she likes tacos."

"Her mom is the artist we're featuring this month. Melanie is the same age as Aiden and works with her mom. She's autistic like Aiden. They hit it off and have been inseparable."

"That's so sweet."

"It is. She asked him to come over and he actually agreed. I'm going to go with him, though, just to make sure he's comfortable."

"I'm done," Aiden announces. "Can Baby Abigail and I go play now?"

Abigail jumps up and grabs Aiden's hand. "I go play." She recently turned one and is now walking.

"Me too!" Hazel adds.

"Go ahead," Lexi says, picking up all the garbage and stuffing it into a bag. I shake out the blanket and fold it up, while she finishes cleaning up, and then we join them over by the slides. Aiden is standing at the bottom, while the girls take turns sliding down. He catches them every time, and then tickles them, making them squeal.

"Again!" Abigail yells, sliding down so Aiden can catch her.

"Be careful," he says when he sets her down and she toddles over to the steps. "Walk, Baby Abigail."

Lexi and I laugh at that. "I think he'll always call her Baby Abigail."

"Probably," she agrees. "Speaking of babies...How are you?"

"I'm okay. The bleeding stopped. The doctor said we can try again after I get my period."

"Are you going to?"

"I don't know," I admit. "I think Hazel is enough for right now."

"Because you're scared?" she asks, calling me out.

"Maybe."

"What are you scared of?"

"For one, losing another baby." I glance at her. "But also, my first thought when I found out I miscarried was, what if I can't have a baby of my own? What if there's something wrong with my body and I can't give Chase a baby that's part me and part him? And that made me feel guilty because in my eyes, Hazel is my own."

"You're human," Lexi says, "and your fears are normal, but you know firsthand that it's possible for a parents' love to be unconditional, even if they aren't biologically related to you."

Lexi's right. Lexi and I aren't biologically related, but you'd never know it. Tristan is my adopted father, but to me he's my dad. And my mom isn't Lexi's bio mom, but she loves her as if she's her real mom. I hope one day when Hazel learns that I'm not her biological mom, she'll still love me the same.

"Do you ever wish your bio mom had come to see you?"

Lexi takes a deep breath. "She was a druggy and she never once stopped long enough to try to see me, so no, I don't." Her gaze swings over to me. "Don't tell me you're considering letting Victoria see Hazel."

"She's clean, has been for several months."

"So what? She gave her up."

"Because she was on drugs. You said it yourself. Your mom never once stopped doing drugs long enough to see you, but what if she did? What if she had gotten sober and wanted to see you?"

Lexi shakes her head. "I don't know. Drugs ended up killing her. Maybe it was for the best I never knew her."

We play with the kids, until they're both wiped out, and then Lexi heads out and Hazel and I walk home. She falls asleep in her stroller, and I leave her in it for her nap, knowing if I move her, she'll wake up and won't go back to sleep.

I stare at Victoria's number for several long minutes before I give in and call her. "Hello," she says, picking up on the second ring.

"Hi, it's Georgia."

"Oh, hey, I was hoping you would call."

"I need to know what it is exactly you want," I tell her, getting straight to the point.

"To see Hazel. To be in her life in some way. I'm just asking for a chance to prove that I can be clean and in her life."

My thoughts go back to Lexi...She didn't get that chance because her mom never stopped doing drugs long enough to want her.

"I'll speak to Chase and let you know."

"YOU TOLD HER, WHAT?" CHASE YELLS, MAKING ME JUMP. "What the hell were you thinking?" He's never yelled at me. Not once—but we've also never fought. But he's yelling now, and I don't like that. Memories from when I was little surface. My dad yelling at me, getting in my face, and then slamming the door closed. Me banging on the door and begging for my mom.

I shrink back, unable to have a conversation with him if he's going to yell. He must realize what he's done because he takes a deep breath. "I'm sorry, I shouldn't have yelled at you."

"No, you shouldn't have." I hit him with a hard glare, making it clear I'm dead serious. "Please don't do that again."

He nods and drops down onto the couch. "Georgia, you can't save the damn world, especially my ex-wife."

"I'm not trying to save the world." I sit next to him. "But the fact of the matter is, she gave birth to her, and when she was on drugs, instead of doing wrong by her, she gave her up, and now she's clean and wants another chance. And if I were in her position—"

"You would never be in her position. You can't even compare

yourself to her."

"You never know what the future holds. Anything can happen, and I'd hope if I messed up and then tried to make things right, I'd be given a second chance."

Chase snorts humorlessly. "You're so fucking naïve. This world isn't perfect. It's not filled with rainbows and unicorns." He grabs Hazel's stuffed unicorn and tosses it to the side. "You just don't get it, and I'm glad you don't. It means you've lived a life without any hardship, and I would give anything to be able to say I've lived a life like that. But what you need to understand is that the big, bad, cruel fucking world is going to eat you alive if you don't recognize that outside your four walls everything is *not* perfect."

"I'm pretty sure there's a dig in there somewhere." I stand, refusing to continue this conversation.

"It's not a dig, it's reality."

"Okay, well, I'm just going to take my reality elsewhere because I don't want to fight with you."

Chase's brows fly up to his forehead. "You're leaving?"

"I'm going for a walk."

He sighs. "Fuck, butterfly." He shakes his head. "Don't go, please."

"I don't want to fight. Maybe it makes me naïve or sheltered, but I want to believe the good in people. Lexi's mom never changed. Drugs are what killed her. But Victoria is trying to change and I want to give her the benefit of the doubt."

"And I think that's great you want to see the good in the

world, in her, but I'm trying to protect my daughter."

His words are a slap to my face. His daughter...like she's not mine. Because she isn't my blood. My baby, my flesh and blood, died before he or she was ever born.

"Your daughter...Right." I nod once.

Chase's face falls, understanding what he's just done, but it's too late.

Without saying another word, I grab my keys from the counter and leave. Chase runs after me. "Baby, please don't go."

"I have to," I tell him. "Because if I don't, things will be said... *more* things will be said. And words are powerful and can't be taken back once they're spoken."

Once I'm in my car, I drive to the closest parking lot and park. I cover my face in my hands and then I cry. I know a part of me is overemotional because of the miscarriage. My hormones are all over the place. But another part of me is hurt by what he said. The accusations he flung at me.

When my phone rings and it shows it's my dad, I pull myself together and answer.

"Where are you?"

"Like you don't know." I laugh. We have a tracking app on all our phones. "Chase called you?"

"He's worried. You've been through a lot recently and you took off."

"Then he should've thought about that when he was yelling at me and telling me how naïve I am."

Dad sighs. "Why don't you come home and we'll talk?"

"Okay."

A few minutes later, I pull up in my parents' driveway. Dad is sitting outside on the porch swing, drinking a beer. I sit down next to him, and he stretches his arm out behind my shoulders, pulling me closer to him. My head drops onto his shoulder and more tears fall. He doesn't say a word, just lets me cry it out until the tears finally stop falling.

"Chase said you want to give Victoria a chance to be in Hazel's life?"

I sit up and nod. "He doesn't agree. It's like he believes if someone messes up they should be given a life sentence."

Dad frowns. "Or he's given her a lot of chances and knows how giving her another chance will end."

"You're talking about Lexi's mom, Gina..."

"She wasn't her mom," he says flatly. "She gave birth to her, but she chose drugs over her. Walked away and never looked back."

"But Victoria did look back. She went to rehab and got better. If Gina had gotten better and wanted another chance, would you have given her one?"

Dad releases a harsh breath and meets my eyes. "At first, yes. I had hoped she would come around, especially when Lexi was little and I was exhausted and confused and lost as hell. I didn't think I was enough. But as the years went on and her drug addiction continued, I wished for her to die."

I gasp in shock. "What?" How could my sweet, caring father

wish for anyone to die?

"If she died, it would mean she couldn't be a part of Lexi's life instead of just choosing not to be. It broke my heart that the mother of my daughter didn't want her, and I never wanted to have to tell her that."

My heart sinks. He didn't want her to die because he's cruel. He wanted to protect Lexi from having her heart broken. Because that's what a good parent does...protects their child. Which is what Chase is trying to do. So why am I pushing so hard for Victoria to see Hazel?

"I'm afraid," I admit, just as I spot Chase driving up the drive. He gets out of his vehicle and then takes Hazel out. Without stopping, he walks inside, and then a minute later, walks back out.

"I couldn't stay away," he says, leaning against the railing. "We're in this together."

I nod.

"Georgia was just about to tell me why she's afraid," Dad says, standing. "I'll leave you two to talk while I go play with my granddaughter." It warms my heart that my parents so easily accepted Hazel as part of our family. He bends over and kisses my forehead. "I love you, sweetheart."

"Afraid of what?" Chase asks once my dad has gone inside.

"I'm afraid that one day when Hazel is older, if we keep her away from her mom, she's going to ask about her and we'll have to tell her she tried to see her and we wouldn't let her, and I don't know if I can live with that. I know there's a chance she might fall off the wagon again, and if that happens then we know we tried and she made her choice. But people make mistakes and sometimes they just need another chance. I want to be able to tell Hazel that we gave Victoria the opportunity to be in her life. I want to teach her to have compassion for others and their situations, to give second chances. If that makes me naïve then so be it." I shrug. "But as you pointed out, she's your daughter and it's your choice."

Chase shakes his head. "When I said she was my daughter, it wasn't a dig at you. I just said it without thinking. When I made the decision for you to adopt her, I took that seriously. She's ours in every way that matters, and I promise you I will never imply again that she's not."

"Thank you. So where do we go from here?"

"We do it your way," he says. "We give her one more chance, but I need you to promise me if she fucks up, we're done. I don't want this to become a thing. I want to live my life with you and our daughter and whatever children we have in the future, and I don't want Victoria's shit to interfere."

"Okay," I agree. "She gets one more chance."

CHASE

"One chance."

"I understand." Victoria nods.

"Only supervised visits."

"Okay."

"And you will *never* get custody back."

She flinches. "I know."

"I'm only agreeing to this because my wife thinks you deserve another chance."

She looks over at Georgia. "Thank you."

Georgia nods. "Please don't make me regret it."

"I won't." She smiles softly, reminding me of a younger version of Victoria. Before the drugs took over her life. Maybe this will work out. Maybe Hazel can have all of us in her life. But the first time Victoria fucks up, she's gone. And I don't give a shit how sweet my wife is, I won't be giving in.

"We need a schedule. You can't be coming over here any time you want," I point out. "To start with, once a week. Then we can add a day or two once we see it's working out. Are you working?"

Victoria nods. "I'm working for my dad, answering the phones." She flushes, her telltale sign she's embarrassed about something. "They didn't know I gave Hazel to you," she admits. "They had cut me out of their life when they found out I was using again."

Her parents are hardworking middle class folks. Her dad owns his own business and makes ends meet. They aren't well off by any means, but they bust their asses making an honest living.

"How did you pay for rehab?"

She flushes a deeper crimson. "Raymond and I signed a prenup. I received a settlement in the divorce."

I nod. "And where are you living?" Not that she'll be taking our daughter anywhere...

"I'm renting an apartment off Cypress."

"That's near the college." I know the area because it's in my station's zone. I'm surprised she can afford to live there on her own. She must've gotten a decent settlement in her divorce to Raymond.

"Yeah, it's in Cypress Gardens. I've applied to go to school too. I'm starting in the summer."

"That's good," Georgia says. "It sounds like you're getting your life back on track."

"I'm trying. My parents even seem to be coming around.

Maybe one day they could see Hazel..."

"How about we focus on you seeing her first," I note. "Then we can consider other relatives."

As Victoria's about to respond, Hazel yells, "Mama, up!" Both women glance at the monitor.

"Georgia is Hazel's mother," I say, not giving a shit how rude I sound. "You're Victoria." Georgia's eyes go wide, and Victoria's lips curve down. "You wanted to be in her life, that's fine. But you gave up your right to being her mother. You're a friend of...Georgia's. Nothing more until we say so."

"I understand," Victoria says. "I just want to be in her life."

"Mama!" Hazel yells. "I want up!"

Georgia laughs and stands. "I'll go grab her."

When she's gone, I look at Victoria, who glances at me. "You might have Georgia fooled, but not me. Never me."

She opens her mouth then closes it like an ugly fish out of water. "Chase..."

"I hope you prove me wrong, but I'm not holding my breath."

Georgia walks out with Hazel in her arms. She looks around and when her eyes land on Victoria, she nuzzles her face into Georgia's neck shyly.

"I'd rather not be around when you visit," I say to Victoria, standing. "So, figure out which day is good with Georgia." I kiss Georgia's forehead then Hazel's. "I need to get to work. I'll see you in the morning."

"Bye, Dada!" Hazel waves, warming my heart. I grab my keys

from the counter and glance at my girls one more time before walking out the door. They're my entire life. My whole world. And if Victoria fucks with either of them...No, I take that back. *When* she fucks with either of them, I'm going to make sure she regrets ever stepping foot back into our lives.

I arrive at the station and find Alec waiting for me outside. "How'd it go?"

"She got what she wanted."

His eyes turn to slits.

"Victoria, not Georgia... Although, I guess she did too."

I walk inside and go straight to my office to check over the paperwork from the weekend. There were a couple house calls and one at the college, an electrical issue. I get started documenting everything, and am doing so when the tone sounds off. I jump to my feet to answer the call, taking down the information so we can head out. It's a single family home that caught fire while the family was out. Turns out they left the dryer running and it caught fire— something that's unfortunately common. The fire has us occupied for hours, between putting it out and doing damage control—the home is lost, but thankfully the family is safe and well.

Hours later, when we finally get back, we all shower and eat quickly, drained and ready for some shuteye. As I'm lying on my bed, Georgia texts me a picture of Hazel and her lying on the couch together, both of them in their pajamas and smiling.

Georgia: Good night! We love you!

Me: Love you more.

I trace the lines of their happy faces and fall asleep thanking God for both of them.

I WALK INTO THE CONDO AND IT'S QUIET, WHICH MAKES sense since it's only six in the morning. A couple of guys from shift A arrived early, so I figured I would surprise the girls with breakfast. I close the door and set the bag of food down, then head back, first stopping at Hazel's room. It's dark and she's softly snoring. She wakes up around eight every morning, which gives me a couple hours of alone time with my wife.

She's sleeping when I walk in, so I strip out of my clothes and climb into bed behind her. I nuzzle the back of her hair, inhaling her sweet scent. Fuck, I can't get enough of her. She's stopped bleeding, but we haven't had sex since she miscarried. She told me she's not sure if she wants to try again so soon, and I'm leaving it up to her, so I bought a box of condoms for when she's ready.

"Mmm... Chase?" she moans sleepily.

"Who else would it be?" I tighten my hold on her hip. "There better not be another man in this bed." It's meant as a joke, but because of my past, it falls flat.

Georgia turns over, framing my face with her delicate hands. "It will only ever be you in this bed," she says, not missing a beat.

I kiss her softly, reveling in how soft her lips are, and my hand skims down her waist, landing on her pert ass. "I missed you."

"What time is it?"

"Six"

Her eyes light up. "We have a couple hours..." She presses a kiss to the corner of my mouth. "Make love to me, Chase."

She sure as hell doesn't have to tell me twice. I waste no time removing our clothes and getting lost in her. We make love, not once, but twice. I could live inside my wife, and if it wasn't for our daughter waking up at eight o'clock on the dot and demanding breakfast, I probably would.

GEORGIA

"I have freshman orientation this morning. Could we meet up at the park afterward?" Victoria asks. We had agreed on Tuesday mornings at nine o'clock, and the last two weeks, she's shown up on time. She mentioned, depending on her school schedule, she might need to switch the days or times, so I'm not surprised when she mentions it.

"Sure, what time?"

"I should be done by one."

"It'll be hot. Why don't we meet at A Cup of Fun?" It's an indoor playground for kids between the ages of six months and six years old. Hazel loves it and when we're there and it's time to go home, she'll even throw a fit that she doesn't want to leave.

"Okay, sounds good."

We hang up and I text Lexi, asking if she wants to meet us there. She's been dying to meet Victoria, so this would be the perfect time. Plus, it'll be on neutral territory, in case my sister gets protective of me and her niece. She of course says she'll be there.

After Hazel's nap, we head out. The place has a café, so we'll get lunch there. After we arrive, get checked in, and put our socks on, Hazel takes off over to the in-ground trampoline.

A few minutes later, Lexi and Abigail show up, and the girls squeal in delight, holding hands and jumping together. They're so cute together. I hope they have the close relationship Lexi and I have.

Lexi and I are taking pictures of the girls jumping when Victoria saunters through the doors.

"That's her," I mention quietly to Lexi, who glances around. I can tell when she figures out who she is because her lips quirk into a grimace.

"Did she not get the memo that this is a kids' playground?"

I look at Victoria again, noting her outfit. Unlike the last couple times we've met up and she was dressed in jeans and a simple top, today she's sporting a skintight minidress and heels.

"She just came from freshman orientation."

"Looks like she came from a strip club."

I cough to cover my laughter. "Be nice."

"Uh-huh."

"Hey!" Victoria says, super excited. "How are you?"

"Good. How was orientation?"

"I actually didn't end up going." Her face lights up. "I applied for my dream job, at LA Models, and they called me in for an interview."

"Wow, how did it go?" Chase doesn't talk a lot about her, but he did mention she used to model. I'm not sure why she quit, but that's good she's finding her passion.

"I got the job!" she shrieks.

"Congratulations!"

"Thank you." She finds Hazel, who has moved on to the pretend kitchen. "Can I go play with her?"

"Of course." When she walks away, Lexi eyes me. "What?"

"A model? I give her a month before she's back to snorting blow."

"What?" I gasp, whipping my head around. "Lexi!"

She shrugs. "Everyone knows most of the models in LA do drugs."

"Don't stereotype. It's rude."

"Whatever."

We spend the next couple hours at A Cup of Fun. The entire time I watch Victoria closely, Lexi's comment stuck in my head, but aside from her outfit being different, she's the same woman she's been the last couple weeks. She plays with Hazel with kindness and patience. We make small talk and, when the girls are wiped out and ready for their afternoon naps, head out, agreeing to discuss when to meet up next. With her new job, she has to see what her schedule will be like.

While Hazel naps, I do something I haven't done in a while—

cook for the guys. After she wakes up, we drive over to the station to surprise Chase. The guys are all outside, sans shirts, washing down the trucks. They're all built and toned, and with the music blaring, they look like they're in the middle of a music video.

My eyes home in on Chase, who's glistening with sweat and water, and my lady parts tingle in anticipation. Since my period showed up a few days ago, we haven't had sex, but it's over now, and I'm most definitely going to be jumping him the first minute we're alone.

"Dada!" Hazel yells, getting his attention. His face lights up, and he drops the rag he was holding into the bucket and bends at his knees, scooping her up into his arms. It's the most beautiful sight, and I quickly snap a picture of them before grabbing the food in the containers and walking over.

"This is a surprise," he says, leaning over and kissing me.

"We brought food." I lift the containers and the guys all cheer.

"You're amazing," he murmurs into my ear, kissing the sensitive spot just underneath. Chills shoot through my body, making me visibly tremble. Chase notices and chuckles.

"I think we need a date night soon," he says, waggling his brows.

"Maybe Lexi and Alec can keep Hazel for a sleepover."

His eyes darken with lust. "Hell yes."

I giggle, shaking my head. "Watch your language."

We eat dinner with the guys, all of them fawning over Hazel the entire time, and then head to the backyard so she can play on the swing set for a little while.

"How was your day?" Chase asks.

"Good. Met Lexi and Victoria at A Cup of Fun." Knowing he hates to talk about Victoria, I don't get into the specifics.

He nods. "She doing okay?"

I'm assuming he's referring to Victoria. "Yeah."

He nods again, then walks over to Hazel to catch her coming down the slide. While he plays with her, I shoot Lexi a text, asking if she can keep Hazel tomorrow night, promising to keep Abigail one night. She texts back she'd love to and to bring Hazel over any time in the afternoon.

While I watch Chase and Hazel run around the yard, laughing and playing, I think about what it would be like to have another little one running around. Lexi and I were close growing up. We're close with Max too, but because he's several years younger, it's a little different. While Hazel has Abigail and they're close in age, I would love for her to have her own brother or sister that she's close in age with. I'm scared of losing another baby, but the one thing Chase has taught me is not to live in fear.

"What's going through your head?" Chase asks, startling me. I didn't realize he and Hazel were standing in front of me.

"I want to try again."

His eyes go wide, then his gaze drops down to my belly. "Really?"

"Do you?" He said it was up to me, but he lost a baby too.

"I would love to, as long as you're good with it."

"I am." I kiss him. "And I think we should start tomorrow night."

———

Victoria: Can I see Hazel?

I STARE AT MY PHONE. WE AGREED ONCE A WEEK, AND she just saw her yesterday. I glance at the time. Chase is due home soon.

Me: I can't today. Sorry.

Victoria: Tomorrow?

Me: We agreed once a week... You saw her yesterday.

Victoria: I'm sorry. I have to work next Tuesday. I was hoping to see her before then.

I sigh, hating the position she's putting me in. Just as I'm about to respond, Chase texts me.

Chase: Running late. I'll be home around five with dinner.

Me: Okay, I'll drop Hazel off with Lexi and meet you at home.

Chase: Sounds perfect.

I switch back to my chat with Victoria. The bubbles show she's typing and a second later a text comes through.

Victoria: Please. I really miss her.

Because I hate confrontation, I give in.

Me: Okay, you can come over this morning.

Victoria: Thank you!

There's a knock on the door while I'm in the middle of feeding Hazel, so I get up and answer it. When I swing open the door, Victoria saunters in wearing another skimpy minidress and heels. Her hair is done, but it looks messy, like it's from last night. And her makeup is a bit smudged.

She's holding a small wrapped gift in her hand. "Morning!" she chirps a bit too loudly.

"Morning." I want to ask her if she slept in that outfit but bite my tongue.

She walks past me and straight to Hazel. "Good morning, sweet girl," she coos. "Did you miss Mommy?"

I'm stunned by her words but quickly recover. "Victoria..."

"Oops! Sorry." She bats her eyelashes at me. "It was out of habit." When her eyes meet mine, I notice they're glassy. My hackles rise. Something is wrong.

She sets the box down and lifts Hazel out of her highchair. "I got you a gift." She kisses her cheek then sets her down on the floor, handing her the box.

Hazel excitedly tears at the wrapping paper. She doesn't really know what a gift is, but she loves ripping paper apart. Losing patience, Victoria helps her rip the paper, until the box underneath is exposed.

She opens the box and inside is a...pacifier?

"This is from Tiffany's," she notes. "A platinum pacifier for my baby girl."

What the hell..."She doesn't use a pacifier," I point out, confused.

Victoria's gaze swings over to me, and for a second it looks like she was about to glare at me, but she quickly reins it in. "She did when she was with me."

I don't like her tone...at all. "That may be so, but she didn't have one when we got her, so we never gave her one."

She scoffs. "What are you saying? That you're a better parent than me?"

I flinch at how crazy she's acting. "Are you okay?"

She stands. "Of course I'm okay. And the last time I checked, you aren't my mother or my babysitter."

"No, but I am Hazel's mother, and I'm going to need you to leave."

Her face falls. "You said I could come over."

"And now I'm saying you need to leave."

I pull my phone out, ready to call the police, but thankfully, she does as I ask and walks to the door.

"I don't know what your problem is this morning, if you're jealous over my gift to Hazel, but I suggest you pull the stick out of your ass. I imagine it's painful."

And with those parting words, she walks out the door, leaving me gaping in shock. Who the hell is that woman?

Not wanting to upset Chase while he's at work, I lock the door and go about my day. I'll speak to him tonight when he gets home. Of course it'll probably ruin our night, but there's nothing I can do about that.

Hazel and I spend the day playing inside. I don't know what's going on with Victoria and the way she was acting has me all sorts of nervous. When two o'clock rolls around, Lexi sends me a text that she's going over to our parents' and will pick up Hazel on her way.

So, a couple hours later, when there's a knock on the door, I assume it's her. Only when I open it, I find Victoria, dressed in the same clothes as earlier, with her makeup running down her face.

"I'm so sorry," she cries, pushing through the door before I can stop her.

"You can't be here." I'm already grabbing my phone, ready to call nine-one-one. Something is wrong with her. It has to be drugs...or maybe she's drunk.

Hazel is finishing up her afternoon nap, so I'm thankful she won't see Victoria like this. Not that she'll remember it years from now. But I don't want her upset.

"I shouldn't have acted that way this morning," she sobs. "I'm just missing my daughter so much, and I got into a huge fight with my parents. My dad got mad when I told him I took the modeling job instead of going to school. And they didn't know about Hazel being Chase's..." Tears slide down her cheeks. "I know we agreed to supervised visitation, but if I could just bring her to their house to visit maybe they'll forgive me…"

Seeing the state of panic she's in, I don't want to upset her further. My goal at this point is to get her out of here so I can lock the door and call the police.

"I would have to ask Chase," I explain calmly. "And he's at work right now."

"Can you call him, please?" she begs. "Please."

"I can ask him tonight, but I can't call him while he's at work."

"That's such bullshit!" she yells. "I was married to him for years! I know damn well you can call him anytime." She gets in my face, and I reach for my phone, now scared.

"Okay. I'll call him."

"Thank you."

I glance down at my phone, debating whether to call Chase or the police, when the side of my face explodes in pain. My body flies backward, hitting the hard ground, and the back of my head smacks against the wall, causing me to become momentarily disoriented.

Before I can get up, a sharp object connects with my ribs—Victoria's heel. She kicks me over and over again. In the ribs. In the face. I'm trying to get up, to move away from her, but she doesn't let up. And when she finally does, and I open my eyes, she's hovering above me, her face inches from mine.

"I'm Hazel's mom, not you, bitch!" She grips my hair and lifts my head then slams it against the hard wood. Pain, like I've never felt in my life, radiates through my body. My head goes fuzzy, my brain feeling like I'm being stabbed with a million knives.

When I finally pry my eyes open, the house is quiet. Too quiet. Hazel! Oh my God, she took my baby. I grab my phone, dialing nine-one-one, as I roll over and climb into a standing position. My entire body groans in pain, but I focus on getting to my daughter's room, praying Victoria didn't do what I think she did.

The operator answers as I step into her room. Her bed is empty. She's gone.

"I need to report a kidnapping," I choke out.

I go through the details with the operator, but it's all a blur. My head is pounding, my side is in agony. I feel like I've been run over by a bus several times.

She tells me an officer will be over right away to get my statement and ask me more questions and that an Amber alert will be sent out immediately.

We're hanging up just as Lexi is walking through the door.

"What the hell happened?" she asks, setting Abigail down in Hazel's crib.

"Victoria," I sob. "She stole Hazel."

Lexi's eyes go wide. "Did you call the police?"

"Yeah. They've put out an Amber alert and an officer is on his way here." I clutch my phone in my hand. "I need to call Chase," I cry out, my body racking with sobs.

"You need to sit. I'll call him." She pulls out her phone and dials him. A few seconds later, she says, "Chase, it's Lexi. I need you to call me ASAP."

She hangs up. "I think you're going to need stitches."

"Forget about me!" I cry out. "I need to find Hazel. She said her parents wanted to see her...But I don't know where they live or what their names are. But Chase will know."

"Let me try Alec. He stayed late with Chase." She dials him on her phone and then says, "Alec, it's Lexi. Call me."

"What time is it?"

"Five o'clock."

"Oh my God," I gasp. "I was out for hours. Victoria can be anywhere with Hazel. I thought..." The room around me spins, and I have to close my eyes briefly to make it stop. "I must've been knocked out."

There's a knock on the door and I rush over to answer it, ignoring the dizziness and pain. Standing at the door are two police officers.

"Please, I need your help," I tell them. "My baby was kidnapped."

CHASE

Today has been a day from hell. First, half of the guys on shift A caught the flu and are all out. Then, while helping an elderly woman put out a fire in her fireplace because she had no idea it was a real fireplace, I dropped my phone and shattered it. I should've called Georgia from one of the guys' phones to tell her, but we got a call about a car on campus that caught fire, which took hours to deal with.

Now, as I'm about to finally leave to pick up food for dinner, hours late, the tone sounds through the station. Stein, the assistant chief, who works shift C should be here by now, but he's stuck in traffic, so it looks like I'll be commanding this one. Dispatch relays the details and the station becomes a whirlwind of activity.

On the way, Alec calls my name. When I glance at him, he looks like he's seen a ghost.

"What's wrong?"

"Lexi called... Fuck! I had my phone on silent, and we were so fucking busy."

"What's. Fucking. Wrong?"

"Victoria stole Hazel. They're both missing."

And just like that, my entire world implodes. "Where's Georgia?"

"At the hospital. Victoria beat the shit out of her and she's getting stitches."

Fuck. Fuck. Fuck!

"They have an alert out for Victoria and Hazel. Lexi doesn't know anything else."

When we arrive on the scene, a clusterfuck of activity is swarming the front of the building. I want to leave to go look for my daughter, find out what the fuck is going on, but a portion of the building is fully engulfed in flames. I can't just walk away.

My eyes find the name of the complex and it sounds so damn familiar...Cypress Gardens...Where the fuck have I heard that name before?

And then it hits me. Victoria said she lived here...Fuck! This can't be happening.

As the guys and I jump out of the engine, we scan the scene, assessing the situation. Since I'm the Battalion chief, it's my job to command. But as I watch half the building go up in flames, there's no way in hell I'm standing out here on the sidelines.

"Hey, Rich!" I yell, as I charge to the back of the rig, grabbing gear and throwing it on.

"Chief," he calls back, looking shocked to see me gearing up. "What's going on?" There's protocol, a way shit gets handled, and by me going in, I'm breaking it. But I don't give a fuck. If that bitch has my daughter in that building, I'm going to find her or die trying.

"I need you to command!" I toss the radio at him.

"What the fuck are you doing?" Alec yells.

"I'm going in! Victoria lives in this building."

Alec curses under his breath. "All right, let's go. You're with me."

Reaching back, I turn on the air on my tank and pull my mask on. Thankfully, it's only a three-story building, and the fire appears to be contained to the east side. I send up a silent prayer that Victoria and Hazel aren't here, and if they are, they aren't on this side.

"Chase, you there?" Rich says over the radio.

"Yeah."

"The fire started in apartment 257. It's leased to a Victoria Burke."

"Fuck," Alec curses at the same time I do.

It's her damn apartment.

Taking my halligan in my hand, I jam it into the doorframe of apartment 257 and pry the door open. When we break through into the apartment, the fire is out of control, thick clouds of smoke curling up toward the ceiling. Thomas and Carter work the pipe to knock down the flames, while Alec and I search the place.

With a thermal image camera in hand, I hold it up, scanning the darkness for any movement. The second I step foot into the master bedroom, my body goes numb. Victoria. She's lying on the bed, her arm draped off the side with a needle sticking out of her vein.

Rushing over to her, I try to shake her awake. Nothing. She's out, whether it's from smoke inhalation or from the drugs, I don't know.

I glance around for Hazel but don't see her anywhere.

Lifting Victoria into my arms, I radio down to command that I'm bringing her out. In the hall, I hand her over to Carter. "Take her!"

The second I go back in, the smoke is thicker, and the roaring of nearby flames can be heard over the piercing alarms. Dropping to my hands and knees, I search for my daughter, desperately throwing shit everywhere. She's not in the master bedroom or bathroom, so I move on to the rest of the apartment. I hear Alec yelling clear throughout the place, but I refuse to take his word for it. I need to see for myself she isn't here. The flames are licking the walls, the ceiling boiling and close to caving, and I know my time is limited. There's no way anyone, let alone a baby, would survive in this heat, in this smoke.

The call comes over the radio. "Command to all units. Evacuate the building. I repeat, all units, evacuate."

"Chase!" Alec calls out, struggling to get a line on the flames. "They ordered evacuation."

"Hazel is in here somewhere. I need to find her."

"The place is clear!" he yells back. "If she were here, we would've picked it up on the camera. We gotta go."

"I need to find her!" I go through a door I haven't gone through yet and find what was the nursery, fire rooted in every corner. Ignoring the command to evacuate desperately coming through the radio, I enter the room, crawling on my hands and knees with the camera in my hand.

Sweat pools inside my mask, the hiss of the tank and my heartbeat the only sounds. Fuck! This can't be happening. She has to be here somewhere. I check the guest bathroom again, then move on to the kitchen. Alec has cleared it, but I need to see it with my own eyes. And that's when I see it...One of Hazel's shoes. Georgia bought them for her last week because her feet had outgrown the old ones. I grab it to make sure I'm not seeing shit, but I'm not. It's half melted, but I know it's her shoe.

On my hands and knees, I search the other rooms for a third time. I'm crawling down the hallway when Alec yells, "We have to get out now! We've searched every part of this place and she's not here."

"She has to be!" I choke out. "She has to be."

His sad eyes meet mine. "Chase..." He can't finish his sentence, but I know what he's thinking. If she's here, there's no way she's still alive.

Command radios in that the fire's made its way to the boiler room, and Alec glances at me.

"Get out of here!" I bark, but he doesn't move. "I mean it! Go!"

With forty pounds of gear on me, sweat clings to my body. It's hard to breathe, hard to move. My hands and knees are burning with the boiling water beneath me.

I don't care about any of that, though. My daughter has to be somewhere in this fucking place. I refuse to believe she's dead. Alec is wrong. I'm going to find her and save her. As he reluctantly exits the apartment, I head toward the nursery again. Maybe she's hiding somewhere. She loves to play hide and seek. What if she's somewhere scared, waiting for me to find her.

A loud explosion shakes the building, stopping me in my tracks. I have to get out now if I want to make it out alive. For a brief moment, as I glance around, I consider staying. Is my life even worth living without my daughter?

"Chase!" Alec yells, shocking the hell out of me. "Let's go! I'm not leaving without you." He grabs me by my tank and yanks me out the door and down the stairs. When we make it far enough away, my feet give out. I drop to the ground and watch as the entire building explodes like fireworks on the Fourth of July.

A second and third engine pull up, working the fire together, but I can't move from my place. I can't stop watching my life go up in flames. And I don't budge until Rich says, "The EMTs called."

Ripping my mask off, I whip my head around, praying someone found my daughter. "Hazel?"

He shakes his head. "Victoria died on the way to the hospital. They don't know the cause of death yet."

I nod and stand. I know what it is. Overdose. She died doing the only thing she loves, the thing she put above everyone in her life, and she took my daughter with her.

"Maybe she wasn't in there," Alec says.

I hold up the shoe I was clutching in my glove and remove my tank. "She was there," I choke out. "This was her shoe."

Alec's face falls. "Fuck, man."

"I gotta go."

"Go," he says. "We'll handle this..."

I don't hear anything else he says. My head is fucking numb. I strip out of my gear, leaving it on the rig, and then start walking. I have no phone, no car, so I have no other choice.

I end up at the hospital. The nurse at the front desk glances at me with wide eyes. I'm sure I look a mess, but I don't give a shit.

I give her Georgia's name and she directs me to her room. When I walk in, she's in tears, crying into her phone. "Please, I just need an update. I—"

When her eyes land on me, her words come to an abrupt halt, before she speaks. "The police located Victoria's parents. She showed up with Hazel, but they got into an argument and she left. They haven't seen her or Hazel since. The police are searching for her, and I was asking them for an update—"

"I have an update," I say flatly, cutting her off.

"You found her?" Her tear-stained face brightens.

I hand her the half melted shoe and her face drops. "Chase..."

"She's dead."

Her head snaps up. "What? Who? How?"

"Hazel...and Victoria. They were in a fire. It hasn't been confirmed yet, but Victoria overdosed, and I couldn't find Hazel's body. I was too late. She's gone."

Georgia gasps. "No." She shakes her head, and it's then I notice she has bruises and cuts all over her face. Stitches above her brow. I should ask her if she's okay, but I don't have it in me to care.

"Yes," I bark out, my grief quickly morphing into anger. "She's dead! Because you, with your rose-fucking-colored glasses refuse to see the world for what it is! Fucked up!"

She flinches. "Chase, I'm..." She breaks into sobs. "I didn't mean—"

"Of course you didn't mean for this to happen. Because you never could've imagined it turning bad because you have no clue about how ugly this fucking world is!" I swipe the tray by her bed, the contents flying all over the place.

"Enough!" a deep voice barks from behind me. Tristan, Georgia's dad, walks inside. "I get you're hurting, but so is she."

"Good!" I bark. "She should be hurting because she caused this." I point my finger at Georgia. "I will never forgive you for this."

Fresh tears fill her eyes, and they're the last thing I see before I walk out of the room and out of Georgia's life. I should've known this would all end badly. She's too good, too sweet, too fucking innocent and naïve. She just doesn't understand how the real world works. How drug addicts like Victoria work. She wants to see the good in everyone and everything, but that's her reality, not mine. In my world, good doesn't exist.

When I get home, I stumble through the door. Robotically, I shower, and once I'm dressed, having no idea where to go from here, I end up in Hazel's room, sitting in her rocking chair and holding her stuffed animal.

I bring it to my nose, inhaling her scent, and then I fucking lose it. With the blink of an eye, I've lost my entire world.

GEORGIA

I can't stop crying. The tears won't stop falling. My body hurts so damn badly. But my heart... my heart has been destroyed. It's all my fault. I wanted to believe the good in her, and in the end, my naivety got Hazel killed. I should've listened to Chase. But I was so hell-bent on wanting to do the right thing, be a good person. I wanted Victoria to have the chance Lexi's mom never got. I didn't want Hazel to one day have to be told that we refused to let her mom see her.

And because of all that, she's dead. She died in a fire by herself. She was probably scared, calling out for us, and I failed her.

"Georgia, I know you're hurting, but you have to calm down," Mom says. "The doctor is going to admit you."

"I'm trying," I cry out, hiccupping through my sobs. "It just... hurts. I never meant for this to happen and now she's gone." I clutch my hands to my chest, wishing for God to take me instead of her.

"I know, sweetheart," Mom coos. "I know." She runs her fingers through my hair, but it does nothing to soothe me. Chase was right. This is all my fault. And nothing I do will make it right. We lost the most precious little girl today because of me.

A couple hours later, the doctor discharges me and I go to the police station to make my statement to get it over with. I can barely hold it together when I recount what happened. They inform me what Chase has already told me, that Victoria died from a drug overdose. As of now, Hazel's body hasn't been found, and until forensics can get in there and investigate, it will remain an open case.

Not wanting to go home and upset Chase further, I instead go to my parents' place. Exhausted and heartbroken, I lie in my childhood bed and, with the help of the prescription the doctor gave me, I fall into a fitful slumber, wishing when I wake up this all will be a horrible nightmare.

CHASE

Knock, knock, knock.

I wake up to the sound of someone banging on the door. I glance around, finding myself sitting in the rocking chair in Hazel's room and everything from yesterday hits me all over again.

Victoria beating up Georgia and stealing Hazel.

Victoria overdosing.

The apartment catching fire.

Hazel dying in the fire.

I consider closing my eyes, not wanting to deal with my new reality, one where I have to somehow move forward without my daughter in my life, but whoever is knocking on the door won't stop. I rise to my feet and drag myself to the front door.

When I open it, standing in front of me are two police officers. I know both of them from working as a firefighter. Have been on calls with them several times. "We were given your number from

Alec at the station. We tried to call you."

"My phone is broken."

He nods. "We have someone that belongs to you." He steps to the side, exposing the other officer, who's holding my world in his arms.

My heart clenches in my chest, and for a second I wonder if I'm going to have a heart attack. It's actually difficult to take in oxygen.

Please don't let this be a dream. It would be the cruelest of cruel dreams.

"Dada!" Hazel squeals, and I release a harsh breath. Her voice, the best sound in the world. A sound I didn't think I would ever hear again.

She wriggles in the officer's arms, reaching out for me to grab her. She's dressed in an overall dress with a pink and white striped shirt underneath. On her feet are pink striped socks and one shoe.

One fucking shoe.

Grabbing her from the officer, I pull her tight into my arms, burying my face in her neck. She shrieks in delight and the sound damn near brings me to my knees.

"She's alive," I breathe through a choked sob. "You're alive."

"She was turned in this morning. A gentleman by the name of Raymond Forrester said he showed up at Victoria Burke's home yesterday to speak with her. He walked in on her doing drugs and barely awake, so he took the child. When he returned this morning and found the building was burned down, he brought her to the station."

I close my eyes, tightening my hold on my daughter. "Please thank him for me," I choke out. Had he not taken her, she might not still be alive.

"Will do."

I close the door behind me and sink onto the ground, refusing to let go of my daughter. She's alive. She's living and breathing and giggling because she has no idea how close she came to having her life taken from her. She's happy and oblivious, the way a baby should be.

"Mama?" she coos, trying to get out of my hold. "Mama!" she yells.

Fuck, Georgia. She doesn't know Hazel is alive.

Thoughts of yesterday come back to me.

She was in the hospital, in bad shape, and I yelled at her, blamed her. She was at her lowest, we both were, and instead of holding her and comforting her, I kicked her while she was down. Fuck. I was so upset, but that doesn't excuse the way I behaved. I never should've said the shit I said.

I stand, scooping my daughter into my arms, and grab my keys. I have no phone, so I can't call her. I'll have to drive over to her parents' place and see if she's there. Unless...Did she come home last night?

No, she would've heard the knock. Just to be sure, I check out the room and then the guest room. She's not in either one. Feeling Hazel's wet diaper, I quickly change it, then put her in clean clothes.

A few minutes later, we arrive at her parents' house. Her truck was still at the apartment, so someone must've driven her to the hospital. I knock on the door and Charlie answers. The second she sees Hazel in my arms, she breaks down into tears, pulling us both into her arms for a hug.

"Oh, thank God." She holds us for several seconds before letting us go. "Is she okay?" She runs her hands down Hazel's arms and legs, checking for herself. Of course, Hazel giggles, thinking she's tickling her.

"She's okay. Victoria's ex-husband found her and took her before the place caught fire. She was never near the fire."

"Hey, Mom, I think—" Georgia's words ring out and then stop. Our eyes meet, and I note how bad she looks. Her eyes are all puffy, and not just from crying, from being beat on by Victoria. Her lip is swollen and her cheek is bruised. Victoria didn't just steal Hazel, she assaulted Georgia.

A loud gasp echoes in the quiet house and tears slide down her cheeks. She moves to come closer but then stops. "She's alive," she whispers.

I nod. "She's alive."

A sob racks through her body, as she shakes her head. "Thank God."

"Mama!" Hazel yells, reaching out for Georgia, completely unaware of what's going on. When Georgia makes no move to come over and grab her, I step forward. Only she steps back.

290

"Georgia...Do you want to hold her?"

She shakes her head. "No."

Charlie sighs. "Georgia, honey..."

"I'm so glad she's alive," Georgia says, her voice shaky with emotion. "I—" She chokes on her sob. "I prayed for this all to be a nightmare..."

"I did too," I admit. "I'm so sorry about what I said. How I—"

"Stop," she says flatly, cutting me off. "You have nothing to apologize for. You trusted me with your daughter and I nearly got her killed."

The way she speaks, her tone devoid of all emotion, sends a chill up my spine. And then it hits me, she said my daughter. As if she isn't Georgia's as well. "I shouldn't have said—"

She cuts me off again. "Yes, you should've because you were right. I *am* naïve and gullible. You trusted me with your daughter and I let you both down."

She can't be saying what I think she's saying.

"I think it's best if you go," she whispers. "I'm going to stay here until I find a place of my own."

No. No. No, no, no. "Please don't do this," I blurt out, stepping toward her. She immediately steps back. "I was upset...I thought she had died and I lashed out. I didn't mean what I said...Hell, I don't even remember what I said." Unfortunately, that's the truth. I was so far gone, I couldn't even recall all that I said to her.

"It doesn't matter what you said. I'm not fit to raise a baby. My only job was to protect her and I failed. You both are better off without me." She glances at Hazel, longing in her eyes. I know she wants to hold her and kiss her and feel her warm flesh and beating heartbeat, but she's resisting because she blames herself. Because I blamed her. When we got married, I vowed to stand by her side, and when shit got rough, I turned on her.

And now she doesn't think she deserves to be Hazel's mom.

I have to fix this. Right now. I did this. And it's up to me to make it right.

Without giving her time to retreat, I cut across the room with Hazel still in my arms, backing Georgia into a corner. Hazel reaches for Georgia and she flinches.

"Chase, stop, please. You need to leave."

"No, you need to hold your daughter." I thrust Hazel at Georgia, not giving her a chance to refuse.

Not wanting her to fall, Georgia grabs Hazel, who clasps on to Georgia, excited to be in her arms.

"You can be mad at me all you want, I deserve it. But this little girl is your daughter. I was wrong for the way I reacted. Your innocence, how you see the world, is what I love about you. It means you haven't experienced the shitty parts of life, and I hope Hazel grows up with the same outlook on life as her mother."

She glances up at me with glassy eyes.

"I hope she grows up to be just like you. You're her mother in every way that counts and regardless of what happens between us, you will always be her mother. You trusted Victoria because it's who you are. You're trusting and good. Life hasn't hardened you yet, and I hope it never does."

"My good almost got Hazel killed," she murmurs, choking on a sob. Fresh tears spill down her cheeks, breaking my heart.

"I should've paid more attention. I knew the way Victoria was and I pawned the entire ordeal off on you. I knew she would fuck up, and to prove a point, I made you handle it all on your own. I should've been your partner. I'm your husband. If what happened to Hazel is anyone's fault, it's mine, because I knew what Victoria was capable of and I did nothing to stop the train wreck."

Georgia shakes her head. "If I hadn't gotten involved, none of this would've happened."

I step closer to her and run my knuckles down her cheek, wiping her tears away. "You don't know that. She still could've come after Hazel. When someone is on drugs, you can't predict what they're capable of." I wipe a falling tear from under her eye. "I know it's going to take time for you to forgive me for what I said, but I'm asking you to please come home with Hazel and me. I love you and I'm so damn sorry. I'm a jaded asshole, and I need you in my life to help me see the world with softer eyes."

She closes her eyes, and I fear she's going to push me away, but instead she moves forward and into my arms. Hazel giggles, being caught in the middle. I wrap my arms around my entire world. "I'm so sorry, baby," I murmur into her ear. "I'm so fucking sorry."

"No more apologizing," she says, resting her head against my chest. "I forgive you."

Of course she does. Because Georgia is good and pure. She's the perfect in this crazy, fucked up, imperfect world. I don't deserve her, but there's no way in hell I'm ever letting her go.

GEORGIA

She's alive. My sweet little girl is alive. When Chase showed up with her, I thought it was some sort of sick dream, but it wasn't. We came so damn close to losing her, but we didn't. At first, I was scared to hold her. After the situation I put her in, I didn't feel like I deserved to. But then he thrust her into my arms and I knew regardless of how I felt, I would never let her go again.

When Chase apologized for the things he said, I had two choices: either hold a grudge or forgive him. Some would choose the former, but I could see the sincerity and apology in his face, in his words, and so I chose the latter. Life is too short and I refuse to live it with a chip on my shoulder. Chase and Hazel are my world and I don't want to be without either of them.

After eating breakfast at my parents' place—where Lexi, Alec, and Abigail joined the second I called and told Lexi that Hazel was alive—we head home. It's odd walking through the door. It's been less than twenty-four hours, but it feels like so much has changed in those hours. While Chase lays Hazel down for her nap, I glance in the living room, where Victoria attacked me, and a shiver runs up my spine.

"You okay?" Chase asks, when he comes out of Hazel's room and finds me still standing here.

"Yeah, I just can't believe what happened. That Victoria is dead and we almost lost Hazel...I could tell something was wrong with her. She was acting weird, like one minute she was on top of the world, telling me about how she's modeling and giving Hazel an expensive gift, and the next she was in tears. I was trying to call for help when she attacked me. I know you'll probably think I'm stupid saying this, but I wish I could've gotten help in time."

Chase smiles sadly. "I don't think it's stupid. I wouldn't expect anything less from you, butterfly. When I found her, she was passed out with a needle in her arm. She had a problem with drugs and nobody could help her but herself. And if she was modeling again, it all makes sense. For Victoria, modeling and drugs go hand in hand."

"Her parents said she got into a huge fight with them. They could tell she showed up high and they kicked her out. They apologized profusely for not forcing her to give up Hazel."

Chase sighs. "When I was searching for Hazel, I found a nursery in her apartment. I think she came here with the intent to take her. Drugs make people think they're invincible and do shit they normally wouldn't do."

He pulls me into his arms. "I know you said no more apologizing, but I need you to know how sorry I am. I fucked up big time and I'm going to spend every damn day making it up to you."

I shake my head. "That's not what I want. Everyone at one time or another says the wrong thing or handles a situation badly. Nobody's perfect." I stand on my tiptoes and kiss the corner of his mouth. "I love you, and all I want is to spend our lives together."

"Jesus, Georgia," Chase growls, lifting me into his arms. "You never cease to amaze me."

I screech, quickly covering my mouth so I don't wake up Hazel. "What are you doing?"

"I'm taking you to our room so I can make love to you." He drops me onto the center of the bed, then starts removing his clothes. When his boxers come down, his dick springs free, making both my mouth water and my thighs clench. It's been too long since he's been inside me.

He climbs up the bed and removes my shorts and underwear, then crawls up my body, pressing his mouth to mine in a searing kiss. "I need to be inside you," he murmurs against my mouth. "I need to feel your tight warmth wrapped around my dick."

His shaft pushes against the inside of my thigh and I assume he's going to thrust inside me, but instead he reaches over and grabs a toy out of the drawer. It's the anal vibrator.

"Lift up." He taps the side of my hip and I do as he says. He slides a pillow under my butt, then places my legs on either side of his shoulders. I'm completely open and exposed like this, but I'm too turned on to care.

His tongue lands on my hole, and I jump in shock. He chuckles, but doesn't stop licking the tight ring. He licks upward, from my ass to clit several times, each time slower, more controlled, and just when I think I'm going come, he stops.

"Not yet, butterfly." He grabs the lube and squirts a little onto the vibrator, then slowly pushes it into me. Once it's inside, he turns it on, and I damn near come.

"Chase," I groan. "I need you in me. Now."

After making sure the vibrator is fully in, he crawls back up my body, settling between my legs, and enters me in one fluid motion. I'm so wet, he slides right in, both of us moaning at how good it feels. He stills for a second, so I can adjust to him, and then he begins moving in and out of me. His arms cage me in, and our bodies connect in the most intimate way. His mouth devours mine as if I'm his lifeline. As if he needs me to breathe, to survive. And I feel the same way. What we went through, it was eye-opening, a reminder of how uncertain life is. I spent so much of my life tucked away in my shell, but now all I want to do is live.

Between the vibrator and him, the ascent to my climax is swift, hitting me hard, and taking Chase with me over the edge. He pulls back, his beautiful hazel eyes locking with mine. They're filled with love and happiness. Butterflies attack my chest.

My path might not be perfect.

Our life might not be perfect.

But our love is.

GEORGIA

Five Years Later

"Fuck, you're so tight," Chase groans, gripping my hair and pulling it, as he thrusts into my ass from behind.

"Harder," I moan, nuzzling my face into my pillow while massaging my clit. The house is filled with people, but I'm horny and couldn't help myself. "Please, Chase," I beg, "harder."

Just because I'm six months pregnant doesn't mean I'm fragile. I like to be fucked and hard. And he knows that.

Thankfully, he listens, and within seconds, my orgasm rips through me. He pulls out, coming all over my ass, and I sigh in satisfaction.

"I never thought I would say this," he says out of breath, "but I think this pregnancy needs to be your last." This makes me laugh.

"I'm serious." He grabs his shirt from the floor and wipes the cum off me. "I'm getting old and can't keep up with you. I'm not sure it's normal to be this horny while you're pregnant."

I sit up, scooting off the bed, so I can get cleaned up properly. "So, what you're saying is, I need to find a younger, more—"

"Don't even think about finishing that sentence," Chase growls, pulling me into his arms. We're both naked and sweaty, and when our bodies glide against each other, my girly parts clench in need.

Knock. Knock. Knock.

We both freeze.

The doorknob jiggles, and I pray to the parent gods Chase locked the door because I know I didn't.

"Mom! Why is the door locked?" Hazel yells.

"Oh, thank God," I mutter, making Chase laugh.

"Mommy! I'm hungry!" Eva shouts.

"Me too!" Hazel agrees. "We want pancakes."

I roll my eyes. "Why are both of our kids calling for me and not you?"

Chase laughs. "Because we all agree you're the cook in the family."

"We'll be right out," we yell at the same time, making us both snort out a laugh.

We take a quick shower—despite me begging him for sex—and after we're dressed, head downstairs.

"About time," my dad grumbles. "You guys spend more time in your room than with us."

Chase raises his palms in a placating manner. "That's all your daughter. She's born—"

I elbow him, making him grunt and stop talking. "Where's Mom?"

We're all staying at their house in Breckenridge for the holidays, and even though it's huge, with enough rooms for all of our families, I'm thinking it's time we get our own place.

"She's sitting on the porch having coffee with your sister and Micaela."

"Ooh! I think I'll join them."

"Mom, wait," Hazel says, her cute little hazel eyes pleading. At six years old, she looks so much like her father. She has Victoria's black hair, but her features are all Chase. "Grandpa said we have to eat cereal." Her button nose scrunches up.

My dad laughs. "There's nothing wrong with cereal. Your mother grew up on it and she survived."

Eva scoffs, her emerald green eyes that match mine glaring at my dad with her four-year-old going on fourteen attitude. "Mommy makes us pancakes and if we're good, she puts chocolate chips and bananas in them."

"Yeah," Abigail says, joining in. "And they're so good."

"The best," Dustin, my cousin Micaela's son, agrees.

"They are," Chase adds. "Especially when she adds peanut butter chips to them."

"Did someone say peanut butter?" Lexi asks, walking into the room. Her hand goes to her protruding belly. At seven months pregnant, she's due four weeks before me. "I love peanut butter."

"Ewww." Micaela gags, waddling into the room. "No peanut butter. It makes me sick." She's due only a week after Lexi.

Ryan groans. "I can't handle this shit. Whose idea was it to let all of our wives get pregnant at the same time?"

Bella, Micaela's mom, laughs. "I think it's adorable. They'll grow up and be close just like Micaela, Lexi, and Georgia are." She glances at my dad. "Just like we were."

Chase encircles me from behind, planting a kiss on my cheek. "I'll make the pancakes. You go sit and drink your coffee."

Mason coughs, "Get a room."

"Good idea!" I grab Chase's hand, tugging him down the hall.

"Butterfly," he groans. "You can't just use me like this. I need sustenance."

"I'm hungry," several of the kids whine.

"I can make the pancakes," Lexi says.

"No!" everyone yells.

The End

ABOUT THE AUTHOR

Reading is like breathing in, writing is like breathing out.– Pam Allyn

Nikki Ash resides in South Florida where she is an English teacher by day and a writer by night. When she's not writing, you can find her with a book in her hand. From the Boxcar Children, to Wuthering Heights, to the latest single parent romance, she has lived and breathed every type of book. While reading and writing are her passions, her two children are her entire world. You can probably find them at a Disney park before you would find them at home on the weekends!

Printed in Great Britain
by Amazon